MOVING TARGET

CATHRYN FOX

Discover other titles by Cathryn Fox at www.cathrynfox.com. Please sign up for Cathryn's Newsletter for freebies, ebooks, news and contests: https://app.mailerlite.com/webforms/landing/c1f8n1

ISBN ebook : 978-1-998943-08-1
ISBN Print: 978-1-998943-07-4

DANE

Man, I love this city.

Having grown up in Bass River, Nova Scotia—AKA buttfuck nowhere—I can't get enough of Halifax and all it has to offer, no matter the time of day or night. As I cruise down Water Street on my Larkspur commuter bicycle, I steal a glance over my shoulder to make sure the road is clear before I cross in the middle of the street, disobeying the signs in the bike lane, of course.

Hey, it's okay. It's Sunday night and the streets are mostly quiet, with everyone home getting ready for a busy Monday morning. Trust me, the commute is way harder, and traffic much heavier, during the Monday to Friday rush hour.

Busy or not, I don't care either way. I love it here in the city, and I love being outdoors, which is why I use my bike as much as I can, even though my older brother left me his car when he went off to play professional hockey for the Boston Bucks. I'll probably use my bike until the snow falls, and maybe even after that since it's off-road detour ready. But it's late September, which means I still have a month or so of good riding ahead of me. Not that I have a lot of free time during hockey season—which is why I'm cruising in the dark on a Sunday night.

I turn back to the street and swerve to the left, long before the lights at the corner, only to come to a dead stop when I run into something or someone. I curse as I tumble off my bike and slide across the hard, unforgiving pavement. Thankfully I'm wearing a long-sleeved shirt, or the pavement would have peeled the skin from my arms, and while I might disobey rules and can at times be reckless—okay, most times—I always wear a helmet.

Breathing rapidly, I finally come to a skidding stop and lay perfectly still as I take a fast second to check for broken bones. A busted-up body is all I need right now. Not only would a broken bone lay me up for this year's hockey season, but it could also put an end to my NHL career path.

Aww, wouldn't that be a fucking shame, Dane.

I quickly shut down my sarcastic inner voice, because yeah, I *have* to make it into the NHL like my older brother and my best friend Jesse, who was drafted when we were in juniors together. I was on the cusp, not quite good enough, much to everyone's disappointment. When I say everyone, I mean my family. I'm expected to make it and can't let them down, whether it's what I really want or not. But if I want my parents' approval and respect...

A garbled noise echoes in the empty street behind me, shutting down my dark thoughts. I turn and wince as my neck muscles rebel. Okay, what the hell did I hit? I scan the dark pavement, unable to see anything. I zero in on the sound of someone moaning, and push to my feet. I scramble toward the sound as a black lump becomes distinguishable.

Shit.

"Hey, are you okay?" I ask the guy huddled in the middle of the street. Why the hell would someone dressed in all black and cross in the middle of a dark street? They should have gone to the lights and used the crosswalk. Rules are made for a reason.

Yeah, and you're one to talk about rules, Dane.

Okay, fine.

As worry erupts inside me, I crouch down and search the black lump, trying to figure out how to help. He's curled into a ball and it's hard to tell which end is up in the dark and I'm afraid to touch him and make things worse.

"Do you need me to call an ambulance?" We're not far from the hospital, but I can't get him there on my bike, and I'm seriously worried he's badly hurt.

"No, I...I think I'm okay."

Shit, it's not a guy, it's a girl, and that voice...why is it so familiar?

"Can you move?"

"I think so." A moan, followed by a crackling sound of joints rebelling, curls around me as she gets into a seated position.

As her small frame comes into view—no wonder I didn't see her—I lightly touch her arm. "Let me help you."

She reaches for me, and I gently take her hand and slowly bring her to her feet. In the distance, I see headlights. "We need to get off the road before we get run over."

"Too late for that."

My gut knots and I wince at the comment, but her words are followed by a soft chuckle. My stomach loosens. "I'm really sorry. I didn't see you."

"Really? You're saying you didn't run into me on purpose?" She waves one hand. "With this long, empty street in front of you, with all kinds of places for you to cross, you pick the one spot where I'm walking and collide with me?"

She doesn't sound angry, so I joke, "Maybe you jumped in front of me. I mean, you could have crossed anywhere, too." I hold her tight as she gingerly walks, grateful that she's not seriously hurt. I guide her to the sidewalk, out of harm's way. "You did say it was a long, empty street," I add playfully, even though my heart is still thundering.

She lowers herself to the curb, and takes a moment to gather herself. "Yes, yes I did." She plants her elbows on her knees. "So what do you think, coincidence or serendipity?"

I take off my helmet and scratch my head. "Aren't they the same thing?"

Her phone buzzes and she pulls it from her pocket. She slides her finger across the screen and the second the light falls over her face, my heart jumps into my chest. Kendra Jaynes. No freaking way. My helmet slips from my hand and lands on the grassy curb. Okay, maybe this unexpected collision wasn't a coincidence or serendipity.

Maybe it was...*fate*.

To me, fate means a person's destiny, the path one is supposed to walk—which doesn't always end pleasantly. That tracks for me, because my future does not include Kendra Jaynes. When it comes to women, I don't commit. Trust me on this, it won't end favorably for me. I've walked in my brother's shadow my whole life. No matter what I do, I'll never be good enough. If I make the NHL, however, maybe I'll finally be worthy of love and respect. Maybe then I'll stop being compared to my big brother Rhys and women will see me as more. Maybe Kendra will...

Nope, not going there...not with her.

"No. They're not the same thing." Her head lifts, and she angles her phone my way. The light falls over me and her jaw drops open. "Dane."

"Hi Kendra." I take in her shocked face. I haven't set eyes on her in nine long months. Not since Jesse and I visited the campus with my brother back at Christmas and I found myself in Kendra's bed. It was a one-time thing—a holiday hook-up. After that, I went back to Bass River, both of us going our own ways. That didn't mean I didn't think about her. I'd yet to run into her on campus and was beginning to wonder if she still went to Scotia Academy. She's our team captain's younger sister, and while I wanted to ask him or one of the other guys about her, I knew better. She's off limits. She was off limits last Christmas, too—even though that didn't stop us that one night.

Her mouth opens and closes as she shakes her head. "What...what..."

As car headlights come closer, I run back to get my bike off the street. I'll check for tire and frame damage later, once I know Kendra is okay. My heart beats a little faster as I drop down next to her. My gaze moves over her face, and something warm ignites inside me. Wow, does she feel the little bolt of electricity between us too? Not that we can do anything about it. I'm a full-time player now, and a hook-up with her is out of the question. I can't risk getting kicked off the team. But there is chemistry here, every bit as much tonight as there was nine months ago.

"What...what..." she stammers again after I sit.

My gaze narrows in on her, and I try to see her pupils in the dark as she repeats herself. It's impossible. "Did you bang your head? I think you might have a concussion." Her hand goes to the back of her head and a pained sound gurgles in her throat.

"Can I touch?" She takes my hand and puts it on the small lump. "I think we should take you to the hospital. I know a concussion when I see it."

"So do I. I'm a nursing student, remember?" I nod. I remember everything about her, even all the little herb plants she likes to grow on her windowsill. Nine months ago, lavender filled my senses when I went to get us a drink of water after a round of sex. As I lean into her, I can still smell it. Does she make perfume out of it? "It's just a small bump. I feel fine otherwise. I'd really like to just go home." I glance up and down the street. She's about ten blocks from home and I'm just around the corner. What was she doing out on the streets this late at night? I'm out here because a hard ride and fresh air always helps me sleep better. I don't suspect it's the same for her though.

I gesture with a nod. "I'm just around the corner. Why don't we go there? I don't want you walking if you have a concussion." Plus, it's dark out, and bad things happen after dark in any city. "Why didn't you call campus security?" I don't want to make her feel bad or stupid. Maybe she doesn't know about the service provided to students. "You have the app, right?"

"I do, I just...it wasn't a far walk."

I glance up and down the dark street. I have no idea where she was coming from, but even a few blocks at night is far enough. "Come on. Let's get inside."

She hesitates for a second and runs her hands up and down her arms. I notice her thin sweater. The night is warm and her shiver is probably from an adrenaline dump. I wish I had a jacket to put around her.

"I...maybe I should call my brother."

A wave of disappointment goes through me. I kind of like the idea of caring for her. She's close to her brother though, and I think that's nice. I guess you could say Rhys and I are tight too, considering how closely I walk in his shadow. "Sure. If that's what you want."

She frowns and glances down, and I sense an internal struggle. "He's probably at study group."

I wouldn't say I was great at reading people. I'm not, so I don't know why I get the sense she's fibbing about study group, and there's a deeper reason that's preventing her from calling her brother.

"Kendra, where were you?" It's not my business and she doesn't have to answer if she doesn't want too.

"I was..." she points to a random spot over her shoulder. "...at my boyfriend's place. Do you know Lance Williams?"

"Yes." I don't know him personally. His family owns the biggest law firm here in the city and their commercials are all over the TV and radio. Personally, I think they're all a bunch of arrogant assholes who think they're better than everyone else. Wait, did she just say Lance was her boyfriend? What the fuck is she doing with that douche?

"Lance is your boyfriend?"

She nods and glances away, like she's embarrassed by that. Or trying to hide something. Maybe she thinks he's a douche too. Christ, the guy walks around campus like he owns the place and I guess in a way he does. His family name is on the law school building. Old family, with old money, and deep-rooted ties to the community.

I'm pretty sure it was just last week, I spotted Lance late one evening, near the track where I was running, having a deep conversation with a girl—using his tongue. Then again, it was dark, and it might not have been him.

"He didn't walk you home?" I work to keep the disdain from my voice. I don't think I'm doing that great a job. She wouldn't be biting back a wince if I was.

"He's very busy. I was helping him study for his LSAT's." Her gaze searches my face. "That's the law school—

"Admissions test. I know."

She wrings her hands together. "Sorry, I didn't mean to suggest you didn't."

I'm sure she didn't. I don't think Kendra is like other girls I know, who think hockey players are dumb jocks who don't know much about anything else. Probably because her brother is a player, and she can see beneath the jersey. Right now, though, all I can think about is Lance Williams and how I'd like to punch him in the face for letting her walk home in the dark. Fucking idiot.

"He writes the test next weekend. He's been very stressed. He has a lot to live up to. His family has huge expectations of him."

I know all about family expectation.

"Come on," I mutter, tired of hearing her defend him. The truth is a lot of people have expectations on them. That doesn't mean the world revolves around them and they get to be an asshole. "You're cold. Let's get you inside and into some warmer clothes. I have something you can borrow. Once you're warm and I'm sure you don't have a concussion, I'll drive you home."

"Okay."

I snatch up my helmet and we start walking. As soon as I put my arm around her waist to make sure she stays upright, her feet come to a resounding halt. Yeah, I get it. She thinks this is a bad idea. Last Christmas during a party at Storm House, her brother pulled her away from me. All the guys on the team have been warned to stay away from her, and her brother, undoubtedly, told her we were all man-whores and to steer clear. Then again, she's probably worried what douche bag would think.

She points to a spot on the sidewalk behind us. "Your bike."

Okeydokey, I guess I called that one wrong. "I'll come back for it."

"No, get it now." She shakes her head and stands her ground. I don't know Kendra very well, but I like that she cares about my bike. "I can walk and I don't want anyone to steal it."

While I love this city, bikes do tend to go missing frequently, even when they're locked up. If I leave mine unattended on the street, it likely won't be there in five minutes. But I can't risk her falling. It's possible she has a concussion. "Are you sure?"

"Yes, get it." I hurry back and pick up my bike, walking it beside me. I reach Kendra and we cross the road. "Is it ruined?"

"I don't think so." I lightly nudge her. "I hit something soft."

"At least one of us did."

She's smiling, but I still feel like an ass. "I really am sorry."

"I know. Strange though," she says. "I haven't seen you around and then we bang into each other, literally."

"Does that mean you've been looking for me?"

She laughs. "I was curious. It's a small city and a small campus. I thought I might run into you."

"And you did...or rather, I ran into you."

We both laugh and I gesture to Storm House. At least her brother moved out, like most players in their last year do, and won't catch me sneaking her to my room. I guess the noise and parties get old after a while.

She grins and I say, "I was wondering if you were still on campus. I guess I've been looking for you too."

She nods and her smile falls away as she glances down. Shit, was it something I said? I pull open the big heavy door to Storm House and the place is quiet. I guess most of the guys are tired from a busy weekend training and of course we did have a big party last night.

"I'm on the second floor." I lift my bike and we go up the big set of stairs slowly and I keep a close eye on her, not wanting her to fall backward. I push open my door when I reach it and gesture for her to enter. She steps in and I follow behind, securing my bike on the wall rack as she glances around. "Looks familiar."

I go still. Is she saying she's been in a lot of the rooms at Storm House? Honestly, she doesn't seem like a puck bunny at all, from what I know of her, that is. Her brother Nate didn't seem to be impressed that she was at the Christmas party last year either. He keeps close tabs on her. When she took me back to her place, he texted a few times. She didn't tell him I was with her, which leads me to believe she has to sneak around. "Same as Nate's room his first year."

"Right," I say and slide open my drawer and pull out a heavy sweatshirt. "This will be big, but it should keep you warm."

"Thanks." She turns her back to me, and lifts her arms to pull it on. The small black sweater she's wearing rises with the movement, and my throat tightens at the dark bruises on her back. Bruises that have yellowed, which means they weren't from tonight's fall.

I take a small step closer, and her body tenses at my sudden closeness. "Kendra, are you okay?"

2

KENDRA

My heart jumps into my throat as Dane's big hand lands on my arm, a light, comforting touch that threatens to flood my eyes with tears. I quickly blink them away and bite down on my cheek to pull myself together. Yes, I'm currently on an emotional roller coaster ride with my boyfriend, and I'm so dizzy I don't know which way is up or down, let alone in or out.

Out.

Yeah, that's what I want. Out. Out of my relationship with Lance. Although I'm afraid of disappointing my brother, and of Lance's temper. But none of this is Dane's concern and I'm sure it's his gentleness and kindness that's doing the weirdest things to my heart.

"Oh," I say quickly and tug the shirt on, pulling on it hard until I stretch it to my knees, wanting to cover all my bruises. "I fell off the bed studying the other day." It's not a lie. I did fall off the bed the other day. I wasn't studying though. I was helping Lance study for his LSAT's, like I have been for a while now. He got annoyed that I stumbled over one of the questions and ripped the book from my hand. His elbow 'accidently' hit me and I fell to the floor with an undignified thud. Much like I hit the ground tonight. I secretly suspect only one of those falls was an accident.

Lance apologized, like he always does after one of his outbursts ends with me getting hurt. Despite the apology, after every incident, I leave feeling like I was the one who'd done something wrong. Back in the beginning of our relationship, he wasn't always so quick tempered, and he assures me that once he finishes his entrance exams, he wouldn't be so stressed or on edge.

My brother set us up at the end of last year. Lance is pretty much the only guy my brother ever approved of. They became friends when they took a business class together, and maybe it's the fact that Lance is studying to be a lawyer that sets him apart in my brother's eyes. It doesn't hurt that he comes from a well-known family of lawyers, who own the biggest firm on the east coast.

Dane turns me, and he puts his palm on the side of my face and this time I can't stop the tears. Dammit. "Hey," he murmurs quietly and tugs me to him. I put my cheek against his pounding heart, and breathe in his warm familiar scent.

I've missed his smell...his touch.

It's true, we were only together that one night and what a wild, reckless night it was. I'd never done anything like that, never hooked up with a guy, let alone a hockey player. My brother would have lost his mind. Most don't understand why I let Nate make choices for me. Most don't understand what we've been through, or how much he's done for me. I trust him and I'm pretty sure his choices have always been the right ones, until...Lance.

The problem is that Nate is stoked about our relationship, and I don't want to disappoint him Maybe I'm wrong about Lance hurting me. Maybe I'm just accident prone. I'm sure that's what Lance would tell Nate if I ever whispered it to him.

A fresh wave of tears prick my eyes, and I let Dane hold me for an extra minute as exhaustion overtakes my body. My legs weaken, and I sag against him. The next thing I know, he's sitting on the edge of his bed, tucking his warm blankets around me.

"I'm sorry," I manage to push out past a tight throat. "I...I..."

"Adrenaline," he explains, and I can't help but think—probably because of the way his brow is bunched—that he's actually asking me a question.

"Yes," I agree. "I've been studying hard, and helping Lance with his LSATs. Late nights and then the shock of running into you."

"Literally," he says with a soft smile, like he's trying to lighten things up. His finger sweeps my cheek, brushing away a lone tear.

"Wait, no. You ran into me," I counter, a small, chuckle bubbling up inside me. I lean into his hand, absorbing his warmth.

He lets out an exaggerated breath. "If that's what you have to tell yourself to help you sleep at night, then so be it." The bluest of blue eyes lock on mine. I hadn't forgotten how gorgeous they were, or how they looked at me with such hunger nine months ago. My entire body warms at the memory, and I reach out and put my hand on his leg. He glances down, and when his shoulders stiffen—a reminder that I have a boyfriend—I ease it away.

"Sorry."

"It's okay," he responds, his voice a bit deeper. He turns his attention to the blankets, and tucks them around me again. "Are you warm now?"

"Getting there."

"Are you hungry, or thirsty?" He points to a small fridge. "I have water and soda, and I can run to the kitchen for some food."

"I don't want to put you out."

"You're not. I'm always hungry after a ride."

"You bike ride for...fun?"

He angles his head and glances at me like I might have a handlebar sticking out of my nose. "Yeah, why?"

"That's what you were doing out there? Recklessly racing up and down the streets because you enjoy it?"

This brings on a laugh. "I don't know if I'd use the word reckless." I purse my lips and his protest dies. "Okay, fine. I thought the streets were empty and why do you say that like it's the most ludicrous thing you've ever heard?"

"I don't know."

"You've ridden a bike before, haven't you?"

I nod. "Of course, I used to have this pink one with these colorful pink and purple ribbons, but I stopped riding it when..." I glance down quickly as old memories rip to the surface and steal the air from my lungs. I take in Dane's watchful eyes, and I shake my head and struggle not to sound breathless as I continue. "It's been a long time since I've been on a bike."

He looks like he wants to ask more questions, and I'm grateful when he turns it back to him. "I used to love my BMX when I was a kid. Had a skate park near my house and used to love to do tricks."

"Sounds risky."

"You don't like risks?" he asks, even though I'm sure he already knows the answer.

"Not really."

He nudges me. "You need to live a little. Have some fun."

I laugh. "Maybe you need to have a little less, before you kill yourself, or someone else," I tease. He might be right though. I do kind of go through the motions in life. I don't take risks, and I don't have a lot of fun—except for that one reckless night nine months ago. God, that was so out of character for me. I want to blame it on the alcohol, but I didn't have that much to drink.

"What do you do for fun?" he asks.

"I give needles at the clinic," I joke playfully, not wanting to admit I don't do anything for fun.

"Ooh, sadist. I like that."

I take in his cute smile. "Did you see the skate park at the commons?"

"Yeah. It's for kids."

"It's not just for kids," I correct. "I've seen adults there too."

"Do it with me," he jokes. "I'll show you how much fun it can be."

"Yeah, sure," I blurt out without thinking. Biking isn't my thing, I don't think. The idea of watching him perform tricks does sound kind of fun. He grins, and gives me a look that says I'm full of...something. "As long as you don't try to run me over again."

He stands and laughs. "On that note. Peanut butter sandwich?"

I put my hand over my stomach. I'd spent the better part of the day helping Lance and he was so grumpy, I could barely eat the pizza he ordered hours ago. "Sounds pretty gourmet right about now."

"Starving?"

"Yeah."

He looks at me for a long second. Does he not want to leave? Is he still afraid I'm concussing and might do something foolish like flee Storm House and get hit by something worse than a bike on the way home?

"Hurry back," I say, and he gives a curt nod. "Wait." I reach out and take his hand. "Are you okay? I wasn't the only one who hit the ground hard."

His face softens as he raps on his head. "Had a helmet on."

"Yeah, but..." I glance at his body, note the way his long sleeve T-shirt hugs his chest and biceps. He looks good. Really good. For the briefest of seconds my fingers twitch, remembering what his body felt like beneath my palms. I let him go and tuck my hand under the blankets before I do something I shouldn't. "You have a small rip in your shirt."

He lifts his arm. "Ah, so I do. Good thing I was wearing long sleeves."

"Maybe not so reckless after all."

He winks. "Maybe not." He fixes the blankets around me again. "Be right back." His gaze holds my attention as he crosses the room, and I glance around, taking in the bare walls. He's been here long enough to make the place his own, but it totally lacks personality. What's that all about?

I snuggle down and roll in his bed, and the smell of him on the sheets fill my senses. I take a few, deep relaxing breaths, and briefly shut my eyes as warmth, comfort and safety, things I haven't felt in a while overcome me.

The next thing I know, my eyes are opening, and I take in the dark room. I shift and lift to check the clock. I groan as my back protests and memories of last night come back in a whoosh. I'm in Dane's bed. I roll over quickly and find the other side empty. I jackknife up and spot Dane sound asleep in one of his chairs. His head is to the side and his feet are up on a duffle bag. Could he be any more uncomfortable?

I push the blankets off and throw my feet over the side of the bed, guilt swamping me. My heart skips a beat at the sight of a peanut butter sandwich sitting on a plate beside the bed, wrapped in plastic to keep it fresh.

"Aww," I say under my breath.

A groan, and then, "Did I wake you?"

I turn and find Dane straining to sit up straight. I'm sure his muscles are achy from the fall and seized from his horrible sleeping position. A groan slips from his lips as he puts his feet on the floor and sits upright.

"No, I think I woke you." I gesture to his nightstand. "I saw the sandwich..."

"It's okay." He rubs his eyes as I stand there. "Are you okay?"

I nod, even though I'm not certain I am. "I should probably get going, and give you back your bed." I point to the chair. "That does not look comfortable."

His gaze moves to the clock and to the dark sky outside his window. "You don't have to go, but if you want to, I'll drive you."

"No, I don't want you going out this time of night."

I make a move to take off his sweater, and a second later his hand is on mine, stopping me. "You can keep this on and I'm not letting you walk home alone in the dark, Kendra."

Okay then. I stand there, secretly liking this protective side of him. "I'll be fine," I assure him, my voice lacking any sort of confidence. "I guess I could use my app and get campus security to walk me." Maybe I should have done that last night. It's always an option here on campus. If I had called it, I wouldn't have run into Dane and I'm kind of glad I did.

He dips his head, his mouth close to mine. "How is your head?"

"Fine, how is yours?"

Did he just roll his eyes at my flippant response? I guess I can't be sure, considering I was staring at his kissable lips. "You think you're okay to walk? You were starving and didn't eat."

Maybe it's my hesitation, or the way I continue to linger as he hovers over me, that lets him know I'm in no hurry to leave.

"You should at least eat something first," he suggests.

"Right. No sense in letting the sandwich go to waste and the sun is going to rise soon, which means it will be light out and you don't have to worry about me walking home in the dark." I plop back down on the bed, instantly missing his closeness, and pick up the plate. Before I open it, I tap the bed. "At least get comfortable, Dane." He stands still and runs his hands through is hair. "It's not like we haven't..." My words fall off as my gaze drops and takes in his boxer shorts, which is all he's wearing.

"...seen each other naked," he teases, finishing my sentence for me.

I gulp. "Yeah."

He looks at his bed with longing. "Are you sure, Kens?"

I grin at the nickname. No one really calls me that and I kind of like that he does. "Positive." I pick up the water bottle beside me, open it and take a drink. I hold it out to him.

"Thanks." He takes a long pull as I remove the plastic from the plate. I bite into the sandwich and moan with pleasure. I truly am starving. Dane shifts beside me, looking somewhat uncomfortable as he pulls the blankets up over his waist. Wait, did my moan...is he hiding...?

Oh, crap.

I bite into my sandwich again, and before I can stop myself, I moan again. "Oh, sorry," I say around a big bite.

"For what?" My gaze drops quickly, and I don't miss the way he follows it. Now it's his turn to groan. "I guess I'm the one who should be apologizing."

"You've apologized enough tonight." I hold my sandwich out to him and he shakes his head. I take the water bottle, and his gaze remains on my mouth as I drink. I set the bottle down and work on my sandwich. Needing my mind on something other than his body, I ask, "Why did they call your brother Cheddar?" I angle my head and take in his cute grin.

"You don't know?"

"If I knew, I wouldn't have asked."

"Wow, smartass." He laughs. "My parents are artisan cheese makers in Bass River. Have you heard of the gouda guy?"

My jaw drops. "That's your dad?" He nods. "I love that cheese."

"Chances are you probably ate some I made. I loved making cheese with my folks."

I always knew Dane was interesting, but this is really something. "I can't believe you make cheese."

"Used to." His eyes dull as he looks at the wall, staring at nothing.

"You miss it," I state.

"Hockey," he explains. "There was just no time."

My throat tightens as I swallow. "Do you like hockey?"

"Sure." Wow, he didn't even try to inject enthusiasm into his voice. He pretends to take a shot with a stick. "My goal is the NHL. Do you go to the games?"

I shake my head and admit, "I don't really follow it, and I don't think Nate wants me at the rink." I crinkle up my nose. "He's worried about—"

"One of the guys liking you."

"Yeah, something like that." I push out an exaggerated laugh. "As if they would, I'm not really the kind of girl they go after."

"Yeah, you are," he says, and a ridiculous thrill goes through me. "I'm a hockey player, and do I have to remind you what happened between us?"

My body heats. "No, I remember." Shoot, I didn't mean for that to come out so breathless. I stare at him for a second, and I'm about to ask if the NHL is what he really wants when he turns the conversation back to cheese. "My brother has red hair, and my parents are artisan cheese makers, so naturally he got the nickname Cheddar."

I laugh. "What about you? What's your nickname?" I reach out and lightly touch his hair, which is blond with some darker streaks. "Your hair is dirty blond."

He feigns offense. "My hair is not dirty, and we don't all have nicknames."

"You know what I mean." I tug on a strand, and he playfully does the same to me. "Since you're on the lighter side, do they call you Mozza?"

"No, they don't call me mozza and if they did, I'd be happy to set them straight, with my fist." I laugh at that. "I don't have a nickname."

"What's your favorite cheese?"

"I like all cheeses."

"Me too," I add. "It's my love language."

He laughs at that. "I guess if I had to pick a favorite, it might be brie."

I nod and look him over. "I think that's fitting. A firm layer on the outside..." I poke his stomach. "Soft on the inside."

"I am not soft."

As soon as the words leave his mouth, my gaze drops lower, to the bulge in his boxers. Nope, not soft at all. I quickly turn my attention back to my sandwich and take big bites to finish it. "It should be light out soon."

"How's the head?"

I lightly touch the back of my head, and the lump is down. "Much better." I take his hand and put it on my head, and as he touches me, sensations rip through my body and settle in a spot it has no right to settle.

"We should have iced it. I don't know why I didn't think of that."

Ice, yeah. Ice is exactly what I need...between my legs. "I can sit in the—" I make a move to get up.

He touches my arm and pulls me back. "You're fine." A long beat of silence passes between us and then he says quietly, "We're fine. We're both adults, we can share a mattress, Kens."

"Okay," I croak out, and sink back down. He lifts the blankets and tucks them around me and I roll to my side, my back to him. He rolls and offers me his back and we both go perfectly still and silent, while I stare at the dark night. As I calculate how long I'll have to lay next to him —and no, math is not my strong suit, oh and did I mention I don't hate anything about this—I try to quiet my heartbeat. What we're doing isn't wrong. We're not touching, or doing anything inappropriate, so I shouldn't be feeling any sort of guilt. Well, okay, my thoughts might be a wee bit shameless, but I'm not going to act on them.

My lids fall shut, and the next thing I know, I wake up, completely wrapped in Dane's arms. *Holy crap, Kendra*! Okay, now everything about this is wrong, and the logical part of my brain is yelling at me to leave. Unfortunately, every other part of my brain and body disagrees and there isn't a bone in my body that will allow me to move.

3

DANE

Movement on the mattress pulls me awake and I open my eyes and find Kendra on her side staring at me, her blue eyes wide and brimming with worry. It takes a moment for my brain to awaken, and the second the fog clears, I jump back, unfurling my arms and legs from around her soft body. Jesus, how did we end up in a twisted mess? Yeah, I was having a hot dream about her, but I wasn't acting on it, was I?

I rub the blur from my eyes. "What...what's going on?" I ask, a stupid question, I know.

"We both fell asleep, and we somehow..." Her fingers tangle in the bedding as her words fall off.

I push up on my arms and glance at the clock. It's a little after seven and I need to get to hockey practice before my first class starts at nine. "Shit, I'm sorry, Kendra. I didn't mean to fall asleep."

"Me neither."

Christ, I need to get her out of the dorm before someone finds her in here with me, and her brother hands me my ass, or worse, makes my life a nightmare on the team. He has a lot of pull with the coach, and if he gives me zero play time, I'll never get scouted, and drafted, and...what then? What then is simple: I can forget about ever being important to anyone.

I run my hand through my hair as she pushes the blankets from her body. "I need to get out of here," she says, a measure of panic in her voice, and I have no doubt she's worried about her brother too, not to mention her douche bag boyfriend. I can't imagine he'd love the idea of her sleeping in another man's bed—even though nothing happened. Not that he should have any kind of a say in what happened last night. Not after letting her walk home late at night all by herself.

I push the blankets off and tug on a clean shirt from my drawer. On the hook by the door, I find my favorite East Coast Lifestyle hoodie and shrug it on. Kendra straightens herself up, and I search for my car keys. Once I find them, I put my ear to the door and listen for sound.

Her brows rise as she restlessly shifts from one foot to the other, and I try not to stare at her curves, or think about how her body felt next to mine. "All clear?"

I open my door and glance up and down the hall, relaxing a bit when I find it empty. I grab my hockey bag. "Let's go." We hurry into the hall and I guide her to the back entrance, where we're less likely to run into someone. Sneaking around like this is...weird. Especially considering I was only trying to help her last night. I'm sure others would put their own spin on things though. Pretty much every guy on the team has a reputation with the ladies and I'm no exception.

We step outside and the cool morning air rushes over us. "I'm right here," I say, and hit the fob to unlock my car. "Not as fun as my bike, but it'll get you home quicker and you'll be warmer."

Her smile is soft and grateful as she slides into the car and touches the sweater she's still wearing. "I'll wash this and get it back to you."

"No hurry."

I pull out of the parking lot and instead of going left, I go right. "Uh, I live the other way." Her fingers tighten on her belt bag. "It's been a while. I can see why you'd forget."

"I didn't forget." Like I said already. I haven't forgotten one single thing about her and in fact, I'd love to learn more.

"Then why are we going in the opposite direction? You're not secretly a cab driver, taking the scenic route to make more money from me, are you?"

I laugh. "This ride is free and the least I can do." I pull into the drive thru at my favorite breakfast place. "Food," I explain.

"Coffee," she responds, her eyes brightening in delight.

"Both."

I order us coffee and breakfast sandwiches and hand her the bag as I drive. She opens it, unwraps my sandwich and passes it over. I catch her grin as she unwraps hers and I bite into mine.

"What?"

She shrugs. "This is exactly what you got me when...well, you know."

"When we had sex last Christmas break."

She nearly chokes on her food. "Yeah, that. Is this your go to meal after every hook-up or something?" She bites into her sandwich and her moan wraps around my cock and tugs.

"When you put it like that, it sounds like we had sex last night, and we didn't. Unless you took advantage of me in my sleep." A pink flush crawls into her cheeks. Wait, were her dreams as dirty as mine?

"Of course not. I have a boyfriend," she shoots back, and pulls the tabs back on our coffees. She takes a drink and there's that moan again.

We both eat in silence as I drive and after a while, I can't help but ask. "You and Lance. How did you two meet?" A law student and a nursing student. I don't know why that sounds like such an unlikely couple. Then again, a nursing student and an NHL wannabe also sounds unlikely.

"My brother, actually. They're friends. He really likes Lance and thought we'd hit it off."

"Have you?"

Her brow furrows at the question. "Well, we're dating."

That really wasn't an answer and I'm still convinced it was Lance I saw that night near the track. Is he fucking around on her? "I saw how protective Nate was of you at last year's Christmas party. I'm surprised he lets any guy close to you."

"He's protective." She glances out the window, that familiar pained expression on her face. "He's a good big brother. He's always been there for me." She smiles, but it's forced. "He's older and wiser, and always knows what's best for me." Her body stiffens and as I watch her quietly, she adds, almost under her breath, "I'd never want to do anything to disappoint him."

Fuck, is that why she's with douche bag? She doesn't want to disappoint her brother? What went on in their lives that he has so much power over her, so much say in who she dates? I can see a parent making decisions for her, and guiding her, but not a brother.

"How would Nate feel about Lance letting you walk home alone at night?"

The sandwich wrapper crinkles in her fingers as they tighten around it. "It's just the days are getting shorter with winter coming. He would have walked me home. He's just swamped studying right now."

I clench my jaw to keep myself from saying something else, something negative. I don't want her to hate me, and really is their relationship any of my business? No. Her safety isn't either, but that doesn't mean I'm not going to make it my responsibility, though. I pull into her driveway.

She toys with the door handle. "Thanks for breakfast."

"Anytime."

She doesn't leave, instead she turns to me. "Thanks for last night too. For…"

After ragging on her boyfriend, I work to lighten the conversation and say, "Running you over with my bike."

She chuckles. "Well, no, but for taking care of me after you did, and for…worrying about my safety."

I take in her blue eyes, the hint of sadness that lives there. "Give me your phone."

"What?"

I hold my hand out. "Phone, please." She frowns, reaches into her belt bag, pulls out her phone. "Unlock it."

She punches in her key code to unlock it and I take it from her. "What do you want with it?"

I punch in my contact information, and jokingly put my name in as Brie. That way if her brother or douche bag sees it, they won't think anything of it. I hand it back. She takes one look at what I wrote and starts laughing. I touch her hand and her laugh fades as her gaze locks on mine.

"No more walking alone at night. Call me. I don't care what time it is. I'll come get you, okay?"

"You don't—"

"Okay?"

She swallows. "Last Christmas. That's not something I do... like ever."

My chest expands as my heart pounds a little harder. I never took her for the kind of girl who did random hook-ups, not that there's anything wrong with that, and while I've never felt special or important before, the fact that the girl who never takes risks did something reckless with me, well...that sort of punches me right in the heart.

"I know, Kens," I say quietly as I put my hand on her face and lightly brush my thumb over her soft cheek.

"I liked what we did," she admits.

"Yeah, me too." I take a breath as she glances at her phone. "No walking alone," I tell her again.

She tucks her phone away. "Okay, *Brie*."

I grin as she exits the car and I wait in the driveway until she's safely inside her house. I back out and head to the rink, working to get my mind off Kendra and on hockey. I need to bring my A-game during practice and during every game if I want to get noticed and make it to the NHL.

I hurry to the rink, and inside, I find Jesse talking with Nate, and I worry he's going to take one look at me and know I was in bed with his sister.

"Hey," I say and open my locker.

"Where were you this morning?" Jesse asks, stepping up to me, and Nate makes his way to the ice. Once he's out of earshot, I pull my skates from my bag and glance around. "I was giving Kendra a lift home."

His eyes go wide. "Are you fucking serious. Are you two—"

"No," I answer quickly. "I actually ran her over with my bike last night, and she fell asleep in my room."

"Oh, so that's why your door was locked last night."

"Yeah, you came by? Did you need something?" I tug on my jersey, and drop down onto the bench.

"Nothing important." He glances around again. "You can't be with Kendra," he says, his voice taking on a serious edge. "You can't fuck up your future like this."

"I know, and I wasn't with her." I pull on my skates. "Do you know anything about her boyfriend, Lance?"

He ties his skates and says, "Who doesn't? His family is pretty well known. I've seen him hanging with Nate a few times, but I've never met the guy."

"I don't like him." Why the fuck would Kendra be with a guy who doesn't even walk her home? I can't understand it. Nor can I understand the control her brother has over her. Sure, he wants to look out for her, she's his kid sister. Handpicking her boyfriend, that's a bit much.

Maybe you're just jealous, dude, and upset that you'll never be worthy of a girl like her...

"You know him?" Jesse asks.

"No, not really."

Jesse shakes his head, a warning look in his eyes as he stares at me. "Just walk away, Dane. You could fuck up your future."

He's right. I know he's right, and I know he has my best interests at heart. I just can't help but think something is off in that relationship, and there's no way in hell I can walk away if he's hurting Kendra. A few more guys come into the locker room and I finish getting ready. As I head onto the ice with Jesse, I work hard to focus on practice, but my mind is on Kendra.

We go through a few drills, and I take my defensive position as my teammates drill shots at me. I spot Coach Jameson and Nate chatting, and from the way they keep glancing at me, I have the sneaking suspicion they're comparing me to my brother. Nothing new there.

Once practice is done, back in the locker room, Nate talks to us about this weekend's home game, and how we all need to be at the top of our game if we want to win against Quebec. After our pep talk, I shower, dress and head to class. I check my phone numerous times throughout the day to see if Kendra messaged, and even though I shouldn't, I make my way to the campus cafeteria, drop down into a chair and send her a text.

Me: How's the head?

Three dots appear and I don't miss the way my heart speeds up. I glance around, and hold my phone closer, like what I'm doing is illegal. It's not, and honestly, I'm allowed to talk and text Kendra. Having a boyfriend doesn't mean we can't be friends, and surely to God her brother doesn't monitor who she talks to. I guess maybe there's a part of me that worries he does. I didn't use my name when I added my information to her phone.

Kendra: Hello Brie. Head is good. Swelling is completely down. Thanks for asking.

Me: Now I want some cheese.

Kendra: I always want cheese.

Me: I'm at the cafeteria. Split a pizza?

Kendra: God, don't eat there. If you want pizza, you should get it from Salvadori's.

Me: Never been.

Kendra: What! It's life changing pizza. You have to try it.

Me: Life changing, huh? Well then, when you put it that way.

Kendra: Try the carnalized onion and brie.

Me: Carnalized? How do you make an onion carnal?

Kendra" You take off the outers skin. HAHA. Autocorrect at its best. Anyway the colors in your world will forever change.

Me: I'll no longer be color blind?

Kendra: You're color blind?

Me: Yup, red/green colorblindness, but it's mild.

I grin, my fingers hovering over my phone as I give myself a mental lecture. I probably should just end this right now. Her head is fine, and spending more time with her isn't conducive for my future. *Put your phone away, dude.*

Me: Salvadori's is just around the corner from you right?

Kendra: Yup.

Me: Great, see you in five...

What the fuck, dude?

4

KENDRA

"Cut it out," I grumble and whack Dane as he holds his hands in front of himself and zombie walks. He looks like a fool, even though everything about him is cute, and I honestly don't need him drawing any more attention to us than he already has. As a hockey player, he already garners a lot of looks.

"I can't help it. The colors are too bright. They're making me dizzy." I roll my eyes. I guess I never should have told him a Salvadori pizza would change the way he saw the world.

As darkness falls over us, we make our way down the sidewalk, and as we approach a streetlight, I step to the side to let a crowd pass. They're all joking and laughing and completely unaware of us. At least I think they are until I hear my name.

"Kendra?"

I turn and find one of Lance's best friends standing there, his gaze going from me to Dane, back to me again. My stomach lurches at the accusatory look on his face, and without even realizing it, I back up, my body bumping Dane's. His hand lands on my side, and electrical sparks dance in my body as he simply holds me in a protective manner.

"Hi James." The crew he's with stop behind him, and go quiet, and I suddenly feel like I'm about to be interrogated.

James hikes his backpack higher on his shoulder. "What are you doing?"

"Oh, I just…" I jerk my thumb over my shoulder. "I'm on my way home." James's gaze drops to take in the pizza box in my hand, and I can almost hear the tumblers falling into place.

"What's up, James?" Dane asks, his warm breath falling over my ear and neck.

"Do I know you?"

"Dane Taylor," he says. "I play for Scotia Storms. Kendra's brother Nate is my captain."

As he glares at Dane, he stands a little straighter, like they're about to get into a pissing contest or something. "I know who Kendra's brother is."

"I was just seeing that Kendra got home safely," Dane responds, his voice an octave deeper, unafraid of the threatening stance James just struck.

My heart hammers at the dig Dane had just gotten in, and I really wish he hadn't said that. It'll come back on me, I'm sure, and nothing good can come from it.

"Yes, just going home," I say again to draw James' attention. I notice the tightening of Dane's hand on my waist, and it nearly takes my breath away.

"See you around," Dane says.

"Yeah, see you around," James responds as he hesitates for a second and pulls his phone from his pocket before turning away from us. I stand still for a second and he and his friends round the corner. I turn to Dane.

"Why did you say that?"

His head dips, his lips close to mine, and he puts his hand back on my side. "Say what?"

"That you were walking me home."

His shoulders rise and fall again. "It's the truth, isn't it?"

"Yeah, but you can't tell me there's a part of you that wanted to criticize Lance for not walking me home last night."

"Yeah, maybe."

I groan. "Come on." I stomp toward my place, and he keeps pace beside me.

"I'm not trying to cause trouble," he says, a sheepish look on his face when I turn to him.

"Are you sure about that?"

His lips quirk at the corners. "Uh, yeah."

"Dane," I warn.

"Look, you're allowed to have pizza with a friend, aren't you, and that friend is allowed to see you home safely, right?"

"Right," I say, and pull my key from my bag. "As long as Lance sees it that way." I open the door and turn back around. Why does my heart react this way every time I set eyes on him? I catch the strange way he's looking at me, like he has something on his mind. He looks over my shoulder and that's when I realize what he's thinking. Last time I invited him inside, it was because I wanted him in my bed.

He steps an inch closer, hovering over me in the doorway. I take a deep breath to pull myself together. I hold the box out. "Are you sure you don't want the leftovers?"

"I'm sure." He reaches out and puts his thumb on the side of my mouth. "You have a little bit of brie on your face."

Oh God, now my brain is exploding with so many visuals. "I... uh...wait here and I'll get your sweater. I washed it this morning."

"Keep it," he says. "It looked better on you than me anyway."

I hesitate. I probably shouldn't keep it, not that anyone will know it's Dane's, and I had a really hard time peeling it from my body this morning and washing it. I really liked breathing in his scent.

"No, I—"

"It was getting too small for me anyway." He jokingly flexes his bicep. "Been working out."

I take in his impressive bicep and resist the urge to touch it. "If you're sure."

He drops his arm and shrugs. "I'm sure."

My phone pings and I don't make a move to get it. Instead, we both stand close at the door, too close for a girl who has a boyfriend, and a guy with a reputation—a guy I was intimate with nine months ago, and suddenly can't stop thinking about again.

Lies.

Yes, it is a lie. I haven't stopped thinking about Dane since the first night I met him. My brother warned me to stay away from him, and it was the only time in my life I went against his wishes. I have no idea why I'm so drawn to Dane. I only know that I am, and right now as we stand close, I'm finding it harder and harder to breathe.

"You going to get that?" he asks and points toward my belt bag, his hand brushing against my hip.

His words and touch pull me back. "Yeah, I should." I smile at him. "Thanks for the pizza and walking me home."

"And the riveting conversation." He leans into me. "Don't forget the riveting conversation, Kens."

I laugh at that. "How could I forget that? It's not every day a girl learns all about cheese making." I poke him jokingly. "You're secretly a cheese maker, and—"

"I believe you mean fromager," he interrupts.

"Right, fromager, if we were French and I was going to say, your talent is being wasted on the ice." I playfully angle my head. "Are you sure you want to be a hockey player?"

His smile instantly dissolves, and he stands to his full height, towering over me. "I should probably get going, and whoever is texting really wants to talk to you."

He's right, my phone hasn't stopped. Although I'm pretty sure it was something I said that ripped the smile from his face. "Night," he says and turns and heads down the sidewalk.

I tug my phone from my bag and my stomach tightens as I read the message from Lance, asking me to stop over. For the briefest, craziest of seconds, I almost call Dane back and ask him to walk me. That would be insane, for sure.

I have an assignment to finish tonight, and I really need to work on it. Lance probably needs help studying and I resign myself to the fact that his test is this weekend and once it's done, he'll go back to being less demanding and stressed. I realize he has a lot to live up to.

I hurry to the kitchen and shove the leftover pizza into the fridge. I turn at the sound of footsteps on the floor behind me. "Hey," I say as my roommate Josie shuffles into the kitchen in her big bunny slippers with the floppy ears. I gave them to her last Christmas because she always has cold feet. I smile at the state of her hair, which is a complete mess. She always runs her hands through it when she's studying. "Left over pizza from Salvadori's. Help yourself."

Her eyes go wide. "You went without me?"

"Yeah, but I brought you some back." She shuffles to the fridge. "It was a last-minute date."

"You were with Lance?" She pulls out the box, and sets it on the table. Her gaze lifts to mine. "I heard a male voice, but it didn't sound like Lance." She picks up a slice and her eyes briefly close as she inhales and brings it to her mouth.

"That's because it wasn't Lance." Josie and I have been best friends since our freshman year. We totally hit it off in nursing school and I'm not about to lie to her.

Her lids fly open and with the pizza inches from her mouth she asks, "Oh. Who was it? The voice kind of sounded familiar."

It should. She was here the morning after I had sex with Dane and the two hit it off. He even brought a breakfast sandwich for her, and while Josie is usually shy around guys, she was completely comfortable with Dane. I think he's just easy to be around. Maybe that's what I like about him. Yeah, sure, he's reckless and wild, but there is just something warm, easy and approachable about him too, "It was Dane Taylor, actually."

Shock and almost...happiness spill from her eyes to her mouth. I'm pretty sure she never liked Lance, not the way she likes Dane. "You were on a date with Dane?"

I swallow. "No, no. I have no idea why I said date. I just shared a pizza with him and he walked me home." A worried look comes over her face and I try to inject lightness into my smile. The truth is, I had no plans to see Lance tonight, and I can't help but worry James said he saw me with Dane. However, like Dane said, I'm allowed to have friends. "I'm on my way to see Lance right now."

She nods and bites into her pizza. "I'm actually going to the library to do some work. Give me a second and I'll walk with you."

Why do I get the sense that she's only going to the library so I'm not out walking alone? "Sounds good." She darts upstairs with her pizza and I put the rest back into the fridge and check my face in the mirror. I debate on bringing my books. If Lance needs help, I won't get any of my work done and will likely be up all night studying for my statistics test. Did I mention I wasn't great at math?

Josie comes back with her hair in a ponytail and her backpack over her shoulder. We head to the door and at the last second, I grab my backpack and lock up. "Are you ready for our stats test tomorrow?"

"Almost," I fib. "I'll probably do some more studying tonight."

The night air is cool, and our breath turns to fog in front of our faces as we walk. "How did you run into Dane?"

I tell her all about him running me over and note the strange look on her face. "What?"

"Are you okay?"

I nod and she nibbles her bottom lip and asks, "Have you uh...seen his friend Jesse around?"

I steal a quick glance at Josie. Ohmigod, does she like Jesse? Is that what the strange look was all about? She's never shown interest in any guy on campus before. I actually had to talk her into going skating with us last Christmas. When she's not in class, she's home, or at the library studying. She tears her gaze away and fusses with her zipper.

"I'm not sure. I could ask."

"No, don't do that." She shakes her head fast. "Jesse wouldn't be interested in me anyway." She snorts out a laugh. "I'm hardly a puck bunny, and did you hear he was drafted?"

No, I hadn't heard because I don't really follow hockey. Josie goes to the games this year, and now I know why. Maybe I'll have to go with her. She's always asking me to. Although that could raise my brother's suspicions. "I'm hardly one either," I say and she grins at me.

"Yeah, I know all about you and Dane. We share a bedroom wall remember?"

Embarrassment floods me. "Sorry about that."

She laughs. "Don't be. I was happy one of us was ringing in the new year with a bang."

"Ohmigod, Josie." I put my hands over my face, ready to die from embarrassment.

She tugs them away from my face as we approach the library. "You know, you and Dane. You guys were cute together."

My stomach squeezes tight. "I'm with Lance now. You know my brother—"

"Maybe your brother should let you make your own decisions." I glance at the dark pavement beneath my boots. "Hey," she says quietly, touching my arm to bring my attention back around to her. "I'm sorry. It's not my business."

"It's okay. He just cares about me."

"I know and I love that. I just..." I stare at her as she stares back, like she's trying to find the right words. "I want you happy, Kendra."

"I'm...happy," I say and work to inject a bit of enthusiasm into my voice.

She stares at me for a second longer, and gives my arm a squeeze. "Okay. I'd better go study."

"Same."

She takes off and I walk a few more blocks until I reach Lance's house. I'm about to knock when the door flies open and he's standing there staring at me like a bull about to enter the ring. My heart drops into my stomach, and my throat squeezes tight.

"You're fucking around with some asshole named Dane?"

"What, no," I counter quickly. "Dane is on Nate's team, and I ran into him the other night when I left your place. We're friends from way back." Not really way back, but still.

He leans into me, his face twisted, like I insulted him and his family name by hanging out with any man other than him. "You were having pizza with him tonight."

A measure of anger grips me, and I straighten a little, which seems to throw him off guard. "We're friends, Lance. I'm allowed to have friends."

"Yeah, so am I. Which is why I invited Jess over to help me study tonight." He widens the door a bit, and I spot Jessica at the kitchen table at the end of the hall. He dated her before me, and her presence is like a slap in the face.

"Why did you ask me to come over, then?"

"To tell you we're over."

I stand there on shaky legs, unable to tell if those five words are making me happy or sad. I think I'm going to go with the former. I fold my arms around my body, my stomach suddenly cramping. Nate isn't going to be happy about any of this.

Lance smirks. "Does your brother know you're fucking one of his hockey players?"

"I'm not...he's a friend," I say again. "That's all."

He leans against the doorjamb, as I stand in the cold. "You know I only went out with you as a favor to your brother. Now he'll owe me one. Tit for tat, you know how that works."

My heart crashes against my ribs as I struggle to make sense of what he's saying. As my brains sorts things out, I glare at him. What the hell did I ever see in him? He's a complete asshole and is no doubt going to make a great addition to his family's firm.

He leans in and whispers. "I was only keeping you around to help me study and to fuck when I needed release. But you weren't even a good lay, Kendra."

I stumble backward and almost fall of the steps, as he closes the door in my face. What the hell just happened?

Kendra is on my mind as I pedal hard and cruise around campus, wanting to clear my head with a bit of fresh air before I go back to my room to study.

Are you really clearing your head, Dane?

Yes, and no. I can't deny there is a part of me hoping to run into Kendra, even though I'd walked her home a little over a half hour ago. I cruise by her place, and it's dark. A wave of disappointment hits. Her phone was pinging and if she's not home, it must mean she's with douche bag. I don't know where he lives, but I do know the direction. I turn around, and spot movement on the sidewalk, a small figure coming around the corner.

My heart leaps, recognizing Kendra's stance and walk. Wait, no, maybe it's not her. This person is bent forward to much, and as she passes by the streetlight, I can almost see her body shaking. I slow and let my feet scrape pavement and the second her head lifts, and her eyes lock with mine, my protective instincts flare to life.

"Kendra," I call and hop off my bike. I take three big steps, moving in front of her and blocking her path. With her body shaking, I put my hands on her shoulders and without words, drag her to me. She doesn't look like she's in any shape to talk and if she wants to tell me what's wrong, she can, if she doesn't, that's totally fine too. Okay, not really.

She leans into me, and her chest is rising and falling quickly. After a long moment, a shiver goes through her, and I put my mouth near her ear. "You should probably get inside."

"Okay," she agrees quietly.

I take her backpack and shoulder it, and guide her to her door. She unlocks it, and I drop her bag inside and stand back on the stoop, waiting until she locks up behind me. She turns, her gaze moving over my face, and when she reaches for me, I take her hand and follow her inside.

"Kens," I murmur, my arms going around her body as my insides soften, wanting and willing to do just about anything to take away the hurt in her eyes.

"I don't want to be alone," she whispers into my neck, her breath hot on my skin.

"I'm here. You're not alone."

What the fuck happened after I left her earlier?

She kicks off her boots and I do the same. Hurried hands go to my jacket and she unzips it and pushes it off my shoulders. She glances at my body as I stand before her, practically trembling with want. She reaches out, and moans as she puts her hand on my stomach. She steps closer. "Stay with me tonight," she murmurs so quietly, I'm not even sure I'm hearing her right.

"Kens?" Her head lifts, and her eyes go wide, like she's remembering something, as they lock on mine. Ah, there it is, common sense. She has a boyfriend, and we shouldn't be doing this.

"Your bike, go get your bike." I hesitate for a second, and take in the panic in her eyes.

"Okay." I dart outside, grab my bike and she backs up as I carry it inside. The second I close the door and set the bike down, she reaches behind me, turns the lock, and takes my hand. I follow her up the steps and into her bedroom. Not much had changed since I'd been here before. She unzips her coat and sets it on her chair, and the lost, vulnerable expression on her face slices into my gut like a sharp blade.

I walk up to her, put my arm around her waist and pull her to me. She lifts her head, her mouth poised. "Kens, what are we doing?"

"I...I just need..."

"You need me?"

She nods, and breathes heavily. "It's over between Lance and me."

My mind races and I back up an inch. "I want you, Kendra. I really do, but it's too soon. I don't want you regretting this come morning, and I think tonight you need a friend."

She steps into me, and puts her arms around my body. "Okay." She sniffs and her blue eyes lift to meet mine. "He was cruel."

My body tightens. "Did he hurt you?" I'm two seconds from storming out of her place and hunting him down.

"He told me he was only with me to do my brother a favor."

"Fucker."

"He was with his ex-girlfriend."

I knew that asshole was cheating on Kendra. I shake my head. "You're better off without him."

"He said I wasn't a good…" She chokes like she can't bring herself to voice Lance's words. The fucker really hurt her and no way am I going to allow that.

"Hey," I say and hug her tighter. "Nothing he says matters." I smooth her hair back. "I guess his friend told him he saw us together."

She stiffens. "Do you think he'll come after you?"

"I hope so," I say. I'd love five minutes with him in a back alleyway. "He's not likely going to do anything to mess up his reputation." A guy like Lance would probably send one of his asshole friends after me.

"My brother—"

"Let's not worry about your brother tonight. You can't be with a guy just because your brother wants you to be with him."

"I know," she whispers. "He doesn't want me with you or any of the guys on the team."

"What he doesn't know can't hurt him," I tell her.

"He could make your life with the team a nightmare." A hard quiver goes through her. "I know the NHL is important to all you guys and we can't let anything get in the way of that."

"Don't worry about me." I cup her cheeks and let my gaze race over her face. "Come on." I back her up until she's on the edge of the bed, a bed I once slept with her in. I can't go there tonight. As much as I want to, I can't. I pull the blankets down. "Slide in."

She swallows hard. "Dane."

"Yeah."

"If I didn't just have a bad break up, would you..." She runs her hand over the fitted sheet and need moves into her eyes. It also moves into my dick, but fuck how can I take her when she's lost and vulnerable. "...you know, like before at Christmas break."

Sadness and something that resembles humiliation settles on her face, and her shoulders curl inward, like her confidence is draining, as she looks back at me. My heart lurches. What the fuck did Lance say or do to her?

"Yes," I answer honestly, and without hesitation, wanting her to know I desire her and that's not what's holding me back from taking her and showing her she has worth.

"Did you...ugh." She covers her face and I drop to my knees, and pull her hands away. My heart is pounding so hard now, I'm almost dizzy.

"Did I what?" I ask, and put her hands on her knees, keeping mine on top of them.

She glances at our hands. Dammit, why is she having such a hard time making eye contact? "Did you think I was bad in bed?"

Motherfucker.

I cup her face and force her gaze on mine, wanting her to know I'm being very serious. "Kens, he's a cruel bastard, and for some reason wanted to hurt you," I tell her. "This is about him, not you."

She swallows. "That's not really an answer."

I shake my head, take her hand and put it over my semi-hard cock. "Would I have this, if I didn't want to sleep with you again? That night with you, Kens..." I briefly close my eyes, my heart thundering in my ears as memories bombard me. I've slept with a lot of women, but Jesus, she was the sweetest, the softest, the easiest to be with. To this day, I still crave her taste. I can't understand it, I only know it was easy to lose myself in her and hard to walk away in the morning. "I haven't stopped thinking about it in nine months."

A smile toys with her lips, a small ray of light back in her gorgeous blue eyes. "Yeah?"

"Yeah," I say, and she doesn't take her hand away from my cock. Instead, she lightly massages it.

"Are you trying to make me harder?" I grumble and instead of shoving her hand away, I push against it. Fuck me, that feels good.

She blinks dark lashes over innocent eyes, and I'm not so sure at this moment she's all that innocent. "I just wanted to touch you. To remember...to feel...something other than numb."

"Fuck, Kens, I want to touch you too." Christ, I want her to *feel,* and why the hell has she been feeling numb?

She pulls her hand away, her mood shifting, becoming darker, somber. "You don't have to."

What the fuck? Did she not believe a word I said about wanting her. Was my hard dick not enough to convince her? I'll be damned if I let her go to sleep and leave here with her thinking she's not every man's dream girl, because she is.

I have no idea what kind of mental mind fuck game Lance is playing with her, making her feel like she's less than perfect. I'm just glad they're not together, and I really fucking hope her brother doesn't encourage her to go back to Lance the douche. Maybe tonight though, maybe if I show her she's everything, she'll never go back to the douche.

"Hey," I say, and she turns back to me. The second she does, I put my hands on her hips, lean into her and a moan. That moan has been sitting at the back of my throat since I first set eyes on her again. It cuts through the quiet in the room as I take her mouth with mine.

"Dane," she protests, her hands on my shoulders. "You don't—"

"I want this, Kens. I want you. I want you so fucking bad, I can't even think straight, and when I first came into this bedroom with you, saw your bed and planned to tuck you in, I was already making plans to jack off fifty fucking times when I got back to Storm House."

Her soft chuckle curls around me, and my heart soars at the sound. "That's an awful lot of times."

"Still wouldn't have been enough." I run my fingers under the hem of her sweater, and groan as my fingers connect with the soft skin on her stomach.

A quiver goes through her. "Your poor hands, wouldn't fifty times make your palms raw?"

"Yup, raw," I tell her.

"How would you even hold a hockey stick tomorrow?"

"Don't know. Don't care."

She lifts her arms and I peel her sweater over her head. I lean back on my heels and almost fucking weep at the gorgeous sight before me. Puckered pink nipples press hard against her white lace bra and I lean in and lick her through the material.

She moans and moves her hips, and I can't wait to bury my face between her sweet legs. "I'd never want to do anything to come between you and hockey, so I have an idea."

"Oh yeah?" I ask and snake my hand around her back and unhook her bra. I slide it off her shoulders and toss it away. "Lavender," I say as I lean in and kiss her neck, breathing in the scent of her skin. "Fucking lavender." I lick her delicate skin and her hips lift as I tug on her yoga pants, dragging them down her legs. I leave her matching white lace underwear on. There are things I might want to do with them.

She puts her hand inside my pants, and my thick dick spills out of her small palm as she rubs. "Fuck yeah." Blood leaves my brain in a whoosh as she tugs on my cock, my pants giving her very little room for movement.

I inch back and open the button and slide my zipper down to give her all the access she could want. "Wait, what's your idea?"

Her grin is full of mischief. "You worry about holding your hockey stick tomorrow," she murmurs, and slides off the bed, mimicking my position by going back on her knees on the floor in front of me. She rubs me from base to crown, and I groan as hot pre-cum fills her palm. "I'll worry about this stick tonight."

She repositions, settling her backside on her heels, leaning forward to take my cock into her mouth. She moans in delight as she laps at my pre-cum. "Sweet Jesus," I grunt, as I glance down to watch my cock disappear between her lush stretched lips. I try not to rock into her, not wanting to choke her. Everything in the way she's sucking me makes it damn near impossible to stay still. I want to push...I want to fuck.

I grip her hair with one hand as I ever so slowly rock into her hot mouth. I'm so fucking close, it's all I can do not to shoot a load down her throat. She cups my balls, and I pant and grip the bed with my other hand, fisting the bedding and mentally doing math to keep my shit together. I'm a grown-ass man with control, not a pubescent youth getting his dick sucked for the first time.

I concentrate and manage to get a small grip on my arousal, and I'm ready to congratulate myself until Kendra changes position and puts my cock between her breasts. What the fuck is this woman trying to do to me? She squeezes me tight and as I move forward, she licks my crown with her hot, wet tongue. A guttural, animalistic sound escapes my throat and vibrates around us. Okay, no man in his right mind—or wrong mind—can take this kind of torture for any length of time.

I inch back, reluctantly sliding my cock from her gorgeous tits, and her eyes are full of lust and bewilderment as I groan and clench down on my jaw. She opens her mouth, like she's about to question me, but all confusion turns to a deep, excited moan as I swiftly pick her up, set her on the bed, and bury my face between her legs.

Now this, right here, is what I've been craving for nine long months...

KENDRA

My God, how can that feel so good?

"Dane," I murmur and fall back on the bed, taking my breasts into my hands as he pulls my panties to the side and pleasures me with the soft blade of his tongue. He eats and laps and licks me, and moans like I'm the best thing he's ever tasted. Lance never much liked doing that—not that I want to think about him or compare the two men—but when he did find himself between my legs, it was quick and rough and not at all pleasurable.

Probably because he didn't care about your pleasure, Kendra.

Yeah, maybe if he had, I'd be more into sex with him, and it would have been less about the physical act and more about wanting to make each other feel good. I can't put this all on him, though. I think there was a part of me that knew we weren't right for one another, and I was numbly going through the motions, much like I've been going through the motions my entire life—well, after the incident anyway—and that's why the sex sucked.

Speaking of sucking.

I go up on my elbows as Dane grips the band on my panties and tugs up on them until the lace disappears in the crease of my pussy, my nether lips hugging the material as it forms a rope and presses hard against my clit. He moves it back and forth, the stretched cord caressing my aching bud, as pleasure grips my core. I lift my hips, craving more...craving every trick he has up his sleeve.

"Like that?" he asks and runs the rough pad of his index finger over my wet lips, teasing my pussy with each delicious stroke. He bends and lightly runs his tongue over my lips and groans with want as he breathes in my arousal.

I toss my head to the side and reach above me, gripping the bedding, needing something to hold on to as I begin to quake. A second later, he slowly peels my soaking panties from my body and discards them. He bends and takes my clit into his mouth and sucks hard, until it's so engorged and throbbing and stimulated that I can't think straight. There's only one thing I know. My body is going to break.

Am I really going to orgasm? Holy, the man has barely touched me, and I'm hovering on the brink and for some strange reason my hormones have been firing on all cylinders these last couple of days. I assume it's because of my crazy attraction to this man. He glances up at me and when he sees the way I'm panting, a smile lights up his eyes. He loves burying his face between my legs. Maybe almost as much as I love him doing it.

I sit up, and put one hand around his head and his chuckle reverberates through me as I shamelessly grind against him. I'm sure this is a one-night thing and I plan to enjoy every-thing. I'm not going to worry about how I sound or look. I don't think he's the kind of guy to make me feel silly for moaning, or grinding, or taking what I want and giving just as freely—all the things I never did with Lance. Just once I want to break out of this shell, and…feel.

"Feel good, babe?" he asks from between my legs, and I rock against his mouth as he slides a thick, callused finger inside me. My nerve endings jump to life, my sex wrapping around his thickness and holding him tight.

"God, yes, Dane. I love the way you touch me."

He slides his finger in and out of me. Slowly, methodically, taking his time to curl around the hot bundle of nerves inside me. I've only been with this man once, but that's all it took for him to understand my needs.

I pinch my nipples and the pleasure/pain response zings through my body and settles deep in my core. The delicious trifecta: his mouth on my clit, his finger inside me and my hands on my breasts, toying with my nipples, is all it takes to nudge me over the edge. I cry out as my orgasm hits like a nuclear blast, pleasure bursting through me. I take fast breaths, struggling to fill my lungs as I spill into his mouth, my hot cum dripping down his chin and my thighs, bringing on a quiver as it tickles my flesh.

He grunts from deep between my legs, his tongue licking and swirling as his finger slows inside me, carefully bringing me down from my high. I fall back onto the bed, gasping like I'd just run a marathon, and while he once joked about seeing color after eating a Salvadori pizza, I'm not joking when I say the world looks different when I'm with Dane, especially after a mind-blowing orgasm. Honestly, ever since my child-hood—the incident—I've been closed off, walking blindly through life. Until Dane. I wouldn't say I was a believer in fate, yet I can't understand what it is about him that fills my life with color.

He lifts his head, a grin on his face, and I crook my finger. He slides up my body, and I moan as his weight presses me into the mattress. His strong heart pounds against my chest, and I revel in his size and power. I'm just glad Josie is out at the library—and I don't even want to think about studying at the moment—because I have a feeling things are about to get wild up in here.

He zeroes in on my mouth, a new kind of intensity about him as he brushes it with his finger and I taste myself on his finger. I shift on the bed and he moves over top of me, his hard cock pressing into my stomach, and my sex quivers in heated anticipation.

I spread my legs and shimmy, wanting him inside me, and making no qualms about it. He groans as he kisses me, hard, like he can't get enough of my mouth. His tongue tastes of my essence, and while I sense he's trying to slow down, I do love the urgency in him. I writhe beneath his rock-hard body, letting him know I'm ready for him to fuck me.

"Condom," he murmurs and rolls to his side. With his pants still around his waist, he pulls a condom from his pocket, sets it on the bed, and tears his pants and boxers off. They land on the floor with a thud.

"Shirt," I remind him, and he grins at me as he peels it over his head, and I take that moment to admire his hard grooves. The man is athletic perfection. On his knees, he moves closer, and I widen my legs and put my hands on his chest, taking my time to touch him. His head falls back and he groans with pleasure. It fills me with a new kind of confidence.

I take the condom from him and eyes brimming with questions jerk to mine. "Kens?"

He must think I'm having second thoughts. "Let me," I say and rip into the foil. He makes a sound, a grunt of sorts, and his face hardens, like me sheathing him with a condom, might destroy any kind of strength or control he has left in him. I like the way I can reduce this man to a quivering mess.

I press the condom to his crown and as I roll it on, he thickens even more and I'm not even sure he's breathing. His gaze holds mine as I fall back onto the bed, opening my body to him.

He falls over me, puts one hand on my cheek and lightly brushes my flesh. I'm pretty sure I've never felt this close, this kind of intimacy with any man before. With every sweep of his finger across my cheek, well, he might as well be caressing my heart.

Careful, Kendra.

"Hey, you okay?" he asks and lightly kisses my mouth.

"I am."

"You still want this?"

I smile, loving the way he's checking in with me. "If you do."

He laughs and presses his cock against my legs. "That would be a big fat yes."

I laugh with him, loving the lightness between us. "I do want it, Dane. I want you inside me."

"Good, because that's where I want to be." He moves his hips until his crown is at my opening, and he puts one hand on my hips for leverage as he slowly slides in. I moan, my eyes rolling back in my head as I take pleasure in each glorious inch, and the man has lots of glorious inches. I remember that from last time.

He slides in deeper, and my muscles ripple as he continues to fill me. Once he's all the way in, he goes perfectly still and does another check in. "Is this what you wanted?" I love the harshness in his voice, the way it's taking effort for him to talk.

"Yes and no."

He frowns. "Tell me what you want, babe?"

Warmth flutters through me. My God, when was the last time any man ever asked what I wanted?

"I want you inside me yes. But not like this." The lines in his forehead deepen, as he brushes my hair back. I give him a teasing grin. "I want you moving," I say and lift my hips to set him in motion. He laughs, his muscles softening as the tension drains from his body. Well, that's not entirely true. One muscle isn't soft. In fact, it's rock hard inside me.

"Christ, you just want it all, don't you?"

"Yeah, I do." Which is the reason I'm being so honest and open. If I only have one night with him, I plan to make the best of it. Asking for what I want, or even thinking I deserve it is so not in my nature. It's different with Dane, and I'm not sure why, nor am I going to overthink that tonight. Nope, tonight is for feeling, something I haven't done in a very long time.

"Fine then," he says and rolls his eyes playfully. He pulls his hard cock almost all of the way out and our moans mingle as he slides back in, his girth stretching me as his crown hits my cervix and sends a fierce, concentrated quiver through my body.

"Dane..." I murmur, nearly delirious as white-hot pleasure grips every inch of me.

"Yeah, I know," he groans, and I sense he feels the intensity every bit as much as I do.

I put my hands around his back and hold him to me, and his firm muscles brush and stimulate my sensitive nipples. I love the way his body quivers beneath my touch, and the way his back muscles tighten and loosen as he powers in and out.

As my pleasure peaks, I wrap my legs around his waist and squeeze. He buries his face in my neck, his breath is hot on my flesh as he grunts. I rake my hands through his hair, and his head lifts, his eyes on mine as my second orgasm takes hold. He groans as my muscles lightly ripple and he shifts position, putting a finger between our bodies to caress my clit. I clench hard around his cock, and curl into him.

"Fuck yeah," he moans, and holds my shoulders with one hand, the other still between my legs as he changes the pace and the rhythm. He pumps into me, rough and raw. This is for him now, and I love how he takes every bit as much as he gives. He rides me hard and fast, an animal in the wild. His guttural sounds are fierce, almost savage, and I love the way he lets go with me.

He could let go like this with every girl. I'm not going to think about that or let it bother me. Right now, I want to concentrate on the pleasure and pretend only the two of us exist.

"Kens..."

His cock thickens inside of me as he drives in deep and goes still. His head lifts, his eyes on mine, a tortured look on his face as he takes gulping breaths, like he wants to keep fucking but has lost complete control over his body.

I squeeze my muscles and he groans. I brush his damp hair from his face. "Let me feel you."

His body lets go and he pulses and throbs inside me, and I love the hot warmth it sends to every inch of my quivering body. He stays inside me, his body relaxing on top of mine as he comes down from his high. I lightly rub his back, and revel in my post-orgasmic bliss.

A door downstairs opens, and we both go completely still. "Tell me your brother doesn't have a key," Dane whispers.

My stomach cramps as he inches up, his cock still inside of me. "He does," I croak out. "But he has no reason to use it."

He shakes his head. "Why does he have a fucking key?" he asks, although it's more of a statement than a question and I get it. People don't understand the relationship I have with my brother. Dane rolls off me, and emptiness invades my soul as he pulls his cock free. Downstairs the fridge opens and closes. He runs agitated fingers through his hair, fingers that had just been inside of me. "Shit, my bike is downstairs. If he catches me—"

"It's not Nate. It's Josie," I assure him quickly, and he relaxes slightly. "She went straight for the fridge like she always does. My brother wouldn't go straight to the fridge."

There's a new kind of coolness in the room as Dane sits on the side of the bed, removes the condom and wraps it in tissue.

"My garbage can is beside the nightstand," I tell him, noting the stiffness in his body. I guess he's kind of right. Nate probably shouldn't have a key to my place, able to check in on me unannounced, whenever he wants. When he finds out Lance and I are over, he'll probably come by to find out what happened. Since he hand-picked him for me, he's not going to be pleased.

"Should I go?" he asks, his back still to me. I shift closer and his muscles bunch as I put my palm on his back. As tension radiates from him, I pull my hand away quickly and he turns to me, his brow furrowed.

"You don't have to go," I tell him quietly and follow it up with, "I don't want you to go."

"I don't want to get you in trouble with your brother."

I fall back onto the bed, as old painful memories flare inside me. I'm not sure why I'm so emotional lately. Maybe it's the breakup...maybe it's seeing Dane again, and having him inside me. I really like this guy, but my brother, well he won't stand for it. I have to listen to him. I just have to. Heck, if I'd only listened to him years ago, our lives would have turned out much differently.

"I don't want you getting in trouble either," I tell Dane. "If you don't get into the NHL because of me, I'd never forgive myself." I put my arm over my eyes and fight back tears.

The next thing I know, Dane is beside me, gathering me into his arms. "I know it's not my business, but it seems like Nate has a lot of control over you."

"He does and it's a good thing." I take a breath, not sure I can let my mind go down that painful road again. Nothing could help Nate and I get back what we've lost—because of me—

and while years of therapy have helped, there's a part of me that lets my brother make decisions because I'm afraid. Bad choices have consequences. I know that firsthand. "You wouldn't understand."

"Try me."

I inch back, and work to quiet my unsteady heartbeat as eyes full of warmth and concern meet mine. "I don't..." My stomach squeezes tight as I think about dredging up the past.

Dane touches my face, and his palm warm and comforting. "It's okay. You don't have to. If you want to just sleep, you can." He pulls the blankets up. "I can stay until you're asleep. Then I'll sneak out."

Don't go.

Those two words barrel through my head like an explosion, and I reach for him, needing his comfort. It's true, I've been numb for many years, and I guess if this man is making me feel things again, not all of those feelings are going to be plea- surable.

I turn to my side, and go up on my elbow, holding my head in my palm. Dane does the same, and he shifts closer, creating a new kind of intimacy, I take a deep breath, and let the tension go from my body.

"Nate and I lost Mom and Dad when I was five and he was eight."

Dane frowns, and puts his hand on my hip, giving it a squeeze. "I'm sorry, Kendra. I didn't know that."

"No, we don't talk about it. We—" Pain swamps me, and squeezes my heart so hard, I choke on my words. "We..." I try again.

"Hey, it's okay." His hand slides up my body, and he curls a strand of hair around his finger. "Take your time and if this is too hard, we don't have to talk."

I nod, and move closer until our bodies are touching, and I'm not sure why, but I want to tell him everything I've kept close to my heart for the past fifteen years. "It was my fault," I confess, my voice low and sad. "I'm the reason they're dead."

● **7**
___

DANE
___

"**K**endra," I console quietly, as my heart lurches, wanting to take away the pain expanding in her eyes, the small quakes in her delicate body. If she was only a child, how could the death of her parents be her fault? Nothing about this is right, but that doesn't mean she's not carrying the weight of their deaths on her shoulders. She's clearly shouldering a heavy load, and her childhood trauma obviously has something to do with her brother running her life. "You were a child," is all I say, and then go quiet to give her the opportunity to continue.

"Exactly." She snorts out a laugh that holds pain, not humor. "I was a stupid child, acting like an adult and...there were consequences."

"You weren't stupid." I have no idea what she did. All I know is five-year-old kids make mistakes, that's how they learn and grow, and she can't be held accountable for the death of her parents. Hasn't anyone ever told her this?

Tears begin to spill, and I don't catch them. I want them to fall, and hope they somehow wash away her pain. Her eyes lift to mine, and she examines my face. What does she expect to see in my eyes. Pity? Judgement?

Fuck that. She doesn't want or need pity or judgment from me or anyone else and she's definitely not going to find it on my face. I put my arms around her and hold her close, offering her warmth and comfort. "What happened?" I finally ask as she remains silent, her past demons still haunting her.

"Mom and Dad were both nurses," she begins. Her lids fall heavily, and she stares at my chest. She zeroes in on an old scar and circles it with her finger. "They used to try to work opposite shifts, so one was always home with us after school and in the evening."

"My parents worked strange hours too," I say. "It's always a challenge. Fortunately for us, the shop where they make and sell cheese is beside our house."

She nods. "When they couldn't get a sitter, Nate would watch me."

I inch back. "Didn't you say you were five and Nate was eight when you lost them?" She nods and I choose my next words carefully. I don't want to criticize her mother and father's parenting methods by any means, but... "An eight-year-old can't, or at least shouldn't, be responsible for a five-year-old."

"It was fine. Nate was very responsible, it was me..."

Her throat gurgles as she swallows, and her body shakes. "Kens," I whisper softly and press a kiss to her forehead. "You were a child."

"Mom and Dad had the same night shift. Sometimes our maternal grandmother would watch us. She never liked to.

She never got along with Mom all that well, and Mom only asked her as a last resort. Dad's parents lived in British Columbia." A deep breath, and I add, "Anyway, my grandmother couldn't watch us, or wouldn't, I don't know, and Nate and I stayed home alone." My eyes widen. "It was fine. We locked up, and went to bed." I nod, not sure where she's going with this story or how the death of her parents was in any way her fault.

"Did they fall asleep at the wheel on the way home?"

She swallows and shakes her head. "Nope, they were both home from their nightshift and were in bed when we got up. It was a Saturday, and I watched cartoons and Nate played video games."

"Saturday cartoons were the best."

A small smile touches her mouth, only to disappear quickly. "I started getting hungry," she whispers. "I asked Nate to make me some noodles." She steals another glance at me. I nod, encouraging her to continue. "When he played video games, he could lose himself for hours, and I really wanted noodles. I kept asking him and he kept saying he needed a minute. I told him I could do it, and he said no, he would, he just had one more level to beat."

My heart jumps and a cold sweat breaks out on my forehead as my blood chills—because I'm pretty fucking sure I know where this is going.

"I figured..."

I run my hand up and down her arm as her body shakes. Even though my insides are a tangled mess, I try to keep my voice calm as I finish her sentence. "You figured you could make it."

She nods. "I'd watched Mom and Dad and Nate do it a million times. I figured I could do it." She shakes her head. "I used to be pretty independent back then."

Now she's not independent at all. She's terrified of the world, of making the wrong decisions and living with the consequences. The puzzle known as Kendra Jaynes and the relationship she has with her brother begins to take shape inside my brain.

"Was there a fire?"

She sniffs as tears spill faster. "I forgot to turn the burner off, and I left the pot on the burner, and it caught fire, then the curtains. There was so much smoke. I was actually in the back yard...playing," she chokes out. "Nate could have died too."

"But he didn't, and it was an accident, Kens. You know that, right? This isn't on you."

Her hair sticks to her wet face as she gives a hard shake of her head. "I should have listened to Nate. I should have waited. He was older, and knew better." Her eyes search my face again. "I didn't listen to him, Dane."

"Oh, Kens." I pull her hard against me and hold her tight to smooth the goosebumps breaking out on her skin. "You were a child, so was Nate, and it's not that he knew best...an eight-year-old can't be responsible for himself, let alone his five-year-old sister."

I get that life is hard and scheduling work around family is even harder, but in this situation, the parents failed the kids, not the other way around. It wasn't even legal to leave children that age alone. Technically at that point, with her parents sleeping, they weren't alone in the home, but they certainly weren't being supervised. I can't say any of this to her, though. It's not what she needs to hear from me right now and I can only imagine how much guilt Nate carries around with him, as well. It has to be why he tries to keep his sister in a bubble, and it's not healthy for either of them.

"What happened after that?" A million questions race through my mind.

"My grandmother took us in, reluctantly. I was terrified we were going to be split up. I heard the social workers talking about it. My grandmother...I don't think she liked kids. I kept quiet, though. I didn't want to lose my brother. He was all I had. He took care of me, Dane."

My heart aches so much it hurts my throat, and it's all I can do not to sob for the little girl who still carries so much pain in her heart. A hard quiver goes through her, and I hold her as she softly cries. I rub her back as her tears soak my chest. After a long while, just when I think she'd fallen asleep, she whispers, "Tell me, what it was like growing up in the country? What were your parents like? Did you and your brother get along?"

A wave of unease moves through me. She just opened her heart and told me all about her horrific childhood and the fact that I'm upset, having to grow up in my older brother's shadow, seems so trivial now. Maybe I'm just shallow, wanting my world to revolve around me and not my brother.

"Did you always want to be in the NHL?"

"That's a lot of questions." She inches back and smiles at me as she rests her head on her pillow.

"Sorry. I'm just curious."

"Don't be sorry." I push her hair back. "Bass River was fine. I had a lot of friends, and we did a lot of biking down old country roads. We had a lot of freedom." Unlike after Kendra's tragedy, my every move wasn't scrutinized.

"You probably got into a lot of trouble," she jokes, and my heart lightens at the small smile on her face.

"Me, no way. I was an angel." I blink rapidly, and she laughs, in no way believing me. She's smart like that.

"Yeah, sure."

Okay, it's possible I acted out for attention. I don't want to tell her that. Wow, I really am shallow. "My brother was really good at hockey, and we spent a lot of time at the rink. I was there so I figured…"

She sits up, reaches for a tissue, and wipes her nose. "That's how you got into hockey?"

"Pretty much."

She sniffs, goes quiet, lost in thought for a long time before she asks, "Your friend Jesse, he was drafted?"

What the hell? She follows Jesse? "I thought you didn't follow the team." *Okay, way to sound accusatory, and jealous, dude.*

"Oh, uh…" As she hedges my back stiffens and a wave of jealousy grips my gut. "I don't think I'm supposed to tell…" She leans into me, and gestures with a nod to the door. "I think Josie likes him. She saw him at the Christmas party. I don't think she spoke to him though, and she doesn't think he even knows she exists."

"Sounds like we need to have a double date?"

Her eyes widen. "Ohmigod, are you serious?" Her enthusiasm is followed up with a fast shake of her head. "No, we can't do that. Josie would kill me and Nate…"

"Let say…if Josie and Jesse went on a date, and we were forced to tag along because they both wanted the company," I pause to let that sink in for a moment.

"It would look like we were only in the same room, or wherever, to help them out. We could even pretend we hated each other," she suggests.

"Yeah," I agree, and even though I came up with the idea, I kind of hate it. Sneaking around sucks ass. If I ever want a real relationship with her, though, I have to prove myself worthy and get scouted. His approval is pretty important to her. At least now I understand the dynamics, even though I still think it's kind of messed up.

Kendra crinkles up her nose. "Wait, I don't think we should use our friends like that."

"You're right. It's shitty."

She toys with the sheets. "She does like him, though."

"Maybe he likes her too. I guess we won't know unless we set them up. It could be good for both of them." I snuggle in. "Are we doing this?"

"I don't know. I guess I can check with Josie tomorrow."

"I can check with Jesse, too."

She smiles and my heart beats a little faster. "Tell me more about your childhood. Did you really love cheesemaking. How is it done?"

"You really are full of questions. I guess it's a good thing it's late. My stories will bore you to sleep." She playfully whacks me. "Okay, well I was a bit of a handful, that's for sure." I point to my elbow. "See this scar here. Biking. I was sure I could do a mid-air flip off a homemade ramp. Learned the hard way I couldn't."

She chuckles and closes her eyes. "Tell me more."

I tell her a few stories about my daredevil days, and eventually talk about cheesemaking. Telling her about the pasteurization process, the draining of the whey, and the different varieties my parents make, with much of the process dating back hundreds of years. "We even have a farm on the property."

Her eyes inch open. "Can we go?"

"Yeah, I guess," I say, although the idea makes me uneasy. I'm not sure my parents would be all that happy with me bringing a girl home. I can hear them now: shouldn't all your focus be on hockey? How do you expect to get into the NHL if it's not?

I close my eyes, and exhale as my stomach sours. Here I am hating the control Nate has over Kendra, and hating that she allows it. How am I any different? Everything I do is to prove my worth to my family.

"How come you didn't follow in your parents' footsteps?" Kendra murmurs, sleep pulling at her. "You've talked more about cheese then you've ever talked about hockey."

"It's a mom-and-pop business." For them it was a means to an end, something to pay the bills. It's not like they want it to be a legacy left to their sons. "They don't need me."

"They don't want one of their sons to take over?"

"They want bigger and better for their sons."

"What about you, Dane? What do you really want?" Her breathing changes, and I try to quiet my mind, and sleep too. When I don't answer, she sleepily murmurs, "Have you heard about the wine and cheese festival coming in December?"

"I heard," I whisper.

"We should go. You could tell me all about the different cheeses."

I lightly brush her hair back. "Yeah, we can go."

"You know, if your parents aren't interested in handing the business down, you could always start your own business. Maybe here in the city."

"Yeah, I could," I say simply to appease her as her mind goes on a journey.

"You could even combine it with your passion for biking and put in a bike trail and call it Bike and Brie Free."

I chuckle softly. Maybe the trauma of her bad breakup tonight combined with painful memories of the past is making her crazy, because the idea of opening a bike and cheese store is simply ludicrous, right?

"I think you need sleep," I tease.

"I do, but think about it."

Joking, I say, "Maybe I could call it Bike and Enjoy the Bries."

She chuckles. "That's kind of long."

"You're right, yours is better."

"Actually, what if we went with, Bike and Bries. You know, like bike, and breeze. Get it?"

I grin at her use of the word *we*, like it's something we could do together, or something she'd support me in doing. "Oh, yeah, I get it." I tap my head. "I know what most people around campus think about hockey players. But I'm not totally dense." I wink at her. "Partially, just not totally."

She whacks me. "I never thought you were dense. Would I suggest running your own business if I didn't think you could do it?"

My mind starts running through possible business names. I like Bike and Bries the best, but I quickly shut it down. I'm not going to think about it, not for a single second. "I have an NHL career to think about, Kens. That's my path." She nods, even though I'm not sure she believes that any more than I do. Nevertheless, it's what I need to do, especially if I want to gain her brother's approval and prove to him I'm worthy of Kendra. Yeah, I need to be thinking about that, not how much fun it would be to combine my two passions.

Okay, I need sleep, and maybe a lobotomy, because now I can't stop thinking about her crazy idea—and it is crazy, and completely out of the question.

Fuck my life.

8

KENDRA

Hushed voices reach my ears, and I roll over to find the other side of my bed empty. I jackknife up, and listen, praying to God it's not my brother downstairs. I relax when I hear Josie laugh. She wouldn't be laughing if Nate and Dane were in an all-out brawl.

I dress quickly. God, what is Josie going to think of me? She doesn't know Lance and I broke up, although she'll probably be happy about it, and now Dane is waking up at our place... again. I run to the bathroom, brush my teeth and smooth my hair before I rush downstairs, taking the steps two at a time and nearly face planting. In the kitchen, Dane and Josie are sitting at the table, eating breakfast sandwiches and it loosens the knot in my stomach and makes me laugh.

My heart wobbles as Dane pulls a chair out for me. "I got you one."

"You really love your breakfast sandwiches, don't you?"

"Hush," Josie says. "I don't want him to stop bringing them." She says that like he'll be spending a lot more time here.

"It's not like he's going to be here every morning."

Josie gives me a grin, and if grins could talk, hers would be telling me I'm very wrong about that. I sit and go straight for the large coffee. Josie goes back to her sandwich and she moans with happiness as she eats, and my stomach lurches when I spot her open laptop.

"I'm never going to pass," I murmur.

"Pass what?" Dane asks.

I groan. "I have a statistics test today, and I didn't get a chance to study." Dane's face falls, like it's all his fault. I quickly shake my head. "I suck at math, and I've been so busy helping..." I let my words fall off. No need to say *his* name.

"Shit." He checks the time on his phone. "What time do you write?"

"This afternoon."

He crinkles up the paper from his sandwich. "Get your laptop."

I take another sip of coffee. "No, you have to get to class, and I'm not going to keep you."

"I have twenty minutes."

"I don't think I can prepare in twenty minutes."

"Now you have nineteen, so hurry."

Josie stands and eyes me, the look suggesting I have some explaining to do. As I dart upstairs, I listen to Dane and Josie's conversation.

"What are you doing after the game on Friday?" he asks her.

A chair scrapes the floor, followed by running water which makes it hard to hear. "Not much. Probably just head home."

"You should come out with us afterward, grab some nachos or something. Jesse and a few of the guys will be there." I go still at the top of the stairs. Is Josie going to be mad, figuring I spilled her secret?

"I don't know. I'm not much into the party scene at The Lower Deck. That's where everyone still goes?"

"Yeah, but I don't think Kendra is into the partying there, either. We can all go somewhere else."

I come down the stairs and set my laptop on the table. I can't really go out with the team. How would I explain that to my brother, and Dane must be thinking the same thing. Nate would also be expecting Dane and Jesse to be at the pub after a game.

"Who says I'm going to the game?" I ask, arching a brow as I stare at Dane. He grins, and my heart tumbles around in my chest.

"I should probably get going," Josie says, no doubt feeling the change in energy as heat arcs between Dane and me. She glances at Dane. "Try to talk her into going. She always says no to me."

"I can probably get her to say yes," he says with a grin that holds so much mischief.

"On that note." Josie laughs, grabs her laptop and heads outside. As soon as the door clicks shut, Dane stands, puts his arm around my waist and drags me to him. "Finally," he murmurs, his head dipping.

"Finally what?" I ask and lift my head, my mouth poised.

"I finally get to give you a proper good morning kiss." His lips find mine and I melt into him, as his hands wrap around me, and hold me close. It's so strange. When I'm with him, it feels like I'm standing on a mountain top, my lungs no longer constricted as I teeter on the rocky edge. I'm not afraid. Which is the craziest thing of all. I'm always afraid, except when I'm with Dane.

He inches back. "Fifteen."

I blink at him. "What?"

"Fifteen minutes, now sit your sweet ass down in that chair and let's cram."

I laugh. Here I thought he was going to take me back to bed. I kind of like that he cares about my schoolwork. "What are you studying anyway?" I ask. "I don't even know what program you're taking. I know it's probably not that important, and most players take easy courses, because they work so hard on the ice, and it's such a huge time commitment."

"Business management, and I'm pretty good at math," is all he says, his voice a little low and somber.

"If you ever decide to open Bike and Bries, you'll have the background to get you started."

He just nods, and opens my laptop, and it kind of sucks that he won't give my idea any consideration. "Okay, let's get at it."

I pick my coffee back up and sip as I open to my study notes. For the next fifteen minutes, we go over some probability equations and concepts that somehow Dane explains in a way no professor ever had, making it sound easy. He gives me a few equations to solve, and I pull them off, easily.

"Any chance you'd like to be my tutor this year?" I ask. "You're pretty smart."

"You're smart too. Math just isn't your thing."

"Math," I groan. "A necessary evil for my nursing degree."

"I'm here to help anytime."

My stomach cramps, and I bend forward and put my hand over it. "Oww."

"Hey, are you okay?" he asks, the concern on his face warming me from the inside out.

"I think the breakfast sandwich hit wrong."

He shifts his chair closer. "I'm sorry."

Oddly enough the cramp disappears, and I blame it on stress. "It's gone now. Just a twinge."

He nods and his voice is low, still concerned when he asks, "Do you feel a little better about the test?"

"I do. Thank you." He checks his phone. "You better get going."

"Yeah." He stands, bends and kisses me like it's the most natural thing in the world, like we do it all the time, and asks, "When will I see you again?"

My stomach swirls at the tenderness—neediness—in his voice. It wraps around me like a gentle hug. "The game Friday."

Hope fills his face. "You're going?"

"I'm not sure. I'm still waiting to see what you're going to do to make me say yes."

He grins at the challenge. "I'll work on that, but I'm not sure I can wait that long to see you again."

No man has ever made me feel as important as Dane does. My pulse beats a little harder and I grab his shirt and tug him back, giving him a kiss that will hopefully hold us over until we can see each other again. I don't know how I can possibly see him on campus or at a game and not touch him.

I inch back after breaking the kiss. "You'd better get going."

He groans in agony and pushes up to his full height. "You kiss me like that and just send me on my way." He shakes his head, and starts down the hall to the front door. "Sadist," he murmurs. "Totally fucking sadistic. You're killing me, girl."

I lean against the kitchen counter, a stupid grin on my face as he mumbles to himself. He casts me a glance over his shoulder, gives me a wink, and takes his bike outside. He closes the door behind him, and I walk to the living room window. He buckles his helmet, jumps on his bike and disappears. The second he rounds the corner, my phone pings, and I laugh when I read his message.

Brie: Miss you already.

I hold the phone to my chest, my inside quivering. I miss him too. I turn back to my computer and my phone pings again. My smile dissolves as my gaze races over the words.

Nate: We need to talk.

. . .

My heart thunders in my ears. He knows about the breakup. Or maybe he knows about Dane. Nate has been so good to me, acting as a mother and father figure since we lost ours. My grandmother didn't have any maternal inclinations. Nate always looked out for me, putting me first, and the last thing I want to do is disappoint him. He's everything to me and it makes me physically ill to keep things from him. He's the last person on the planet that I'd ever want to hurt.

Me: I have a test at three and can meet you here afterward.

After he agrees, I glance around my place, to make sure there are no signs that Dane had been here. Other than my bedding, which still has his scent, all is good. I quickly dispose of the sandwich wrappers and put the paper cups and plastic lids into the recycle bin. My stomach is one big knot of guilt by the time I pack my backpack and head outdoors. As I head toward campus, the cool morning air swirling around me, my mind races and my steps slow.

You need to stay away from Dane, Kendra.

I take a quick breath as that reality chokes the air from my lungs like a raging house fire. Dane is a good guy, and I can't mess with his future, for my own personal selfish reasons. There's no way this relationship can go anywhere. I can't come between him and Nate, or do anything to risk Dane's future, whether the NHL is his passion or not. He's clearly not giving up on it.

Tears fill my eyes, making the sidewalk blurry. As I blink them back, I hurry to my first class, resolving myself to the fact that I can't carry on a secret relationship. Nothing about it is right and it's not fair to either of us. I work to close myself off, much like I have for years. Numbness is always better than pain.

By the time afternoon rolls around, I grab a salad at the cafeteria and spot Josie heading my way. She has a grin on her face, which just intensifies the cramping in my stomach. Maybe I'm coming down with something.

"Sooo," she says as she plunks down across from me, leaning in all conspiratorial like. "Dane Taylor."

"It was just a one-night thing," I say quickly and stab my fork into a cucumber. "Lance and I broke up, and I ran into Dane, and he didn't want to leave me alone because I was sad, so—"

"So you slept with him."

I cover my face with my hands and croak out, "Yes."

Josie takes my hands away. "I think he's the best thing that ever happened to you."

"Josie, I can't." I go quiet for a moment as a group of students walk by us. I lean in closer once they're gone, "My brother, hockey…"

Her eyes narrow as she lays her arm across the table and takes my hand. "You have to do what's right for you, Kendra."

"This is what's right." My heart might not know it, but my brain, however, does. I stare at my best friend, who knows about my parents and the guilt I carry. She doesn't usually press too hard about my brother, and I appreciate that.

"I like seeing you happy." She softens as she gazes at me with worry. "I don't remember the last time I saw you smile like I did this morning." She holds a finger up. "No wait, that's not true. Last time was Christmas break when you hooked up with Dane." She leans back and states, "You like him, Kendra."

I don't bother denying it. "It's a little more complicated than that."

"Uncomplicate it."

"The only way to uncomplicate it is to end it." Her lips turn down and I hold my hand up to stop her, not wanting to talk about this anymore. I turn the conversation to her. "Are you going to join the guys for a beer after the game?"

Her eyes go wide. "I can't believe you told Dane I liked Jesse."

I scrunch up my face as I reach for her hand. "Don't be mad."

"I am mad." She doesn't look mad, she looks embarrassed. She snatches a cherry tomato from my salad and tosses it into her mouth. "It was nice of Dane and all, but Jesse doesn't even know I exist. I don't want him doing something he doesn't want to do, and honestly I'll just end up making a fool of myself."

I pop the cucumber into my mouth. "No, you won't, and now's your chance to get to know him."

Her head bobs and I don't like the challenging look on her face. "Fine, I'll go if you go with me."

"Did you not just hear anything I said?" I groan and let go of her hand. "I can't do this with Dane anymore."

"Yes, you can. We either go together or I'm not going at all."

"Did you really just put your love life in my hands?"

She stands, and puts her backpack on her shoulder. "Tell me you'll think about it."

"I'll think about it," I say, and what I mean is, I'll think about not going, even though I want to more than anything. But I just don't want to talk about this anymore. I need to get mentally prepared for my test, my brother, and the text I need to send to Dane.

9

DANE

It's dark as I cruise down the street toward the dorm. I haven't heard from Kendra all day. I thought she might have messaged after her test to let me know how she made out, and her silence has me worried—in more ways than one.

At tonight's practice, her brother seemed off, pointing out all our mistakes and nearly ripping our heads off at nothing. Something tells me his ranting had less to do with his teammates' fuck-ups and more to do with his sister's break-up with Lance. The guy comes from a good, well-known family with ties to the community, and Nate clearly thinks he'd be good husband material. Someone to watch out for Kendra and take over the role of protector when he goes off to the NHL.

The problem is Kendra is quite capable of taking care of herself, and needs to break out of the bubble her brother keeps her in. As far as Lance, he's not the guy for Kendra. He never was. My guess is there was a lot of shit that Nate didn't see, a lot his sister never told him and while I'd like to fill him in, it's not my business. Even though I'd like it to be.

Why hasn't she texted me?

As I approach Storm House, my phone buzzes in my back pocket and my heart jumps. I stop my bike, and pull my phone from my pocket, a smile coming over my face as her name pops up. I quickly swipe my finger over the screen and read her text. My mood shifts fast, bile punching into my throat as her words sucker punch me, hitting like a wayward puck to the gut.

What the fuck?

I stand over my bike on shaky legs in the dark as cars speed by on the street. Voices reach my ears as the doors to a local coffee shop open and close, and I glance around, debating my next move.

Go home, Dane.

I put my feet back on my pedals as a million questions race through my mind. I get it. I do. I understand why Kendra sent that message. It doesn't mean I have to like it. The night air grows colder, and I zip up my jacket, my breath coming faster now. I set my bike on the road and aim toward Storm House, only to make it a couple feet before I spin back around.

I should go home. I want to go home. Going home is the right thing to do, especially if that's what she really wants. Then why can't I? Oh, probably because every fiber of my being craves Kendra and I can't let this—us, whatever the hell we are—end over a text.

I bike faster, a new kind of urgency driving me, and as I come to a rolling stop, I jump off my bike, set it on her lawn with my helmet and hurry up her steps. I knock hard, and shove my hands into my pockets as footsteps sound on the other side of the door.

It swings open and I come face to face with Josie. I try not to sound breathless when I ask, "Can I come in?"

"Um..." Her eyes widen, and she stands there shifting from one foot to the other, not knowing how to answer me. I guess Kendra must have filled her in on what was happening between us. "I should get Kendra."

"Yeah." We both shift our attention as the stairs behind Josie creak, and the second I set eyes on Kendra, Josie heads to the kitchen, and I bolt toward Kendra, taking the steps two at a time until I reach her. My heart hammers as energy arcs between us, hot and volatile...demanding to be addressed. "Can we talk?"

I take in her puffy eyes, and I want to drag her to me, make everything all right. I don't because I'm not sure if she's going to kick me out or not. "Dane," she whispers and nearly fumbles backward. I reach out to stabilize her, and her warm lavender scent fills my senses.

As I hold onto her, she tenses and I swallow, my heart sinking into the pit of my stomach. Fuck, I shouldn't have come here. I should have listened to what she wanted. I'm such a selfish bastard.

"I'll leave." I turn to go.

"Wait." She grabs my arm and the second I turn back to her, the need inside me intensifies.

I can't breathe let alone think as she steps into me, and I drag her to me, my arms around her body, my mouth on hers, eating, devouring, terrified this is our last kiss.

"Kens," I murmur into her mouth. "What are we doing?" If she doesn't want me, I need to leave. Now. This kissing, touching, is only drawing me in deeper, and I don't want to fucking hurt more than I already do.

"I don't know what we're doing." She takes my hand, and guides me to her room. We're both breathing heavily as I kick the door shut and lean against it. She backs up and as she puts distance between us, I ache for her. She grips the knot on her cute, frilly pink robe and nervously toys with it.

"Kens," I growl. "You can't fuck with me like this. Last night...you wanted me." I run my hand through my hair. "Then tonight you text, pushing me away. Jesus Christ. You could have at least talked to me in person." I grab my phone and hold it out to her, so she can see what she sent me. I thought something special was happening between us, and when I first read it, I couldn't tell if she was mad, or angry because I'd done something to hurt her, or if she was trying to let me down gently. "If you think I'm not good enough for you, fine, but at least say it to my face." She glances at my phone and we both read the text.

Kendra: Hey Dane, it was really nice running into you... literally. Thanks for everything. Good luck at the game on Friday.

She gulps and tightens her belt even more. "Dane, no. It's not that."

"Then why did it feel like a slap to the face?"

"I'm sorry. I thought a text would be easier. It's just...my brother...I thought breaking up this way, although it's not really a break-up..."

"Right, it's not a break-up, because we never were a couple." My breath comes faster, harsher. "It was a hook-up. I get it."

"Dane," she murmurs. "We shouldn't be together, your career, my brother, and I thought...this was the right thing to do. Until I saw you at the front door."

I push off her bedroom door and walk toward her. "The right thing? For who, you or your brother?"

"For you." she says quietly, and I grab the belt she's wrapping around her finger, and pull her toward me.

"How about I worry about me?"

"I don't want—"

I press my finger to her lips to hush her. "Right now, I want you to tell me what you do want, not what you don't want."

She swallows, desire reflecting in her blue eyes as they search mine. "I can't offer a future. My brother, we had a talk today." She tears her gaze away, and looks at my chest, as my heart thumps away. "He found out about our pizza and you walking me home. He's determined to find me the right kind of guy."

Yeah, I get it. I live in my brother's shadow, and in her brother's eyes, I'll never be good enough for her. Unless I make the NHL.

I touch her chin and lift her eyes to mine. "Tell me what you want tonight."

Her breath comes faster now, and she wets her bottom lip as her hands tentatively move to my shoulders. "Dane," she whispers. "We both know we can't go any further with this relationship, but maybe we can have some fun as we ride it out."

"What are you saying?"

"I want you."

That's all I needed to hear. I cup her face, and press my lips to hers, my body aching to touch and kiss her, to put my cock inside her. It's insane how much I want her, how fast I'm falling. Although, I've never stopped thinking about her since I took her to bed last Christmas. She's so fucking sweet and vulnerable, and I want to be the guy to bring fun and color into her life—even if it can only be for a little while.

I slide my hands down, and try to keep them steady as I untie her robe, and it falls open, showcasing the curves of her breasts, right down to her soft, damp curls. I growl as I take her in, and I run my fingers down her exposed skin, and nearly lose all ability to think as my fingers meet with her hot wetness.

"You need me, Kens?" I slide a finger into her, and her muscles clench around me.

She grips my arms tighter, and my body heats. "I do," she answers, her voice low, needy and breathless. I work my finger in and out of her, and her hands move to my coat zipper. She drags it down, and puts her hands on my chest. Fuck, I love the way she touches me.

She rocks into me, and I hold my hand still as she rides my finger. She's so hot and wet, I could come in my pants just from knowing how much she needs me.

Anxious fingers move to my shoulders and she works to push my coat off. I reluctantly remove my hand from between her legs to undress. I tear my coat off, followed by my shirt, pants and boxers. She whimpers as I take my cock into my hand, and move toward her. She backs up, and I take in her perfect naked body, I swear I'm the luckiest guy on the planet.

"You're beautiful."

She drops her robe, turns around and points her perfect heart-shaped ass at me as she climbs onto the bed.

"Fuck, Kens."

Still on all fours, she looks at me over her shoulder. "That's the idea." My cock throbs as I take in her mischievous grin. Dammit, I like this playful—free—side of her. How can I help her release it more often?

A little moan escapes her lips as she extends her arms and legs, and she flattens herself on her stomach. I rub my cock harder at the gorgeous sight. She rolls and goes up on one elbow, her sweet body beckoning me.

"Are you going to stand there and stare or are you going to come over here and let me give you a hand?"

"Jesus Christ," I murmur and slide onto the bed. She pushes on me until I'm flat on my back and repositions herself, going to her knees between my legs. I can't stop staring at her, can't stop reveling at the way she's blossoming before my eyes. "I love you like this," I murmur, and her eyes lift.

"Like this, between your legs you mean?" she asks as she bends forward to lick pre-cum from my crown. My dick jumps beneath her tongue. Fuck, that feels good.

"Yes," I admit. I'm a guy. Of course, I like what she's doing. "But you and me, Kens. Just us, doing what we want."

"I like this too, Dane." She leans forward and takes my cock to the back of her throat, and I groan. She moans around my throbbing dick, enjoying what she's doing to me. The vibrations settle in my balls and reverberate through my body. Jesus, I'm too close too fast. She works her hands and mouth over my long length and I grow shaky.

"Babe," I murmur and tug her off my cock. She whimpers in protest until I move her over my body, her legs straddling my hips. Her gorgeous nipples are everything a man's fantasies are made of. I sit up and groan as I suck one into my mouth. I wrap my arms around her, balancing her body as her nipple grows harder beneath my hungry tongue.

"God, yes," she cries out, as I move to the other breast, leaving a wet trail on her quivering flesh. She squirms and I grip her hips pulling her down onto my hard-as-steel cock. She sinks down, and I curse under my breath as I bury myself in her, balls fucking deep. My cock throbs as her muscles squeeze tight, and I take fast breaths to keep it together.

I try to hold her still as I work not to shoot my load off, but she's on a mission of her own, lifting herself up and coming down hard. I fill her, stretching her tight channel and she moans and takes everything I'm giving. There's a new kind of wildness about her, and I fucking love it.

"Yeah, babe, take my cock, take it just the way you need it. Ride it, fuck it, whatever you want, you take."

She whimpers and slams down, leaning forward to grind her clit on my pelvis. I stare at her in pure awe, loving the wildness about her. Honestly, I'm getting off simply from watching her let go. As my cock thickens, reaching the end zone, I grip her hips to help take the weight off her legs. I lift her, and bring her back down again, following her pace, and her gaze meets mine as she begins to pant.

"Dane…"

Fuck, she's gorgeous like this. "Come all over my cock, Kens."

She whimpers, throws her head back, free and unguarded, as she explodes around my pistoning cock. Her wet heat melts me, and I pound into her, wanting to wring out every sweet clench. Her whimpers curl around me and tease my release and the second she stops throbbing, I let go, high inside her. Pleasure grips my balls as I fill her, each pulse sweeter then the last.

"I feel you," she murmurs and sits up high on my cock, her back arched as she takes her breasts into her hands, which makes me come a little more.

I grunt, and she whimpers, our bodies so hot and slick as I pull her down and hold her there, never wanting to leave her sweet pussy. She falls over me, her breasts to my chest and I lightly run my fingers up and down her back. Her lips brush my chest before she rests her cheek on my heart. We both fall silent, our breathing ragged, and I close my eyes, soaking in this moment, and praying to fuck there will be more.

After a long while, she shifts, and groans as she stretches out beside me. "You okay?"

"I don't think my legs are working."

I roll to her, and grin as I take in the glazed, yet contented look in her sleepy eyes. As I come down from my post-orgasmic bliss and my brain starts firing again, I reach down to rub the kink from her legs and that's when I realize I fucked up. I jackknife up and blurt out, "Oh, shit."

"What?" I ask as I take in the worry in his dark eyes. My heart jumps into my throat. Is he regretting what we just did? No, that can't be it. He was into the sex as much as I was. Maybe he hears my brother. I break out into a cold sweat, because that would be a disaster. As my body chills, I grip the blankets and tug them up, listening for noise downstairs as I search his face for answers.

"Kens, we..." He shakes his head and runs his fingers through his mussed hair. "I didn't use a condom." He growls, and the muscles in his jaw tighten. "Fuck, I always use a condom. I just...I wasn't thinking straight."

My heart settles a bit. "Yeah, me neither." We were both in a frenzy, unable to think about the consequences of our actions. I can't speak for him. I only know, up until I met this man, my actions were always careful and calculated.

"Shit, Kens, I'm sorry. I'm clean, we don't have to worry about that, but birth control. Fuck."

I reach out and put my hand on his chest. "It's okay. I have an implant. Nexplanon, and I'm clean too." He frowns. Obviously he has no idea what I'm talking about. "It goes in the arm," I explain and lift it to show him where it was inserted. "It's an etonogestrel implant." Now he looks worried. "It's like the pill and it's painless."

He relaxes. "Oh good. I am so not ready for a baby."

He drops back down next to me, and fixes the blankets around our bodies. "Are you saying someday you'd like to be a father?"

"I don't know. I guess I never gave it much thought before. Probably someday, when I'm older, and established." He brushes my hair back. "What about you?"

"No, I don't want to be a father." I laugh as he grins, then turn serious. "A mother...I don't know." I snort out a humorless laugh. "The world is a scary place." I snuggle against him, loving the way he makes me feel safe in a world I'm afraid of. "I don't think I want to bring a child into it. Plus, what do I know about parenting? I was raised by a grandmother who didn't want me."

"The world's not that scary," he whispers as he drops a soft, comforting kiss onto my forehead. "I understand where you're coming from, though, and why you think that. But maybe negotiating the world with someone who will be there for you and look out for you would make it less scary in your eyes."

A wave of uncomfortable heat hits me in the center of my chest and spreads outward before it churns in my stomach. Ever since my parents' deaths, I've been sheltered by my brother, and I've kept myself guarded, kept control of my environment, too afraid to step out of my small comfort zone for fear of failing someone I love.

His voice is low and soft when he adds, "Don't forget, you were also raised by a brother who really cares about you."

Guilt swamps me. In a way, being here with Dane, isn't that failing Nate once again? It's not what he wants for me. He doesn't think Dane is good enough to be my partner. No college hockey player is. Then again, did he really even know what Lance was like, outside of him coming from a well-known, well-respected family?

What do you want, Kendra?

I'm not sure. All I know is I'm tired of being scared all the time. Tired of living in a bubble and being told what to do. Something about this man beside me makes me want to take chances.

"How did you get here?" I ask.

His brow furrows at the change in topic, then his eyes go wide. "Shit. My bike. I left it on your lawn, and it's probably gone by now."

"Come on." I kick the blankets off, completely comfortable in my skin, as I walk naked to my dresser, secretly smiling as Dane's tortured groan curls around me.

"Where are you going?" he growls.

"To get your bike." I tug on a clean pair of panties, followed by yoga pants. I turn to find Dane with his tongue hanging out and I laugh. "Come on."

He shakes his head. "I can get it. You stay here."

"Nope." I pull on a T-shirt, not bothering with a bra. "Are you just going to sit there and drool?"

"Yes."

Laughing, I cross the room, pull his blankets down and notice he's semi-hard. "Dane," I squeal and laugh playfully. "Seriously?"

"Uh, yeah." He mocks indignation. "You just walked to your dresser naked, what do you expect? You have seen yourself, right?"

I shake my head at his foolishness, but the truth is, I love how much he wants me, how special—alive—he makes me feel. "You have three seconds to get up and get dressed."

He folds his arms like a petulant child, and it makes me smile. I can just imagine what a handful he was as a kid, and I've heard her can be reckless around campus. At least that's what my brother told me after he heard about Dane walking me home after pizza.

"Or what?" he asks, his brows arched.

I tap my chin, pretending to be deep in thought. "Or...I don't let you back in my bed with me tonight." It's a lie. Short of cheating on me, and really, since we're not in a real relationship that can't happen, there's very little he can do that would stop me from letting him in my bed. In fact, I plan to drag him back between the sheets, but first, we're going to do something completely out of my comfort zone, and I'm insanely excited about it.

He jumps up like I just threatened to castrate him, and I burst out laughing. He grabs his clothes off the floor and now it's my turn to admire him as he dresses. It's strange, this new giddiness inside me. I'm not sure I've ever felt it before. Maybe when I was little, before...well, I'm not going down that road tonight. Nope, I'm going down a different one, literally, with this man I could very well be falling for.

Not smart, Kendra, not smart at all.

Ignoring that inner voice, the one who's kept me safe all these years, I walk to my bedroom door, and gesture for him to follow. He snatches his coat off the floor, and we quietly head downstairs. I grab a coat from the closet and pull it on.

Dane opens the door. "Wow, my bike is still there."

"Go get it."

He heads outside and I search the top of the closet for one of Josie's old helmets. I'm sure she won't mind me borrowing it. I put it on my head as Dane lifts his bike, his eyes narrowing as I snap the pieces of the plastic buckle together.

"What are you doing?"

"I thought we'd head to the skate park, and you could show me a few tricks. I doubt there'll be any kids there this time of night."

He throws a leg over his bike and puts on his helmet. "There won't be."

I place my hands on my hips, and challenge, "And you know this because you go there?"

"Maybe." I laugh and step up to him, trying to figure out how we can both get on his bike. He gestures behind him. "You take the seat."

"Not the handlebars?"

"Baby steps, Kens. Baby steps. Now hang on to me, and keep your feet in tight, but don't get them caught in the spokes."

"So bossy."

He laughs as I settle onto the seat and put my arms around his body. He jumps onto the pedals and my feet go flying forward as he starts down the road. I right myself, and let the wind wash over me as I watch his cute ass rise up and down in front of my face as he heads toward the Halifax commons.

He's keeping close to the sidewalk, being careful with me on the back, and I'm grateful for that. Will I even remember how to ride a bike when we reach the park? There are a few people hanging around the Oval, a rink that I like to skate on in the winter, but other than that, the place is quiet.

Dane stops the bike by the ramps, and I slide off the seat. "Show me what you got, big boy," I joke, giving his ass a slap.

He grabs me, pulls me to him and kisses my mouth. My heart thumps, a little thrill of excitement racing through me. I really like when he does that. "I thought I already did," he growls. I'm about to correct him, and his head rears back playfully. "Oh, you mean on the ramps."

"Yes, on the ramps." I walk over to a bench, sit on the cold plastic and shove my hands into my pockets. Dane circles the ramps, biking on the grass. He hops up, putting one foot on the seat and one foot on the frame of his bike, showing me a trick. He grins and I clap.

"Kid stuff," he says.

"Maybe, but it looks hard enough that I'm not trying it. I'll be lucky just to keep the bike upright."

He stands on his pedals and let's go of the bars. "Look, Kens, no hands."

"Get your hands back on the bar," I say, when he begins to wobble. He laughs and takes the bike onto the platform that has a ramp on either side. He starts at the further end of the platform, and pedals fast, going to the top of the ramp, where he puts one foot down, does a one-eighty with the bike and comes back down. "Looks fun."

He stops the bike, balancing it by keeping his feet on the pedals, moving them ever so slightly back and forth. It's easy to tell how much he loves all this. "Come on, give it a try."

I stand, hardly able to believe I'm going to get on a bike and attempt a stunt. "I won't let you hurt yourself."

He jumps off when I reach him and I get on, gripping the warm handlebars tightly. "It's been so long, Dane."

"Bike around the ramp first, get used to it." I put my feet on the pedals and push off. "Look at that, just like riding a bike," Dane teases, laughing as I fall right back into it.

I bike around the ramp and he runs with me, keeping close in case I fall. I pedal faster, forcing him to run harder and I can't help but laugh as he struggles to keep up. There's a freedom in riding hard and fast, and I guess I can see what he loves about it.

"I think you've got it," he yells and slows down. He jumps onto the platform, and I do a few more circles before joining him. "Going up?"

I frown and calculate the risk. "I don't think I can do that."

He comes closer, putting the front tire between his legs. Gripping the handlebar, he leans in and kisses me. "It's okay. You don't have to."

I shrug and glance at the ramp. "Actually, maybe I want to."

He laughs. "I wasn't trying reverse psychology. Not everyone loves doing stunts and it can be intimidating and scary."

"That's just it, though, isn't it, Dane?" He angles his head, his face scrunched, not at all sure what I mean. "How can I know if it's for me or not, if I don't try it." He moves the front wheel back and forth between his legs, and I exhale, a strange kind of exhaustion racing through my blood. "I think I might be tired of being afraid."

His eyes narrow in on me, a careful assessment. "You sure, Kens?"

I look to my right. "All I have to do is get a good amount of speed and that should take me right to the top."

"That's right and when you reach the top, just stay there. You don't have to do a spin turn like I did. That takes practice, and that's something we can work on another time, if you want."

I pull the bike back, out from between his legs, and I go to the end of the platform, as far back from the ramp as I can. Dane keeps a close eye on me as I start pedaling, and the next thing I know, I'm halfway up the ramp and my foot slips off the pedal. "Oh no," I yelp as I begin to slide backward.

I hit something solid, and tumble off the bike. It goes one way, and I go the other. Fortunately for me, I land on something soft. Well, relatively soft.

Dane wraps his arms around me, using his body to cushion the fall, and I have no idea why, but I start laughing. My body jiggles on top of his and he laughs with me, and I'm sure if anyone can see or hear us they'd think we were two drunk idiots about to kill ourselves doing stunts.

I turn in his arms, unsnap my helmet and remove it. My hair falls into his face. "That didn't go according to plan."

He removes his helmet, and it bangs against mine on the ramp. "Most things don't," he responds, and tucks my hair behind my ears to get it out of his eyes.

"It was fun...until I fell." I wiggle on top of him, and all softness leaves his body—and his face. He grunts as I rub his cock with my pelvis, and he widens his legs, holding me between them. I breathe in his scent, my pulse jumping as my body warms all over.

"You're not having fun anymore, Kens?" There's a new measure of heat in his voice as his gaze drops to my mouth. Honestly, everything about this is fun. Just being around Dane is exciting, arousing...freeing.

I wet my bottom lip and he growls as his head lifts, his mouth finding mine. I push against his cock, writhing, practically dry humping the hottest guy on the planet at the park, where anyone can see us—which is completely out of character for me. My God, what have I become? I'm not sure. I can't say I don't like it, though. I do like it. Very much.

He growls as his tongue slips into my mouth, tangling, playing, and searching for more. My panties grow damp as my nipples harden. My God, I need to get this man back to my room and naked before I do something really out of character. Like have sex with the hot hockey player in the middle of the city.

I break the kiss and meet his hungry, tortured eyes. "I guess falling can be fun," I say, my voice a breathless whisper, and yeah, I'm not at all talking about my tumble off the bike.

The truth is, falling can be fun but it can be scary too, especially when it's with a guy who's off limits. Then again, didn't I just say I was tired of being scared?

DANE

The energy is high in the locker room as we get ready for the game. I catch sight of Nate out of the corner of my eye and two things hit at once. Guilt that I'm seeing his sister behind his back, and anger that he has so much control over her. I'd imagine he's carrying guilt too, but to twist Kendra's guilt into obedience...that shit is just wrong.

Maybe he doesn't even know he's doing it, so I can't get too mad. It's possible he's just terrified of losing her, like she is with him, and he keeps her in a bubble because of that fear. Either way, they both have a lot of issues to work through—who am I to judge? I do too—and they're probably going to continue down the same fucked up road if one of them doesn't break the pattern.

Is Nate going to lose his shit if he spots Kendra in the stands?

Kendra...

Fuck, it's been too long since I've seen her.

"Something on your mind?" Jesse asks and slaps me on the back.

"Nope, I'm good." I don't normally lie to my friend.

He rubs his hand over his face, and tugs on his helmet. "Worried about the scouts?"

"Yeah," is all I answer, and finish lacing my skates. I stand, tug on my helmet and he puts his hand around the back of my head, bringing my helmet to his.

"Head in the game, bro."

Fuck, he can read me too well. "Yeah, got it." We head toward the doors. "Do you know who Josie is?" He eyes me. "Remember we met her at the party when we were here at Christmas, and she was at the oval when we went skating."

"Yeah, why?"

I pull open the locker room door and he heads out first. "She's Kendra's best friend."

"Don't be fucking dragging me into this shit, Dane."

He's right, I shouldn't be doing this, and I wouldn't if I didn't think they'd make a good couple.

Is that why you're really doing this, bro?

"I just thought you two might hit it off."

We make our way to the ice, and I search the stands, my heart doing a little flip when I spot Kendra and Josie.

"Is she here?" Jesse asks through clenched teeth, as he glares at me.

"They both are."

"Jesus Christ, Dane. Are you out of your fucking mind? You're going to blow your chance at the NHL because of some girl."

That's just it. She's not some girl. I really like her.

"We're just hanging out, and I think you'd like her friend." I steal a glance into the stands again, sensing Kendra's eyes on me. "We're going to meet up later, after we hit The Lower Deck."

"Play the best fucking game of your life and I'll go," Jesse says, and I knock helmets with him again.

"You got it."

"What the fuck is my sister doing here and why is she looking at you?" Nate asks, his voice hard and gruff as he skids to a stop in front of me.

Shit.

I struggle to answer, and Jesse pipes in. "She's with her friend, Josie. Josie and I kind of have a thing."

Nate glares at me for a second, and I just shrug. He turns to Jesse. "Fine, just keep your head in the game tonight. You," he says turning to me. "You have big skates to fill tonight, and you'd better fucking fill them." He skates off and I exhale, happy my secret is still safe, yet tied up in knots at the reminder I'll never be as good as my brother.

I pat Jesse on the back and exhale. "Thanks, man, I owe you."

"Yeah, you fucking do." He skates off and starts warming up. I do the same and for the next two and a half hours, I give the game everything I have, aggressively chasing pucks, blocking players and shots, our team winning the game in a shutout. The crowd goes crazy when the game ends, and we all hug each other on the ice.

Nate skates up to me and tugs on my helmet. "Bring that game every time, Dane."

"Thanks," I say, proud of the way I played. Maybe I can be as good as my brother, when I have something important I'm playing for. I can't help but search out Kendra, and she's on her feet clapping and jumping with Josie. I grin, anxious to be with her tonight. Then I remember Nate is watching me and I tear my gaze away.

"You played as well as your brother tonight," Nate continues. "Keep that up and you'll get scouted." Scouted, yes, that's exactly what I need. Then maybe I'll be good enough for his sister. Sure, playing in the NHL might not be my calling, but it's a means to an end and I want it more now than I ever did.

We line up to shake our opponents' hands and the energy is high in the locker room after we all file in. I strip off and jump in the shower, wanting to show my face at the Lower Deck, and get out as fast as I can. I'm not sure what Kendra wants to do tonight. We never solidified a plan and it doesn't matter, just as long as I can be around her.

I dress and wait for Jesse. He's grinning as he opens his locker and pulls on his clothes. "You killed it, man."

"Thanks. You too." He scored two of our three goals. It's no wonder he was drafted in Juniors.

"Keep it up and hopefully we'll be playing for the Bucks together."

I push enthusiasm into my voice, because playing in the NHL is what I need, not necessarily what I want. "Yeah, we better."

"Let's go get a cold one."

We lock up our gear and outside there's a group of girls waiting for us. They come running up and we hug them like we always do, and we also give them piggyback rides to the pub. It's tradition. I glance around, but Kendra is nowhere to be found, and I guess I never really expected her to be. Jesse has a shit ton of girls hanging off him by the time we reach the pub. We all pile in and grab our usual big table in the middle of the room.

My phone buzzes in my back pocket, and I try to reach for it. It's a bit hard with a girl sitting on my lap, her tits in my face as she practically straddles me. Any other time, any other night, I might have gone for it. Right now, there's only one girl on my mind, and it sucks that she can't be here with me.

"I'll be right back." I lift her off me and set her on the long bench, and head toward the hall, searching for a moment of privacy. I pull my phone from my pocket and my heart speeds up as I read Kendra's message.

Kendra: You nailed it tonight.

Me: Thanks. Can't wait to hang out with you later.

Kendra: You didn't look like you were lacking company.

Me: Not the company I want. You know I don't want any of those girls, right?

Kendra: How long do you have to put in an appearance at the pub?

Me: I'll be out of here as fast as I can.

Kendra: Come to my place when you're done.

I stand in the hall like an idiot, grinning at my phone until someone bumps into me. "Shit, sorry," I say, glancing over my shoulder as I'm tugged into the little girls' room by two puck bunnies. Seconds before the door slams shut, I catch Nate in the hall, his phone out, grinning at me, and fuck, now I have to play along, otherwise he'll be suspicious. What single hockey player wouldn't want to get with two bunnies in the bathroom right?

Cassie pushes me against the sink and I reach behind me and grip the cold porcelain. "Dane, you were so on tonight. It was hot."

"Yeah you were totally *on*," the other girl, I think her name is Becca says, as she drops to her knees. "Now it's time to get off."

Oh, shit, shit, shit.

She rips into my jeans, and tugs. I jerk backward, but the sink prevents me from moving. "Wait, no." I grip her shoulders and confused eyes blink up at me. I get what they're doing isn't uncommon. I've heard the stories. I'm not usually a recipient in the bathroom. I guess my stellar game tonight changed all that. The thing is, I'm not a cheater. It's true, Kendra and I aren't a couple. That doesn't matter to me though. She's the only girl I want to be with, which means, in my mind if I fucked around, I'd be cheating.

Becca pouts. "Don't you like me?"

"Sure, I like you." She smiles and goes for my dick again. "I just...I have a girlfriend." Fuck. I need to get better at thinking on my feet before I dig a hole I can't climb out of. I shift my body and tuck my dick back into my boxers.

"Who?" Cassie asks, the look on her face accusatory, and doubtful. I get it, most rookies on the team don't commit. As I've heard it said numerous times: why would we when we can get so much pussy.

Becca still doesn't look like she intends to stop. "Since when?"

"You guys wouldn't know her and it's all pretty new," I squirm, trying to get away. No fucking way is this happening. "We're keeping it low key right now."

Becca tries to take my dick out again. "She never has to know."

"I really like her," I say, much firmer this time. "I'm not going to do anything that would upset her." I move away and zip up my pants. "I appreciate the offer. I just...can't." I hold my hand out, and Becca takes it. I pull her to her feet and she smiles up at me.

"I didn't know you were so sweet," she says.

I shrug at that, and they go to the mirror to fix their hair and makeup, and that's when I head out the door. I go back to the table, and Jesse is eyeing me, so is Nate. I guess Nate must have told him what was going on. I pour a beer from the pitcher, and swallow half of it in one gulp. Conversation breaks out around me, and some guy takes to the stage to play guitar. With Nate occupied, he has three girls hanging on his every word, I get Jesse's attention, and nod to the door.

He stands and we both step into the dark night. "What the fuck, dude?" is the first thing Jesse says when we're alone.

"Nothing happened."

He shakes his head. "You must really like Kendra."

"I do," I admit, as our boots slap the pavement, my footsteps hurried as I grab my phone and text Kendra to let her know we're on our way.

"This isn't fucking good."

"Not good at all," I agree and cast him a quick glance.

"I'm only tagging along because you kicked ass at tonight's game. Maybe Kendra is good for you. For your motivation, anyway." He glances at the path as he zips his coat up. "Where are we meeting them, anyway?"

"At their place."

"Jesus," he grumbles and I get it. I am not making good decisions. We hurry through the busy city streets, and I find Kendra and Josie on their front steps waiting for us. She stands when she sees me coming and it's insane how happy I am to see her. Before she can even speak, I lean in and kiss her on the mouth, not caring that the other two are watching, and this could be awkward for them.

I can't tell in the dark, but I think Kendra is blushing after I break the kiss. She clears her throat. "Great game tonight." She turns to Jesse. "Jesse, we met briefly last Christmas at the party. I'm Kendra, and this is my friend Josie."

"Yeah, I remember. Hey Josie," he says, and Josie smiles back. "Thanks for coming to the game."

"I love watching you..." She winces and gives a fast shake of her head. "I mean, I love watching the team play."

Okay, now it's awkward.

I change the subject and ask Kendra, "What do you guys want to do?"

Kendra and Josie exchange a look. What the hell are they up to? Kendra takes my hand and gives a little tug. "Come on, I'll show you."

12

KENDRA

Going anywhere in town with two guys as popular as Dane and Jesse after a hockey game is risky. Half the students on campus are out partying after the win, which is why we need to get off the city streets, or more accurately, out of the city altogether. Which is exactly what I have in mind...sort of, anyway.

We walk ahead of Josie and Jesse, and it seems to me like they're hitting it off. Josie was losing her mind tonight after the game. Pacing our house like crazy, sure Jesse wasn't even going to show up. The second she saw him coming down the sidewalk with Dane, I thought she was going to swallow her tongue. I figured she'd be tied up in knots when he talked to her, and I was pleasantly surprised at how easily she fell into conversation. I have to say, I'm impressed at how fast Jesse put her at ease.

She might not have a lot of experience with guys, but deep down inside, when push comes to shove there's a quiet confidence and strength about her. Unlike me, when push comes to shove, I back down and let my brother make decisions for me. Not recently, though. I've been making them on my own. Maybe I'm stronger than I realize.

I glance behind me and smile as I hear their banter. Even though they're different people, from different worlds, a bookworm nursing student and a hot hockey player on his way to the NHL, I hope they find common ground. Heck, it can happen. Dane and I are living proof that opposites attract, and I have to say, I kind of like the adventurous side of him. It's opening up my small world.

My phone chimes and I recognize the special tone. It's my brother texting. I debate on reading it, as Dane watches me. "My brother," I say.

"You should check."

He's right. It's odd for him to message me right after a game. If he noticed Dane and Jesse disappear from the pub, I can't have him thinking they're with me. I tug my phone out.

Nate: Let's have dinner Sunday.

Me: My place or yours?

Nate: Mine.

That one word knots my stomach, a reminder that he doesn't like it when I cook and we all know why. Does he do that on purpose? A reminder of what we lost because of me. No, I can't think that way. He only has my best interests at heart.

. . .

Me: Sounds great. See you then.

I tuck my phone away. "Everything okay?" Dane asks, his big body brushing mine as we go down a big hill, headed toward the busy waterfront.

"Yeah, he just wants to have dinner."

He casts me a glance. Is he worried Nate knows? "Do you guys do that often?"

"Yeah, we try for once a month. Just to catch up." My gut warns this might be about more than catching up. I think my brother is determined to find me a proper guy and when he sets his mind to something, there's no stopping him.

Maybe you're the one who needs to stop him, Kendra.

A wave of guilt swamps me. He has no parents because of me and took on the role of mother and father. I owe him so much.

Dane nods and smiles as we walk by a popular downtown restaurant that has outdoor firepit seating. We do love to extend our patio season here in Halifax. "That's nice."

"I guess you don't get to see your brother much now that he's in the NHL."

His hand finds mine, and he holds it tight. "No, not much."

It's strange. I can't tell if he's happy or sad about that. He glances around. "Where are we going?"

Okay, so he doesn't want to talk about his brother. "It's a surprise."

"You don't look like the kind of girl who likes surprises, Kendra."

I laugh. "I don't, and this surprise isn't for me, it's for you."

"Something I'll like, huh?"

"I think so."

"Does it involve you naked?"

"Dane," I yell and whack him.

He jumps back. "For a tiny thing, you sure do pack a punch."

He takes my hand again, and my body tingles as we continue along the waterfront, following the trail of white lights guiding the way along the long stretch of wooden boardwalk. The moon is high and I lean into Dane, simply enjoying his company as light glistens on the still water. Our steps slow and Josie and Jesse walk past us. She comes to a stop on one of the ramps leading to a boat moored on a wharf below.

"We're going on a boat?" Dane asks. He frowns as he glances at the chain and padlock meant to keep intruders out. "Are we stealing it?"

Josie laughs and slides a key into the padlock. The durable chain clangs as she releases it. "No, my grandparents own it."

"You know how to drive this thing?" Jesse's voice is full of surprise as his gaze jerks back to Josie.

She lifts her chin. "Yes, I grew up around boats."

"Impressive. I grew up around farm equipment." The ramp rattles and sways as he steps onto it. "Tell you what, you show me how to pilot this and if you ever get to our farm, I'll show you how to ride a tractor."

Josie laughs. "Riding a tractor is impressive too, and that sounds like a plan." Jesse angles his body to let her lead the way. "Tell me more about what kind of farming your family does," Josie says as she and Jesse walk down the ramp and climb onto the cruiser.

I'm about to follow them, stopping as Dane puts his hand around my waist and dragging me to him. Light falls over us, and his head dips. That's when I see the lipstick on his neck. A painful wave of jealousy rips through me, cramping my stomach as I reach out and wipe it away.

"What was that?" he asks.

"Lipstick."

He grunts. "It's not what you think."

I try to inject lightness into my voice. "You were pretty popular tonight."

He rubs a spot on his forehead and groans. "What did you hear?"

"I saw all the rides you were giving the girls."

"What you didn't see was that I was dragged into the bathroom by two at the pub." I stiffen and inch back. He pulls me to him and holds me tight against his hard body. "Nothing happened. I promise."

"I believe you." I do believe him. The problem is, something could have happened and while we're having fun, we're not committed. He can be with whoever he wants. Right now, it's me, and I just want to enjoy that while it lasts. We don't have a future, not one I can see working out, anyway.

I lift my chin and his head dips, his mouth on mine, kissing deeply, proof that it's me he wants to be with tonight. Footsteps sound on the wooden walkway behind us, and someone shouts, "Get a room."

I chuckle as I inch back, instantly missing his kisses. "I think that's good advice."

"Agreed." He takes my hand. "Let's get out of here before we get caught."

Now it's my turn to say, "Agreed."

We head down the metal ramp. "This is one hell of a big boat." He frowns at me. "You don't really strike me as the boating type."

"I've never been on it, so I don't know." I'm doing a lot of things I haven't done before and so far I've been enjoying all of it, except for the sneaking around. That's not so much fun. We can't risk Nate finding out. He wants what's best for me, I get that, and Dane can't risk Nate hating him. It could be detrimental for his future career. "Have you been boating before?"

"Yup, just not on anything this fancy."

I hold the rails as the ramp wobbles. "Is there anything you haven't done?"

He puckers his lips in thought. "I never had sex on this boat."

"Ohmigod, you've had sex on a boat before?" I ask my voice low as I hear Josie and Jesse talking inside the cabin. She's giving him instructions on how to pilot the boat and I like that they're hitting it off.

"I think we should talk about something else," he grumbles.

"You brought it up," I shoot back with a laugh.

He throws his hand out. "Because I want to have sex with you on this boat."

"Is there anywhere you haven't had sex?" I ask, thinking how we nearly did it on the skate ramp.

He looks a bit skeptical when he answers with, "Probably."

I shake my head at him as I step onto the boat, loving the way Dane puts his hand on my waist to help me balance myself. He's always thoughtful. He follows behind, and we enter the cabin. I quickly catalogue the space. "This is gorgeous." I drop down onto the leather seat and spread my fingers over it. I note the way Jesse is standing behind Josie at the wheel, his body pressed against hers as she explains how things work.

"Are we actually taking it out?" Dane asks and drops down next to me, lifting my legs and putting them over his.

Josie casts a glance at us, and it's easy to tell from the way her eyes are glistening that it's going well between the two of them and I'm happy for her. "Sure, if you want to."

"I do," Jesse says excitedly.

"Okay." She pulls a band off her wrist, ties her hair back and smiles up at him. It's funny how much he towers over her. All power and protection. Is that how Dane and I look standing next to each other? "Come outside with me, Jesse, and I'll show you how to release the lines and secure the boat fenders."

He salutes her. "Yes, ma'am."

She laughs at him. "You have to do everything I say, otherwise, these two could be drifting out to sea while we remain on the dock."

"Wow, smart, bossy and take charge." He gives her a teasing grin. "Where have you been all my life?"

"Do not let us drift out to sea," I warn, although the idea of Dane all to myself for a few hours does sound nice. The getting rescued by coast guard part, not so much.

As the two of them disappear, I stand and check out the two small bedrooms. One has a single bed and I like the idea of being in such close quarters with Dane. I turn around to talk to him, only to find him right there, standing over me, hovering, one hundred percent strength and power that takes my breath away. I can see why I threw caution to the wind back at Christmas and took him home with me—despite my brother's warning.

Maybe your brother isn't making the right decisions, Kendra.

"Oh," I murmur, as the heat in his body warms my blood. Or maybe it's the new feral look in his eyes as he glances over my head and takes in the small bed. My God, I want him. I crinkle my nose and ask, "Would it be rude of us—"

"No," he answers quickly, so quickly, a happy chuckle climbs out of my throat. Catching me by surprise, he picks me up by the waist and sets me inside the room, closing the sliding door behind us. "They're into each other and won't even notice we're missing."

My knees wobble, partly because the boat is rocking against the dock, and partly because I'm here with Dane. Everything about the way he's into me—even if it is just physical—cocoons me in warmth, and it's been a long time, maybe since childhood, that I've felt like this.

Tender fingers brush my face. "I liked you watching me tonight." The low deepness in his voice curls around my heart.

"I liked watching."

"Oh, a sadist and a voyeur," he teases.

"I believe you just admitted you were a voyeur too." I poke his chest and he grasps my wrist and brings my finger to his mouth. He kisses them, and I take a fast breath.

"Is it voyeurism if you like being watched?" he murmurs, absently as I back up in the small space and turn on the lamp.

"I'm not quite sure. Let's see if you are a voyeur." As the room fills with a soft golden glow, I peel my coat off. His breathing changes as I toy with the top button on my shirt. His eyes move back to my face, and I honestly can't believe what I'm about to do. I am so not myself with this man, and I love everything about that.

He stares at me and I pop the first button. I'm pretty sure he does like watching and I'm going to give him something to watch. Noises sound from outside the boat, a splash followed by a gasp and then laughter. What the hell is going on out there? Did they drop one of the boat fenders the into the water? I'm not sure and I can't think about that, not when Dane is standing there, looking like a delicious snack, and my entire body is ravenous. An impatient growl rumbles in his throat and sets me into action.

I slowly work the buttons on my blouse, and he is completely still, mesmerized as he watches my movements carefully. I steal a glance down and take in the big bulge in his pants. I love how hard he gets for me. I slip my shirt off my shoulders and make quick work of my bra.

"Fuck," he murmurs, his gaze racing over me like it's the first time he's seen me naked. "Sadist."

"Are you hurting, Dane?"

"Yes."

"Why is that?"

His eyes narrow. "I want to bend you over that bed and fuck you—that's what happens when you make me wait three long days to see you—but I don't want you to stop what you're doing."

"A conundrum for sure," I tease.

"Yeah, Keep going." He unzips his coat and lets it fall to the floor.

I do as he asks, and pull open my pants, slowly releasing the zipper. He swallows and the sound does something to me, makes me want to step even further out of my comfort zone. Instead of taking my pants down, I slide my hand inside my damp panties and Dane's deep, tortured groans reverberate around me. I find my swollen clit and close my eyes as I tease it. Pleasure zings through me. My God am I really masturbating in front of Dane?

"Babe." That word is so low and tortured I love it. He takes a step toward me, ripping into his jeans to pull out his cock, and I work my finger faster. Two big steps close the distance, and he takes my hand from my pants, replacing it with his, and my head rolls back.

"Dane..." I take his hard cock into my hand, and he leans down and presses his forehead to mine. His breathing is as rough as mine as we stand there touching each other, and there's a strange new intimacy curling around us.

He slides a thick finger inside me and I clench around him. I swear to God, ever since he came back into my life I've been in a constant state of arousal. My hormones are a complete mess

"You really liked watching tonight, huh?" he teases as he dips into my soaked sex.

"I can't believe what I've been missing. I should have been going to the games."

"To see me, right?" he asks, and while I get he's joking, there's something else there too.

"Yes, Dane to see you. You were amazing."

I stroke him and dip into the pre-cum on his crown. He grunts. "What was that you said about bending me over the bed?" His body goes tight, and his eyes lock on mine. I'm not even sure he's breathing. I wet my bottom lip, letting him know just how much I like that idea.

"Fuck, Kendra."

"Yes, fuck Kendra." He tugs his finger from my panties, and moans as he puts it in his mouth. "I've been thinking about tasting you all fucking day."

"What a coincidence, I've been thinking about that all day too."

13

DANE

I forget how to talk as Kendra turns her back to me, slowly, teasingly, inches her pants down her legs, shimming her sweet ass my way as she tugs off her pants, tosses them away and goes down on her knees.

Sweet Jesus.

She positions herself at the foot of the bed, pressing her breasts into the mattress as she presents me with every man's fantasy come to life. I grab my dick and tighten my fist around it to prevent myself from shooting all over her plump ass cheeks.

"Kendra, babe," I murmur and shove my pants to my knees. I want to take them off, but that will take too long. Sliding my hand between her legs, I circle her clit and part her soaking wet lips, opening her up. She wiggles and whimpers, and who am I to keep her from what she wants?

I guide my cock to her opening and breathe in her intoxicating lavender scent. "Yes, God yes, Dane." She grips the bedding and curls it in her fingers as I jerk my hips forward and drive home. Home. Yes, home without fighting for my place, without competing for love or attention, that's exactly what she feels like to me. I could fucking sob as her gasp of pleasure tugs at my balls and they tighten, a load building inside me.

I grunt and try to quiet myself when I hear water turn on in the bathroom beside us. The bed is rocking, but I'm not even sure we've left the dock yet. I pull out and the second I see my dick, wet and glistening from her hot juices, my cock spasms. Fuck, this thing between us, everything about it feels so good, so right, it's going to take a shit-load of control to hang on.

"Babe," I whisper and fall over her, putting my mouth near her ear as I drive back into her. "I don't know how I made it through the week without touching you." I moan, inch out and piston back in again. "Actually, that's not entirely true. I do know. I whacked off every fucking day, babe."

"Really?" she asks, her body vibrating around me as she speaks. She glances at me over her shoulder and it's easy to tell she likes what she hears.

"Yeah, babe, really." My cock aches for release with each hard thrust, and I bite it back, needing her pleasure first. "I must have taken you six hundred ways in my dreams."

"Six hundred. That's a lot of ways," she teases. "I can't wait to try them all out." My body throbs at the idea of playing out my fantasies. I grab her ass cheeks and tug her open, striving to get in deeper, to make her as delirious as I am. I power back in, and she groans and tugs at the sheets...mission accomplished.

The boat rocks, and I move with it, allowing it to help me slide in and out of her hot, gorgeous cunt I'm easily losing myself in. When has sex ever been this good? I lightly run my fingers over her sides, tracing the outer edge of her breasts as I press my chest to her back. I slide my hands along her arms until I capture her hands. I thread my fingers through hers, put my mouth near her ear and whisper, "I really missed you, Kens."

Her fingers tighten in mine, and as I fall silent her gulp cuts through the quiet. Christ, is she feeling this thing—whatever it is—between us too? My heart thumps against her back, and I slow the pace, fucking her gently now, using long, even strokes to help me make this night last forever. I don't want to think about it ending, or us ending. I don't want that to happen. I pinch my eyes shut, not wanting to go there, but my one working brain cell speaks to me.

What are you going to do about that, Dane?

"Dane," she cries out, her voice high and frantic as I create a rhythm between our bodies. Our fingers clench tighter and my dick swells as her pussy muscles lightly ripple around it, a good indication her orgasm is going to be a powerful one. Fuck yeah, I love making her come.

"I feel you." I press hot kisses to her neck and back, as I let go of one hand, and reach around her hips to apply pressure to her aching clit. "Nice," I murmur as she gasps and pushes her ass against my body, taking what she needs. I put my palm between the bed and her body, letting her rub up against it as I fuck her.

"That...yes..." She whimpers and drives her ass back, and a second later, her hot cum spills all over my fingers and dick, taunting my orgasm to the finish line.

Pleasure grips every inch of my body, and I give into it. "Babe," I grunt, and grip her hips, driving in as deep as possible as I fill her body with my seed. I throb as I unload inside her. Pinching my eyes shut, I jerk forward, wanting every last drop of my cum in her hot cunt. I love the idea of it dripping out of her all night, a reminder to her how insane and perfect sex is between us.

She whimpers, still spasming, and I keep my dick high inside her until we're both sated and spent. I press hot, open-mouthed kisses to her back, and lightly run my damp finger over her side. She quivers.

"That tickles."

I chuckle against her back and the boat moves. We both groan as my cock slides almost all the way out of her. I don't want to leave her body, I don't want to move until...ever. Her knees must be killing her, though. I slowly inch out, go back on my heels to watch my cum drip out of her hot center and down her legs.

"So goddamn hot," I groan, my dick twitching again. She glances at me, confused, and my heart nearly stops beating as it fills with the things I'm feeling for her. "Watching my cum drip out of you," I say, answering the query in her eyes as I put my finger between her legs, and rub my cum all over her hot pussy.

She moans as I touch her, and while I'd like to finger her again, she must be a bit sore. "I love how you touch me." She collapses back on the bed, and it's all I can do to stop myself from telling her how I feel. I'm not enough for her. She might say otherwise, but I know the truth. Until I am, I need to keep my damn mouth shut. The last thing I want is for her to run the other way.

I spot a box of tissues on the nightstand, and push to my feet, pulling my pants up. She watches me cross the small space and stays still, content to let me clean her up. Not wanting to make a mess of Josie's boat, I tuck the tissues into my pocket to discard later.

Kendra puts her hands on the bed, to push herself up and I grab her hips to help her. Once she's standing, I turn her to face me and push her hair off her shoulders. We bang into each other as the boat wobbles.

"Feel good?" I ask, a ridiculous question, I know. I shouldn't be seeking approval, but it's a hard habit to break. I've spent my whole life doing it. In my family love is conditional. Not that I'm talking love here.

She cups my cheeks. "Did you not feel my orgasm?"

I laugh, bend and kiss her sweet mouth. "I don't think we got off."

She frowns. "Wait, I just said I orgasmed, and I'm pretty sure you did too." Her eyes go wide, and I love how she worries about me too. "You didn't?"

"Oh, yeah, I did." I gesture toward the small round window. "I mean, I don't think we got off the wharf."

"Oh no, I hope everything is okay?" She frowns. "I thought I heard a splash earlier." We both go quiet, and I cock my head, listening for sound.

"Shit. We'd better check on them." I tug my pants up, and zip them. Kendra scrambles for her clothes and I find her shirt as she tugs on her pants.

I take a fast glance at her to make sure she's ready before we exit the room. She nods and the second I slide the door open, a laugh bubbles out of my throat.

"Dude, what the fuck?" I ask Jesse, when I find him standing there in a too-snug Hawaii shirt, and a pair of shorts. He shakes his head, and glares at me.

"Just don't."

"What happened?" Kendra asks Josie, as I take in her flowery dress, one she wasn't wearing earlier. Her hair is wet. Come to think of it, so is Jesse's.

Josie holds both hands up, palms out. "Please don't ask."

"Is that your grandmother's dress?" Kendra asks.

"What part of don't ask, didn't you get?" Jesse says.

I glance at Kendra and we both try not to laugh. "Okay, no questions," I agree. My phone pings, and I tug it from my pocket. I read the message and my stomach tightens. "Fuck," I whisper under my breath.

"What?" Kendra asks.

"It's Nate." I cast a fast glance at Jesse as his phone pings. "Party at Storm House and he's wondering where we are."

Jesse holds up his phone. "Yeah, got it, too."

"You should go," Kendra says quickly and while a part of me knows she's right, there's another part that wishes she'd tell her brother she could see whoever she wanted to see. I have to bide my time here, though. Once I get scouted, Nate will surely look at me differently, and then Kendra and I can come clean. Until then...patience.

"You're going to freeze outside in that dress," Kendra says.

She points to the room we just came out of. "I have clothes in the bedroom."

"Oh, sorry," Kendra says and winces.

Josie smiles at her. "Don't be." I grin back. I like Josie. She disappears into the room.

"We'll walk you home before we head to Storm House."

"You don't have to do that," Kendra says and I dip my head and give her a look that suggests she might have just arrived from outer space.

"You really think I'm going to let you and Josie walk back in the dark?"

"Nope, I don't." She laughs, and I bend to kiss her as Josie comes from the room with warm clothes for herself.

"Good." It's nice that she knows who I am, and that I'm always going to be there for her. Unlike the last douche bag in her life. I can't believe he was fucking around on her. I guess it's to my advantage he had no idea what a good thing was when he saw it. Otherwise, I wouldn't have had a chance with her.

We gather up our things, and Josie grabs the keys. Outside the wind is cooler off the water, and I tug Kendra to me. The boardwalk is busier now and she pulls up her hood, and I'm not sure if it's because she's cold or doesn't want to risk being caught with me. I try not to let that bug me. Even though I understand where she's coming from, it still stings a little.

We quickly walk the girls home, and once they're safe inside, we turn and head back to Storm house. "Jesus, let's hurry. I'm freezing my fucking balls off," Jesse groans.

We pick up the pace. "Thanks for coming tonight."

"You owe me."

"Yeah, I do." Shit, I guess maybe they weren't getting along as well as I thought. "Are you still headed back home next month, when we finally get a free weekend?"

"Yeah, you still driving me?"

I nod. Jesse left his car behind and traveled to Halifax with me. It needed a few repairs and his Dad, a jack of all trades, was fixing it for him.

"You okay if I ask Kendra and Josie to come along?" He eyes me. "Hey, you're the one who said something about teaching Josie to ride a tractor if she taught you to drive the boat."

"We didn't even get off the wharf." Our footsteps slap on the pavement as we hurry down the sidewalk, passing by a few people who start chanting our names as we pass them.

"It's still an arrangement."

Jesse casts me a fast glance, concern on his face. "You're getting yourself in deep, bro."

"Is that a yes? The girls can come?"

"Fine. She did say she'd take me another time."

"So that is a yes."

"I don't like being your accomplice, Dane."

"Dude," I shoot back. "How many times did you tell your folks you were sleeping at my house when you were out fucking all night?"

"Yes." He snarls at me. "It's a yes."

I laugh as we hurry down the sidewalk, even though there's a part of me that does feel guilty for dragging him into my business like this. With any luck, he'll see Josie is sweet, and realize having that one special person is so much better than fucking around with a different girl every weekend.

We hurry into Storm House, the party already in full swing. Guys and girls are laughing and dancing, and in the kitchen, keg stands are happening. Christ, I couldn't wait to live here, to party with the guys, and now I'm already tired of it.

"Dane," some girl I don't recognize calls out.

"Fuck, I need to get out of these grandpa clothes," Jesse tells me.

Before we can get upstairs, Nate comes out of nowhere, and blocks our path. "Hey," he says, his eyes narrowing as he takes one look at Jesse. "What the hell, Soup…"

Jesse shakes his head. He hates the nickname Soup, which comes from his last name Campbells. "Had an accident. Borrowed a friend's clothes."

Nate chuckles as he reaches out and tugs on the elastic waistband barely holding up the shorts. "That's the best your friend could do?"

"Apparently."

"This friend…did he lose his bifocals at his assisted living home?"

"Something like that and before you say anything about the fashion police, I'm going to get changed." He darts upstairs, and I'm about to follow, not wanting to partake in our post win party. I turn, about to bolt. Nate puts his hand on my shoulder, squeezing to stop me.

I turn back to him, trying for casual. "What's up?"

"You did good tonight."

"Thanks."

"Keep it up. You're getting your name out there, so don't do anything to fuck up your game." There's a warning in his tone, and I try not to tense.

"Don't worry about me. I'll impress the scouts." It hasn't happened yet, but my motivation has never been higher.

"Good. You have someone who's been looking for you all night." He crooks his finger, and I turn to spot Emma coming my way. Emma has never paid me any attention before. Either I impressed her tonight, or Nate knows something is up and is testing me.

"Hey Emma." I smile at her, feigning interest. How the fuck am I going to get out of this one? If Nate is setting me up and I tell her I have a girlfriend, Nate will be keeping an eye on me. I can't have that. Maybe I'll tell her I have crabs.

Nate pats my back. "Have fun, bro."

KENDRA

It's been close to a month since Dane and I have been sneaking around. I didn't go to last night's away game in Cape Breton. I wanted to, but traveling to an away game would raise all kinds of suspicions, and the truth is, I haven't really been feeling that great. I probably shouldn't have eaten that leftover pasta that's been in the fridge forever.

I check my phone as Josie comes bursting into the living room. She wasn't at last night's game either. We both had a test to study for and we have the whole weekend away with the guys to make up for it. I told Nate I was having a girls' weekend away, and that's sort of the truth. When I had dinner with him a few weeks ago, he talked about Lance and me getting back together. Lance told him he'd consider it, and I have no idea what my ex is up to, but I don't want any part of it. Now that I know how a girl should be treated, I'd never go back to him.

I straight up told Nate no, which is unlike me. I am proud of the way I stood up for myself. I never would have done that months ago. I think Nate might give up on Lance after I refused to even consider it. What I'm worried about is that he's not going to give up on finding someone for me. Someone to basically take over his role of watching out for me when he's gone—like Dane secretly does now, even while Nate is here. Although, I'm beginning to believe I don't need anyone to take care of me. While I like Dane being there, I'm pretty sure I can take care of myself.

I can't tell Nate about Dane, of course. He'd lose his mind. There was a point where Dane was pretty sure he knew and was testing him—like when he tried to hook him up with some bunny named Emma. I like that Dane comes right out and tells me the truth about those things. Dane ended up downing a bunch of alcohol that night, and pretended to pass out. So far we've been able to keep the secret and I'm just going to ride it out, and have fun while we can. I'm not really sure how long it will last, or if we'll even be together when Nate goes off to the NHL. One day at a time, I guess.

"Why are you freaking out?" I ask Josie as she runs around the room, looking for God knows what.

"Why aren't you freaking out?" she shoots back.

I chuckle. "It's fine, Josie. He wouldn't invite you to his farm for the weekend if he didn't like you."

"I just...I can't believe I'm going to his farm. I barely know him. This is all happening so fast."

I understand that. Things are happening fast with Dane and me too. "Now is the time to get to know him." She picks up a sofa cushion, and searches beneath it. "You really like him, huh?"

"I can't find my phone."

I pick up my phone, and call her number. It rings—from her back pocket. "Ohmigod," she yelps and pulls it out. "I don't think I can do this." She plops down onto the sofa.

"Josie, stop. You like him, he likes you."

"I've seen the girls he's been with, Kendra. Guys like him don't pay attention to me. I'm always the sidekick, the supporting cast. I am in over my head here. I'm going back to bed and staying there for the weekend."

I sit on the coffee table and face her. "You're overthinking this, and Josie, you're every bit as gorgeous and desirable as any of those girls who throw themselves at Jesse. Listen, if you're uncomfortable at any time, I'm just down the road and you can come stay with us, or we'll just head home."

Tires crunch as a car pulls into the driveway and while my insides are jumping, I work to keep a calm and even demeanor for Josie's sake. Her eyes go wide, and pretending my heart isn't bobbing up and down inside my throat I say, "You've got this."

I'm going to spend the weekend away with Dane.

My stomach squeezes tight and I'm not sure if it's from excitement, or the old leftover pasta. Now is not the time to get sick. I hurry to the kitchen and take some antacids, and nearly gag on the chalky texture. I toss them into my belt bag and go to the door when I hear boots on the steps.

I try to calm my racing pulse as Dane stands there, legs wide, one arm raised to knock, looking like sex incarnate. "Hi," I whisper, trying not to sound breathless.

He stares at me in silence for a second. Is something wrong? I'm about to back up until he slides his arm around me, drags me to him like he's laying claim and plants his mouth on mine.

"Get a room," Jesse mumbles from behind, and I break the kiss and chuckle. I glance up and down the street, noting the way Dane is watching me. Kissing me on the steps like this is risky, and he knows it.

"Are you ready?" he asks, his body close, his voice low, holding all kinds of promises that send shivers straight to my girly parts.

"Ready," I tell him. Honest to God, was I ever ready for a guy like Dane. I back up so the guys can get out of the wind. I reach for my overnight bag and Dane snatches it up first.

Jesse pushes past Dane. "Hey Josie. I'll take that." He removes her bag from her hand and shoulders it. "You all set?"

"All set," she chirps out, her voice a little too high. My God, is she going to be okay? I'm sure Jesse will put her at ease. He has a knack for doing that.

We go outside and after I lock up, I spot Dane's car. "We're not biking?"

"Little hard to fit all four of you on the bike," he teases.

I make a disappointed tsking sound. "I thought you could do anything on that bike."

He grins at me as the guys toss our bags into the trunk. A moment later, he slides in next to me, his arm touching mine on the center console, and I like it. Since his place is only a couple of hours or so away, we decided to leave Friday night after classes to make the most out of the weekend.

"You sure your parents don't mind me visiting for the weekend?"

He reaches over and puts his hand on my thigh. "Of course not. As long as I'm kicking ass at the games, they don't much care about anything else."

Okay, that's a strange thing to say. I'm not sure he has the best relationship with his folks and the reason he's working hard for the NHL is because that's what they want from him. Personally, I still love the idea of him combining his love of biking and artisanal cheese and opening his own business. I realize that will never happen. He has his mind set on the NHL, and oddly enough, seems even more determined lately.

A song comes on that I like and I turn the station up and sing along. Josie and Jesse talk quietly in the back seat, and I'm happy that she found her voice again. We drive through the city streets, and I point at a few houses that are decorated for Halloween.

Twenty minutes later, I watch the city disappear as Dane pulls onto the highway, and I push back in my seat, a sense of calm coming over me, despite the churning in my stomach, which I'm determined to ignore. Stupid pasta.

"How was your test today?" he asks, casting me a fast glance and my heart swells.

"It was hard, but I think I did okay. How were your classes today?"

He shrugs. "Not too bad. I'm not loving economics and I don't think my professor likes hockey players all that much."

"Why not?"

For the next hour and a half, we fall into conversation and traffic slows as we enter the sleepy town of Bass River. I sit up a bit straighter. I can't say I've been anywhere in Nova Scotia. I pretty much stick to the city, and my grandmother gave up driving in her early sixties, which meant Nate and I bussed everywhere. Money was never an issue. We were left an inheritance, which I'm able to tap into this year. Money was also left for Grandma to take care of us.

"A Christmas tree farm," I blurt out and point to a sign on the road.

Jesse leans toward the front seats. "Do you know Carter Gillis? His family owns it."

"I don't think I know him. Is he on the team?"

"Yeah, left winger," he tells me.

"I think I know him," Josie says and Jesse leans back.

I nod. "I can't believe little old Bass River produces so many hockey players."

"Hockey is big in this town," Dane says. "Everyone wants their kid to be the next big thing in the NHL."

"I can see. You'll have to point him out to me next time."

Dane squeezes my leg and catches Josie's gaze in the rearview mirror. "It's okay if you don't."

I laugh at his jealousy. "There are a lot of family run businesses here?"

Dane nods. "Lots."

"Carter's family also does a haunted house and a haunted corn maze," Jesse tells me.

"No way." I shiver, not wanting anything to do with that.

Dane grins at me. "We'll go tomorrow."

My eyes go wide at the thoughts of ghouls jumping out at me. "It's okay if we don't."

He laughs, and Josie says, "I actually think that would be fun."

"Way to have my back, ex best friend," I playfully shoot over my shoulder. The truth is, I'm trying to be more open, trying to do things that frighten me, trying to live a little. Dane makes me feel safe and as long as I'm with him, I'm sure I'll be fine. Besides, haunted houses and mazes are for kids. How scary can they really be?

We go a little further down the road and Dane pulls into a long gravel driveway. We pass numerous weeping willow trees and as the road opens, Jesse's big farmhouse comes into view. I lean forward to take it all in. "Wow, your farm is huge."

Dane stops the car in the big driveway, and kills the ignition. "Need some help?" he asks as he presses a button to pop the trunk. I turn and catch Josie's eyes. My God, she looks like a deer in the headlights.

I give her a nod to let her know she's got this and we also have our girl code, so I'm not going to leave her. "Have fun. See you tomorrow for the haunted corn maze."

Josie exits the car as Jesse puts both their bags over his shoulder. She stretches and looks around. A woman who I assume is Jesse's mother, comes out the front door.

"Hey, Mrs. Campbell."

"Dane, I told you a million times to call me Carol."

Dane laughs. "I told you a million times not to exaggerate."

She throws her arms in the air to wave us off, and I laugh. "Ohmigod, I thought I heard someone at the game call Jesse, Soup. Now I finally get it."

"Don't call him that to his face, he hates it."

"They really don't have a nickname for you?" As he heads back down the driveway, I look over my shoulder and watch the way Mrs. Campbell pulls Josie in for a hug. I'm sure she'll like that. Her parents are both busy surgeons, and so is her grandfather, hence the fancy boat they own, and Josie was practically raised by efficient nannies.

"She's going to be okay," Dane reassures me.

I frown and pluck at lint on my jacket. "I feel a bit bad, using her as an excuse to get away."

"I think they make a cute couple," he assures me. "I'm sure by the end of the weekend, they'll be crazy about each other."

I'm crazy about you.

Instead of saying that I just smile, and glance out the window, ribbons of nerves threading through me. "So you rode bikes for fun as a kid, and played hockey. Anything else?"

"Cheese, don't forget the cheese."

"I can't believe you like making cheese."

"Why, does that sound cheesy to you?"

I groan and whack him. "Oh, Dane, you can do better than that."

"What, you didn't think that joke was gouda?"

I groan again. "What have I gotten myself into?"

We don't go very far down the road when he pulls into another long driveway. I sit up straight, my nerves jumping to life. I've never gone home to meet a guy's parents before. Lance never introduced me to his. Not that Dane is my boyfriend, or that he'll be introducing me as his girlfriend. But I do want them to like me. Obviously, I'm a people pleaser.

"See the shed over there?" I follow his pointing finger. "You'll probably have to sleep there. That's where all guests go."

I take in the old shed, which looks like it's been around for two hundred centuries and about to collapse. "Okay," I say quietly.

"Oh my God, Kens, I'm kidding. Shit, now I feel bad. You'll sleep in the house, with me."

I whack him for teasing me, and he captures my hand and kisses it. "With you?"

"In my bed."

My gaze strays to the quaint shop with a sign that reads Gouda Guy over the door. "Your parents will be okay with that?"

"Yes," he says without hesitation, and I curse at the knot of disappointment tightening in my stomach. Then again, maybe it's just the bad pasta fighting back. I should not be this jealous and should have known he'd brought girls home before and they'd slept in his bedroom. If he's so sure his parents have no problem with it, it's something he likely does on a regular basis.

"You good?"

I plaster on a smile. "Yes, excited to see your place, and the animals and how cheese is made. You are going to teach me, aren't you?"

"Cheese is your love language, Kens. Of course, I'm going to teach you."

He slows and pulls in beside a big SUV and I eye him and try to read what he's saying. Does he want me to love him, or am I being totally ridiculous? We both know we can't go any further with this relationship and we're just going to have fun as we ride it out.

"I'm looking forward to learning, and to eating." Chuckling, he takes the keys from the ignition and climbs out. I follow him to the back of the car as he gets our bags.

"Let's put these inside and then we'll go say hello to Mom and Dad." We take the three steps up to his front door, and he pushes it open. I follow in behind him as he drops our bags on the floor. The house is old, but it's very neat and tidy inside. I take a fast peek around, glancing at a toothless picture of Dane on the wall.

"My God, you were adorable."

"Still am," he says and throws one arm over my shoulder. I turn into him, and his gaze heats as his eyes drop to my mouth. "The price to see my cheese mastery skills is a kiss."

I go up on my toes, and lightly press my lips to his as he wraps both arms around me and practically lifts me off my feet. My heart pounds against his chest, and my earlier nausea is now gone, thankfully.

"Did that cover entry costs?"

He sets me back down, slides his hand around my ass and tugs me against his growing erection. "For now. I might want more later."

"I definitely want more later."

He chuckles. "Let's go say hello."

The sun is low in the sky as we make our way to the little shop beside the house. A car pulls in as we walk, and when an elderly gentleman opens his door, Dane runs over to help him.

"Dane, son, I didn't know you were going to be home."

"Drove Jesse back. He needed to get his car." The man pulls his cane from his car and balances on it. "Who do you have here?"

"Hi." I smile and hold my hand out. "I'm Kendra. A friend of Dane and Jesse's. I'm here to check out the cheese and animal farm."

"Kendra, this is Mr. Baker. He's a loyal customer."

I smile at him as Dane makes his way to the door, holding it open for Mr. Baker. He enters and Dane and I follow behind.

"Look who I found outside," Mr. Baker says, and Dane steps out from behind him. His mother smiles. What she doesn't do, is open her arms and hug him. Not that my grandmother ever did that either.

"Dane," his dad says, coming from the back as Mr. Baker goes to one of the refrigerated cases to browse the cheese. "Nice to see you, son."

"Mom, Dad, this is Kendra, the friend I mentioned who would be coming home with me. Kendra this is my mom and dad, Terri and Bill."

"It's nice to meet you both," I say. They both eye me, staring so long and hard, it's all I can do not to fidget. "I love your cheese." Oh God, now I sound like an idiot.

"So happy to hear that," his dad finally says. "What is it you do, Kendra?"

"Nursing student," I answer proudly.

He nods, not at all impressed. "Dane here is going to follow in his brother's footsteps right into the NHL and make us proud." He eyes me for a second, telegraphing a message that nothing or no one, including me, can get in his way. "Aren't you, Dane?"

Dane stiffens. The movement is so slight, if I wasn't standing next to him, I might not have noticed it. But as he does, two things occur to me. One, his parents won't settle for anything less than the NHL—their love and respect might actually depend on it. And two, I can't do anything to jeopardize his chances.

I shouldn't have come here.

15

DANE

As Dad's words ring loud and clear in my brain, I cast a quick glance Kendra's way, and note the fake smile. I eye her, and actually, upon closer inspection, she looks a bit pale. Is she nervous? I brush her hand with my knuckles, a caress of comfort and support, wanting to put her at ease. My father can intimidate me all he wants, but he's not going to do it to my girlfriend.

"Samples?" I ask Kendra as Mr. Baker walks up to the counter with his weekly supplies.

She nods and her smile is less fake as she aims it my way. "Of course." I put my hand on her back and walk her up to the counter, where little pieces of cheese sit in small white cups.

"Kendra," Mom says, and Kendra looks at her. "How long have you and Dane known each other?"

"Oh, we met last Christmas when he was visiting the college with Rhys." She naturally keeps out the part where we went back to her place and spent the night in bed. My body warms at the memories.

Mom's smile is big at the mention of Rhys. "Did you know Rhys?"

"Not well. Just his reputation. He's quite well..." Her body tightens, her words falling off, like she might have caught herself before she said the wrong thing. I get it. She meant his reputation with the ladies.

"Yes, he's quite the hockey player and very well liked." Mom's eyes gloss over with pride. "I'm sure everyone on campus knew him."

"Yes, exactly," she answers, relaxing. "You must be so proud of him."

"We are, we are," Dad pipes in after ringing in Mr. Baker's cheeses and packaging them in a brown paper bag.

"Dane is doing great things too." Her eyes warm as she glances at me. "He was amazing at last week's game. He blocked so many shots."

"That's what I like to hear," Dad says. Unfortunately, in this house, love is conditional. I need to be something great or I'm not worthy.

"Have you talked to your brother?" Mom asks.

"Not lately, been busy." I love Rhys, and I feel guilty for not calling, although my parents love to message me to let me know how he played each game, which is always amazing. I'm happy for my brother, I really am. It's just hard, always being compared to him. Now being out on my own without my parents' constant judgments has been kind of nice. I've been enjoying the space and also, a phone works both ways. Rhys could call me. He could be tired of always looking out for me —heck knows, our parents put the burden on him to show me the ropes and teach me all his skills—so he could simply be enjoying the freedom too.

Mom casts a look at Kendra, her lips thinning. "Yes, busy. I see."

I use a toothpick to stab a piece of cheddar and hold it out to Kendra. "School and hockey take up all my time." I grab a cube of peppered gouda and toss it into my mouth.

"What do your parents do?" Mom asks Kendra and the cheese I just put in my mouth sours.

"Oh, I lost my parents when I was young. I was raised by my grandmother."

Mom frowns. "I'm sorry to hear that." She wipes her hands on a towel and pulls out a fresh block of cheese. "Try this?" She cuts off a piece of jalapeno cheese, pokes it with a tooth-pick and hands it to Kendra.

Kendra takes a bite and her eyes go wide. "That is so good." She turns to me. "You have to teach me how to make this."

Dad clears his throat. "I'm sure Dane is too busy to be fussing around in the shop."

"Yeah," is all I say. I kind of do want to show her my skills in the shop, and impress her a little, but I guess that's not going to happen.

"Are you headed back to the city tomorrow?" Dad asks.

I shrug. "I was actually planning to stay until Sunday. I'd like to show Kendra around, and we're going to meet up with Jesse and his friend to do some things tomorrow."

Dad puts his hands on the counter, and leans forward. "You mean like head to the rink in town here, to practice?"

Jesus Christ, do I have to eat, sleep and breathe hockey? "Yeah, I'm sure we'll get a practice in." I jerk my head toward the door. "I dropped our bags at the front door. I'd better take them upstairs. Kendra and I are going to grab a pizza for dinner. Do you want me to bring you guys one back?"

"It's card night with the Millers," Mom points out. "There's some leftovers in the fridge if you want them."

"No, I think we'll head out."

"Are you sure? It's meatloaf, your favorite."

My mother does make a mean meatloaf, and it was always my favorite childhood food, but I don't think Kendra would enjoy it quite as much as I would. The bell over the door jingles as another customer comes in. "We'll get out of the way."

I turn to leave and Kendra says, "So nice meeting you both and thanks for letting me stay here for the weekend."

Mom and Dad both smile, and turn their attention to their customer. Outside, I take Kendra's hand and give it a squeeze.

"Sorry," I murmur.

"For what?"

I take in a breath of fresh air, my insides heavy, my shoulders tight as we head toward the house. "For all the hockey talk."

"It's okay. They just want what's best for you." She glances down at the ground, and I can only imagine she's thinking of the way Nate runs her life.

"I don't know. Maybe they want what's best for them." We step inside the house and I'm about to reach for the bags. She stops me, and puts her arms on my shoulders, lightly massaging out the tightness.

"I know I'm the last person who should be saying this, but maybe you have to do what's best for you, Dane."

I want to tell her she's right—that she's the last person who should be giving advice that contradicts her actions. I don't. Instead, I cup her face and give her a kiss. "You're right." What she doesn't realize is that I have to make the NHL. If I want to win her brother over and be with her, I have no choice.

"Now show me your room."

I chuckle and pick up our bags. "Follow me."

"Is it a shrine?" She laughs. "Left like it was in high school, with all your trophies?"

I snort. She's going to be sorely disappointed. "Come see."

She heads up the stairs and I follow, enjoying the view from behind as she hurries up the steps. She stops outside Rhys' room and her eyes go wide. "Ohmigod, it really is a shrine."

"Keep walking." I nudge her and she gives me an odd look. "That's Rhys' room."

"Oh." She moves down the hall and stops outside my room. Her gaze goes from my room, to me, back to my room, and there's warmth and compassion in her eyes.

I nudge her. "Go on in."

She steps in and I set our bags on my bed. She sits down next to them and catalogues the trophy-free room. Understanding eyes meet mine and the compassion there wraps around my heart. "Not easy living in your brother's shadow, huh?"

"I'm doing okay." Am I though? Am I really doing okay? I drop down in front of her, widen her knees and shimmy in between her thighs. "At least I am now," I say and kiss her deeply. She rakes her hands through my hair, and a new sense of urgency grips me. Fuck, man, I don't want this thing between us to ever end.

"I don't think your parents like me."

"It's not you, Kens. They just don't want anyone or anything to interfere with the NHL."

"They sort of made that clear." She shifts uncomfortably. "Maybe I should go."

I put my hands on her legs, my heart squeezing. "If you want, I can take you back. If you stay, we can have some fun. I'd love to show you around, and we have the haunted house tomorrow with Jesse and Josie."

"Like that's an incentive," she says with a laugh. It dissolves quickly, and she frowns. "You're right, though. I don't want to leave Josie." Her chest rises and falls as she fills her lungs. "Are you sure I should stay? I don't want your parents upset with either one of us."

"I can handle my parents, Kens. We won't see much of them anyway."

"Are they like this with all the girls you bring home?" I eye her, and arch a brow as I go silent. She angles her head, her eyes clouding with confusion. "What?"

I circle my thumbs on her thighs. "Remember when you asked me if there was anything I haven't done?"

She nods. "Yeah, that night on the boat."

"Right, well, the answer to that is yes. I've never brought a girl home before, and..." I pause and poke the mattress. "...never slept with a girl in this bed."

A big smile overtakes her pretty face, like I'd just given her a gift, and dammit, I couldn't be happier that we can do something special together. "Are you sure they're not going to care where I sleep?"

"They might be my parents, and this is my childhood room, but I'm a grown-ass man, Kens. They at least know that much and as long as I'm working hard to make the NHL, and not letting anything get in my way, it's all good."

Her lips turn down. "They think I'm in your way."

I touch her coat. "The only thing in my way is your clothes." I push her back and fall over her.

She squirms beneath me. "We are so not doing this. What if they walk in? I'd die of embarrassment."

I roll off her. "Let's go get pizza and then I'll strip you naked and fuck you so hard when they go out to play cards, you'll be too busy having mind-blowing orgasms to worry about anything."

She gulps. "Um...okay...yeah."

I laugh and push upright. "Let's go get some food. Do you feel like pizza?"

She rubs her stomach. "I'm not that hungry. I think I ate some bad pasta. I'm sure I'll find something on the menu, though."

"We don't have to go out if you're not up to it."

"I am. Should we check with Josie and Jesse?"

"If you want. My guess is they'll all be sitting down to a big family dinner." A look of longing comes over her face, and I wish things were different in my home, wish I could give her that sense of family that she deeply craves.

"Josie would really like that," she murmurs almost under her breath. "Let's not call them."

"We'll see them tomorrow and I kind of want you to myself tonight anyway," I tell her, taking her hands and pulling her to her feet. My dick twitches as she bumps against me. I marshal my cock into submission and take her hand. We make our way outside, and as the sun sets low on the horizon, she glances off into the distance to where the pigs are squealing.

She crinkles her nose. "What's the noise?"

"The piglets. Playing in the mud."

She grins. "You have piglets. Do you have a Winnie the Pooh, too?"

"No, but we do have horses, donkeys, ducks, rabbits, geese, chickens, cows, and even an emu."

"Wow, do they all get along?"

"There's a pecking order, for sure, and they're all kept in separate areas. It's the emu you have to watch out for. Rocky is a mean motherfucker. I have no idea why that bird doesn't like me. I don't know what the fuck I ever did to offend him."

"Rocky?"

We head to the car and slide in. "Yeah, that's what I call him because all he wants to do is fight me." I eye her. "Between you and me, I'm scared shitless of the bird."

She laughs, hard. "How does he fight you? I mean, it's a bird. He has wings."

"He runs at me, and tries to kick me." I hold my hand out and make a claw. "Fucker has these toe claws." I eye her as she works hard to bite back a chuckle. "It's not funny." Okay, I guess I can see the humor in that—when I'm a good distance away from the asshole.

"No, not at all." I start the car and back out of the driveway.

"Why do you keep him?"

"He only hates me, Kens. I'm not sure what I ever did to him."

"I have an idea. On our way home, let's get a bucket of chicken and eat it in front of him."

"That's just wrong," I tease. "I like it, though." I snort and give her thigh a squeeze.

"Okay, show me your old haunts," she says sitting back and glancing around, looking more relaxed and happier now since our exchange with Mom and Dad.

I drive and start pointing out all the places Jesse and I hung out when we were teens. She smiles and takes it all in.

"Do you miss living in the country?"

"I love the city, and all it has to offer. Of course, I've only been there a few months and it could lose its appeal." I thought I'd like living in the dorm for years too, and now, after having met Kendra, the idea of privacy is much more important than partying every weekend. Maybe the country would be nice...quiet. Christ, what am I thinking? My plan is the NHL and there will be no country living until retirement. "How about you? Have you ever thought about country living?"

She narrows her eyes, deep in thought. I don't think she's ever considered the possibility of living anywhere but the city. Like it was never really a thought that passed through her head. "They do need nurses in these rural areas."

"Maybe you could get a big old farmhouse and fill it with kids." Then she could have the big family dinners she seems to long for. She laughs at that as we drive by the lake.

"Did you swim there?"

"Yup, want to go later?" I ask.

She looks at me like I have a hockey stick growing out of my neck. "No."

"Why not?"

She holds her finger out. "One, it's cold out, and two, I don't have a suit."

I wink at her. "Don't need one."

I pull into my favorite pizza joint—nothing is too far in this small town—and we unbuckle. We head inside and the place is packed, like it always is on a Friday night. This is a local hangout joint and I notice some of my high school friends. Ones who didn't go off to college and instead went to work on the farm, or at the lumber mill.

"Dane," someone calls from the back and waves me over.

I wave back to the crowd at the table. "That's Colton, an old friend. We don't have to join them if you don't want to."

"What, and not hear about all the trouble you got into as a teen? Oh, we're definitely sitting with them."

I laugh, my heart full with all the things I feel for her as she walks away, giving a little shake to her sweet backside, which I totally plan on ravaging later.

Man, I've got it bad.

16

KENDRA

"You mooned a cow? Really, Dane?"

He laughs and feigns innocence. "What? It was a dare, how could I not?"

I shake my head, enjoying the easy comfort between us. "Do you do everything you're dared to do?"

"It's how the game is played, Kens," he says as we walk along the shoreline of his favorite lake. "I knew we shouldn't have sat with those guys."

"Oh, I'm so glad we did." I glance at the waves lapping against the shore. "If I dared you to strip off and swim, would you?"

Beneath the full moon, he wags his eyebrows. "If you want me naked, all you have to do is ask." I whack his stomach and laugh. "The thing is, if you want to play the game, I could make you strip and dunk, too."

I pucker my lips in thought. "Hmm, maybe I'll pick truth."

His steps slow as he angles his head, his gaze moving over my face like he has something very serious he wants to ask me. I suddenly suspect it might be a question I can't, or don't want to answer.

"I'll probably pick dare," I say quickly, needing to hide from the truth.

He unzips his coat, and I go still. "Dane, don't. It's too cold." His coat falls to the ground, and he tugs off his sweater. "Wait, no, let's moon a cow instead, or even Rocky."

"I'm not mooning Rocky. God knows what he'd do to me. Besides, haven't you heard of cold-water shock therapy?"

"Heard of it yes. Done it no, and have no desire."

"I double dog dare you, Kens," he says, with a smirk, and I can't believe my eyes as he tugs his pants and boxers off. He hops, all his parts dangling as he tugs his socks off and heads toward the water.

I stare at him, hardly able to believe he's doing this, but loving how fun, wild and reckless he is. Since I vowed to try new things and step out of my comfort zone, I unzip my jacket. My God, am I really jumping in a lake, in Nova Scotia, in October? I must be out of my damn mind.

I shed my clothes, shivering as he hurries into the water, yelping the whole way. "Way to make it enticing," I call.

"It's actually...wwwarm. Like...bababath water."

"If it's so warm, why are your teeth chattering, and your words coming out garbled?" I dip my toe in and wince. "I don't think I can do this."

"You don't have to if you don't want to."

I stand there naked. I guess if I've come this far, no use backing down now. "Actually, I think I want to."

"That's my girl."

"You'll warm me up later?" I ask.

"With my tongue."

I laugh at that, and clench down on my jaw and run in until I reach him. He puts his arms around me. "Ohmigod, Dane, it's freezing." I wrap my legs around him, trying to get some of his body heat. He holds me tight, and his lips find mine. He kisses me deeply, and for the briefest of moments I forget I'm naked, in freezing cold water.

He breaks the kiss. "That's probably long enough. I think there might be a fine line between shock therapy and hypothermia."

He starts walking and carries me to shore. He sets me down, and we run to our clothes and try to get into them, not an easy task when we're wet and shivering. Once I'm dressed, Dane throws his arm around me.

"My legs are tingling, but that was actually kind of fun."

He guides me to his car, which we parked on the side of the road, and once we're in, he blasts the heat. Five minutes later, we're pulling into his parents' driveway. "Are your parents home?"

"No, the car is gone."

"I don't think your dad would be too impressed with us jumping in the lake."

He shrugs. "If I told him it was part of my therapy for hockey, he'd be happy."

I turn my head so he doesn't see my frown. I really hate the pressure his parents put on him. You know what? I'm also getting annoyed with the pressure my brother puts on me. But what if Dane doesn't make the NHL? What happens then? Will they disown him?

"Want to go see the animals?" I ask.

"Fuck no. If Rocky sees me coming in the dark, fuck knows what he'll do to me."

I laugh and slide from the passenger seat. "I can't believe you're afraid of an emu." I close the door quietly. "Do you think he'll hate me because I'm with you?"

"No, he likes women."

"Maybe he really likes you. Maybe that's his mating call or something."

We head toward the house and Dane angles his head, his brow furrowed. "Are you suggesting Rocky wants to fuck me in the ass or something?"

I laugh. Hard. Although he doesn't seem to find the humor in it. "I'm just saying. Maybe he's sexually fluid."

"Maybe and I don't care who he gets his bro on with, as long as it's not me." We enter the house, and Dane turns on the light as the cool night air chills my body. He nods toward the stairs, as we take our coats off and hang them in the closet. "Why don't we have a warm shower?"

"Ah, I guess you figured out why I dared you to jump in the lake." He arches a questioning brow. "It was my way of getting you naked in a hot shower."

He leans in and brushes his lips over mine. "There are easier ways."

His warm breath sails over my goosebumps. "Such as?" I ask, my body tingling all over but for different reasons this time.

"Just ask. Your wish is my command."

"Really?" I pucker my lips. "Anything."

He takes my hand and we start toward the stairs. He casts me a quick glance and when I grin, suggesting I'm up to something he won't like, he shakes his head. "Within reason of course, and as long as it has nothing to do with Rocky."

A laugh bubbles up inside me. When was the last time I felt this happy, this light inside? Upstairs we go straight to the old farmhouse bathroom, which has wallpaper with light blue flowers. It's kind of quaint and cute. Dane opens the shower curtain, and turns on the spray. "These old pipes can take time to warm up."

His cold hands brush my stomach as he reaches for the hem of my sweater. I quiver as I lift my arms, to let him peel from my body. My bra quickly follows and he puts his hands on my breasts and I yelp.

"Sorry," he chuckles and pulls his hands back and blows on them to warm them.

"It's okay. It was just shocking." I take his hands and put them back on my body, and reach for his zipper. He winces, and after I pop the button and slide his zipper down, I blow on my hands to warm them too.

"Whew," he teases, and bends to take my nipple into his hot mouth as I wrap my semi-warm hands around his semi-hard cock. He thickens beneath my strokes, and with unhurried touches we explore each other's body's. Once the room begins to fill with steam, we hurry out of our clothes, and Dane takes my hand to help me into the old-fashioned tub.

Hot water falls over me, and I moan in delight. Dane takes a bar of soap that smells a little flowery from the ledge and lathers me up, and I warm under his touch. I put my head back, and water runs over my face as he puts his big hands on my body warming even the darkest edges inside of me. He repositions me to rinse off the soap, and once I'm clean, I reach for the soap.

"My turn."

He groans as I clean him, taking extra special care with his cock. I stroke him and he grunts in pleasure. "Keep that up and I'll shoot off in your hand, Kens."

I shrug. "Maybe I'd like that."

"You think you'd like that more than this?"

Before I realize what's going on, he spins me, and puts my hands on the wall. One arm goes around my waist and tugs as he shoves a foot between my legs to widen them. "Oh, God," I moan, my breath coming much quicker.

"Well, do you?" he asks, and slides a hand down my stomach to toy with my throbbing clit.

"No," I say quickly. "No, I think I like this more."

He puts a finger in me, to prepare me. I'm already wet, soaked actually and it's not from the shower water. I practically claw at the tiled wall as he positions his cock at my opening, and in one long thrust, enters me.

"Dane," I mumble, my legs weakening as he fills me. He grunts and I love the animalistic sounds he makes when he's inside me. "So good," I tell him. He grips my hips for leverage, and his fingers bite into my skin as he pumps. Each hard pump lacks any sort of eloquence. Fucking me from behind in the shower is simply all about the end game, and I can get behind that—or rather Dane is getting behind that.

That thought makes me chuckle, and Dane puts his mouth near my ear. "Having fun?"

"Yes," I push out and he drives in deep. "I always have fun when I'm with you."

"Good," he grunts out and goes back to his fast thrusts. A loud garbled noise crawls out of my throat and I don't much care. I guess he really meant it when he told me earlier that he was going to fuck me so hard I'd be too busy having mind-blowing orgasms to worry about anything.

One hand leaves my hips, and the rough pad of his finger finds my clit and swirls around it. My head rolls back, and Dane's mouth is right there. He kisses the side of my neck, and it's all I can do to fill my lungs as pleasure grips my entire body.

"Dane..." I groan, and push back, meeting his thrust and I'm rewarded with a deep, guttural groan. He's close, and holding back, for me. My heart thumps, fully committed to every-thing we're doing and while that's a dangerous thing, maybe for one second, I'll embrace it. The second I do, the most powerful orgasm rockets through my me, and as my legs give out, his arm goes around my body, holding me up and keeping me close.

"Fuck." He grunts as I squeeze around his cock, and he holds me tighter as he spurts inside me, filling my body with his seed and warmth. His deep breaths fall over my back, and he rests his cheeks between my shoulder blades. I hang onto the wall until he straightens and pulls me up with him. He goes quiet as he backs me up and puts me under the spray with him. There is no need for words. I think our bodies just expressed everything that needed to be said—everything that was felt.

As the water grows cooler, he inches his cock out of me, and I whimper at the loss. There's warmth in his eyes, a small smile on his mouth as he turns me. I smile back, and he brushes the back of his hand over my face, moving my damp hair away.

"Can you walk?" he asks quietly.

I nod, even though I'm not sure I can. He nods and turns the water off before it turns as cold as the lake, and helps me from the tub. I shiver and he grabs a towel and wraps it around me.

"Better?"

I nod, and he towel dries himself and wraps it around his waist. I yawn as he gathers up our still damp clothes, and takes my hand. We hurry from the bathroom, down the hall and into his room. He drops the clothes, and pulls back the bedding, waving his hand for me to climb in.

I drop my towel and slide between his warm flannel sheets, a moan catching in my throat as I snuggle in. He drops his towel, and I can't take my eyes off his beautiful body as he climbs in beside me and gathers me into his arms. I breathe in the fresh scent of his skin and as I do, his earlier words hit me.

"Oh no," I say, and inch back to see his face.

"What?" His worried gaze moves over my face and when I curl into myself a bit, he reaches down. "Your stomach? Not feeling good again."

"That's not it." I glance around his room. "It's just...the night is over, and this afternoon you said you never had sex in this room and I thought, well, I thought it was kind of nice if I could be your first."

His grin is playful and mischievous as he wraps his arm around my waist and tugs me back until my body is meshed with his. God, he feels so good. "Who said anything about the night being over, Kens?"

17

DANE

"Please don't make me," I teasingly joke as we make our way through the farm on our way to see Rocky. Kendra laughs and while I get she thinks this is funny, I really am terrified of the damn emu. I still don't know what I ever did to piss him off. He loves Rhys. Then again, who doesn't?

I slow my steps as we approach his area of the farm, and put Kendra in front of me as a human shield. "Nice, Dane," she says.

"It's not you he hates."

She reaches into her bag of pellets and takes a handful. "What if you feed him?"

"He'll likely take my hand off." From the corner of my eye, I spot the emus, and they're at the other end of the tall fence. A couple are hanging out, and Rocky, of course is running around like a turkey with its head cut off. Crazy bird.

"Does he answer to the name of Rocky?" she asks.

"No, that's just what I call him. His name is Mike."

"Mike?" She laughs. "Really?"

"I didn't name him."

"Hey Mike," she calls out and holds the pellets out.

"Are you crazy?" I stand behind her, as a couple of kids come over to grab handfuls of pellets and the birds all flock to them. Rocky struts over and eats from the kid's hands, and I stay hidden, happy he hasn't noticed me yet.

"Hey Mike," Kendra says, her voice soft and alluring, and Mike trots over. He dips his head and eats from her hand.

"He likes you," I whisper, and the second I do, the bird's head lifts—obviously recognizing and hating the sound of my voice. I suck in a fast breath as we stand there, eye to eye, in a standoff with Kendra in between us. "Oh, shit."

A deep rolling grunt echoes around us and the kids start laughing. Rocky starts running in circles and I take off, only for him to come running at me. I hear Kendra shriek and the kids and their parents are laughing their asses off—at my expense.

I duck behind a bale of hay, and Kendra calls out, "Hey Mike. Over here." The dumb bird—or maybe I'm the dumb one—stands there for a moment, before he turns, deciding he'd rather be with Kendra. Yeah, okay, he's not dumb.

I jump up onto the pile of hay, and sit there as Kendra and Rocky bond. I shake my head, not at all surprised. What's not to like about Kendra? She pets him and he nibbles at her belt bag, then almost nuzzles her neck. Damn, am I really sitting here jealous of a ridiculous emu? Yes, yes I am.

Once she's done, she brushes her hands on her jeans, and starts my way. I sneeze as she gets close, the hay playing havoc with my allergies. "I love Rocky."

"I can tell."

She grins. "You were right. He doesn't much like you."

"Believe me now?"

"I think it's a domination thing. He's the big bad alpha male and you threatened him with your big bad alpha maleness."

I laugh at that and jump down from the hay, pulling her to me. "You think I'm a big bad alpha male, Kens?" I toss a piece of hay into my mouth to complete the tough look.

"Rocky's got nothing on you. I can see why he's threatened."

"You're very good for my ego."

"Oh yeah, what else am I good for?" she asks, rubbing up against me in a teasing manner, and my chest tightens. Christ, we're just having fun here, having sex while we ride things out for as long as we can. I guess she must think that's all I think she's good for when it's the furthest thing from the truth. Do I tell her? Tell her how much I want her, in and out of my bed, today, tomorrow, next year? Fuck, I want to but I can't risk frightening her off.

"What am I good for?" I ask instead of answering.

Her face softens as her gaze holds mine. She opens her mouth, and when I get the sense she might say exactly what I'm feeling, I stop breathing. I wait, and one second turns into two, as she works to formulate her words. She's about to speak when a kid's scream penetrates the quiet around us.

"Mom, a piglet," he yells, repeatedly, and the little piglets all start squealing as he chases them.

Kendra closes her mouth and chuckles. "Looks like someone found the piglets."

I nod and smile despite the storm inside me. I really wanted to hear what she had to say.

"Let's go see them."

She inches back and I hold her arm. "For the record, you're good for more than my ego, Kendra," I find the nerve to explain.

She smiles and doesn't answer. Instead, she takes my hand and tugs, and for the next hour we walk around the farm, and she feeds all the animals. She honestly looks like she's having the time of her life and she probably is. She's been pretty sheltered in the city, and I want to be the guy who introduces her to new places and new experiences.

After we complete the entire loop around the farm, Kendra's phone pings and she pulls it from her belt bag. A smile lights up her face. "It's Josie."

"Everything good?" Jesse texted me earlier. He set up a pick-up game with the high school team, first thing tomorrow morning.

"She's asking if we want to grab dinner before we go to the haunted house and maze." Her eyes are big and hopeful, and I shrug.

"Sure." Mom and Dad are in the shop. I talked to them for a few minutes this morning over coffee, while Kendra was still sleeping. It's not like they'd take any time off to spend with me. Shit, I sound like an asshole. They have a business to run, and can't put up the 'Closed' sign simply because I'm home. They have a job to do, and so do I—make it to the NHL. We all play our part in this family.

Kendra smiles as she texts back, and I put my hand on the small of her back and guide her to the house to wash up. Mom and Dad were up and in the shop by the time she got up. Maybe later tonight, after the shop is closed, I'll be able to sneak her in and show her around. I think she'd like that, and maybe I'm just looking for approval. I am kind of good at cheese making.

Inside the house, we scrub our hands together in the bathroom, and she smiles at me in the mirror. "I think Josie and Jesse are hitting it off." She nudges me playfully. "Double wedding." My mouth drops open. Did she really just say double wedding? My shocked reaction has her shaking her head fast. "I'm kidding of course. It's not like we can ever get married, and Jesse will be leaving once he finishes his degree. I can't imagine anyone having a long-distance relationship like that." She reaches for the towel and dries her hands, before putting them on her stomach, like the thoughts of marrying me makes her physically ill. Jesus. "They're probably just having fun, like us."

All I can respond with is, "Yeah."

She stares at me for a second, and I think she's going to say more on the subject when she begins with, "Are there any other restaurants in this town, or are we going back for pizza?"

"There are other places." I shut off the tap and dry my hands. "Let's see what Jesse and Josie feel like having."

We head downstairs, and I gesture toward the shop. "I should let Mom and Dad know we're headed out." A knot tightens my stomach. I don't want to be rude and just drive off. But the thoughts of seeing their disapproving scowls, to know I'm out having a bit of fun instead of focusing on hockey isn't what I need right now.

"I'll come with you."

We walk side by side, and the parking lot is full of cars. Inside, Mom and Dad are both chatting up customers. They worked hard their whole lives to provide for Rhys and me, and I feel like a little shit for being selfish.

"Do you need help?" I ask Mom. I could always give Kendra my car and she could meet up with our friends without me. I'd hate to do that to her and I want to spend time with her. I can't not offer to help though.

"We have everything under control," Mom answers. Ever since I began to show a lot of interest in the business, they forced me out, afraid I might want to make cheese instead of playing hockey.

"Shouldn't you be practicing?" my father asks, scowling at me.

"Jesse and I are hitting up the rink first thing tomorrow morning, before we head back to the city."

He nods, pleased with that. "Good to hear."

I jerk my thumb over my shoulder. "We're meeting Jesse and a friend now for dinner, then we're headed to the haunted house. Do you need anything?"

Dad wraps a slice of cheese in brown paper and hands it to the customer. "No, we're good, son. Don't stay out too late now."

"Right." Kendra gives an awkward little wave, and we leave the shop.

"I didn't know you had a pick-up game tomorrow."

"It's early, you don't have to go."

"I want to go."

I eye her. "Really?"

"I loved watching you play the other day. I'm kind of mad that I never went to any games before."

"Do you think your brother will be wondering why you're suddenly going now?" Fucking Nate. I love the guy, I do, but dammit, he needs to cut his sister some slack. She's a smart girl, who made one bad decision when she was five for Christ's sake. Does she have to carry that with her for the rest of her life?

"No, because Josie is into Jesse, and wants me with her, remember?"

My stomach tightens even more. I shouldn't be using my friend like that. "Yeah, I remember." I open the car door for her. "Do you think we're doing the right thing?"

She slides in. "All I know is Josie really likes Jesse and she never would have met him or talked to him if it weren't for us."

"That's how we're spinning this? That's what we're telling ourselves to sleep better at night?" I ask jokingly but not so jokingly.

"I think they make a good pair."

"I do too, actually." Although I'm not so sure Jesse is in the market for a relationship. I owe him big time for helping me out like this. I slide into the driver's seat and negotiate the busy parking lot carefully as I pull onto the back road. I drive the short distance to Jesse's. I park and we exit the vehicle, turning when a loud revving sound comes from the backyard.

"Let's go check it out." I take Kendra's hand and we circle the big farmhouse to find Jesse and Josie inside the tractor. They're both laughing and it eases some of the tension inside me. I catch Kendra's grin. "Want to try?"

She crinkles her nose, and for a second I think she's going to say no. "Why not? Hey, when in Rome."

"We are far from Rome, Kens."

She nudges me. "You know what I mean. I think I'd like to go to Rome someday, though."

"That's on your bucket list?"

"I've never done one, actually. Have you?"

"The only thing on my list is the NHL."

She nods, but there's a hint of worry in her eyes. What, does she think I won't make it, too? "Yeah, of course."

"Hey," I say and Jesse looks my way when I call out to him. The tractor squeals, coming to an agonizing halt under Josie's guidance, and they both hop out.

"Ohmigod, that was so much fun."

"She's a natural," Jesse says with a laugh.

I laugh with him. "Yeah, looked it. Mind if we give it a go?"

"Wait, you know how to drive a tractor?" Kendra asks. "I thought Jesse was going to give me a lesson."

"Any lesson you need, you can get from me, Kens," I tell her, and my words come out sounding far more sexual than I intended.

She grins. "Oh, is that right?"

I throw my arm around her. "Whatever you want." She smiles up at me, and I realize I might be what she wants, right now, but am I what she needs? Will I ever be good enough for this woman?

18

KENDRA

"Catch of the Bay," I read as I glance up at the sign hanging over the restaurant.

"You sure seafood is okay?" Dane asks as we walk down the wharf to the restaurant Josie said she wanted to try.

My stomach turns, and honestly, I'm not sure any restaurant sounds appealing to me. I'm not going to complain, though. Josie is having an awesome time. She and Jesse really seem to like each other, and if this is where she wants to eat, it's the least I can do. I am using her as an excuse to hang around Dane. That thought brings another pang to my stomach. I'm sure it's all this stress of sneaking around that's getting to me.

I squeeze Dane's hand as Jesse pulls open the door for us all. "It sounds perfect." I glance at Jesse as he waves his hand for us all to enter. "Jesse, did you use to moon the cows too?"

"Jesus," Dane groans. "Really, Kens?"

Jesse laughs and Josie spins around. "Did you?" she asks.

"No, I'm not a moron."

"It was a dare," Dane says, like that explains everything and I just laugh.

"He told you that?" Jesse queries as I walk past him.

"No, we ran into some of your old high school friends last night."

Jesse cringes. What, is he worried about the stories they might have told about him? Now I'm really curious. Inside the smell of seafood overtakes my stomach, and a wave of nausea grips me.

"Are you okay?" Josie asks.

"Just have to run to the bathroom," I tell her and put on a big smile. "Late night last night."

She grins and nods. "Lucky girl."

"I'll be right back."

"We'll grab a table," Dane says, as I make my way down a long hall and step into the bathroom, needing a reprieve from the smell of seafood, which I usually love. I take a look at my pale face in the mirror. Good God, I look like death warmed over. Yeah, the stress is really getting to me. After splashing some cold water onto my face, I pinch my cheeks to give them a bit of color and add a dab of lipstick to my lips.

Once I appear semi-human, I step back into the dining room and find everyone sitting at a table overlooking the water. The place is quite quaint, actually. I never thought about living in a small town before. Heck, I never left the city, but the idea of nursing in a rural community does hold a measure of appeal. Although it could get lonely. Then again, I'd probably make lots of friends at the clinic.

Unease hits my stomach. The truth is, thinking about a future without Dane in it is going to be lonely no matter where I live or how many friends I make. I sit, and Josie stares at me, wide-eyed.

What the hell? Do I have something on my face?

"You went swimming last night. Are you crazy?"

"It was fun." I take a sip of water after the server pours it.

"No wonder you're pale today."

"I'm not pale," I say and touch my cheek. "The cold water was invigorating, and shrunk my pores and gave my skin an invigorating glow. You should try it."

"I think I'll pass," Josie says.

I grin at her as the server takes our drink orders. I stick with water, as the idea of alcohol makes me a little nauseous. My stomach eventually settles and I'm able to enjoy a seafood casserole, while the others all dig into big servings of deep fried fish and chips.

"Are you going to the pick-up game tomorrow?" I ask Josie, as I bite into my food.

She groans. "Does it have to be so early?"

I laugh. She's not much of a morning person. "Is that a no?"

"That's a yes, but does it really have to be so early?"

"Yeah, it does," Jesse explains. "It's the only time the school has rink time, and then we need to get back to the city."

I'm anxious to get Josie alone to find out how things are really going between them, but I suspect she'll drive back with Jesse and I won't get to interrogate her until we're back at our place.

"I'm going," she finally says. "Are you?"

"Of course," I tell her, wanting to support Dane, and beneath the table, he gives my leg a squeeze, a sign he knows I'm on his side.

I take a big drink of my water, thankful that my stomach has settled, and that my food wasn't greasy. I'm not sure that would have done me any good. After I wipe my mouth with the napkin, I set it down, and ask, "Who's ready for the haunted house?"

"Me," Jesse says, excitedly.

Josie groans and rubs her stomach. "Maybe I shouldn't have eaten so much. I don't want anyone to scare that meal back up."

I laugh at that. "You don't have to do it."

"Oh, right, and then you'll all call me a chicken. If you're doing it, Kendra, I'm doing it." I'm the chicken in the coop here and everyone knows it. Since I'm turning over a new leaf, I'm not letting anyone do anything fun or scary without me.

"Let's go then." The guys pay for our meals, despite our protests, and Josie and I wander outside. I breathe in the fresh country air. "It's nice here, isn't it?"

"I thought you loved the city."

I nod. "I do." I step a bit closer, feeling conspiratorial. "Now tell me everything going on with you and Jesse."

She grins and if I'm not mistaken, I think I see a flush on her face. "You really like him, don't you?" She nods. "And it's mutual."

"It's new, Kendra." Her shoulders shrug and there's a weariness about her. "We just met. He barely knows me and vice versa. I think we're just having fun, you know. I don't want to read any more into it. Know what I mean?"

"Oh yeah," I say. I totally know what she means.

"You say that like it's the same between you and Dane. Just having fun?"

My stomach tanks. I don't see how we can have a future. "Just having fun," I tell her. "My brother thinks no one is ever good enough, and he only wants what is best for me."

She groans. "Does he know best."

My stomach tightens as old memories bombard me. "Josie..."

"Kendra, you have to do what is best for you." I nod. She's not telling me anything new here, and I'm not in the mood to rehash this same old argument.

"If Dane makes it into the NHL..." My words fall off as Dane exits the restaurant, and from the look on his face, I have a feeling he heard the last part and knows what I'm saying. My problem is, I'm not sure the NHL is right for him. He needs to do what's right for him too, not what others think is right. What a pair we make.

Dane puts his hand on the small of my back, and I spot a hint of pain in his eyes. He blinks it away and my heart pinches tight. "All set?" he asks.

I nod. "It's not really that scary, is it?" I ask, trying to lighten the mood.

Jesse laughs as we walk to the car. "Are your socks on tight?"

Dane takes my hand. "Just stick close to me. I won't let any big monsters hurt you."

What he doesn't realize is he's the only big monster who can hurt me, and when this thing ends between us, I have no idea how I'll plaster on a smile and use only the memories of us to keep me warm.

We jump into our seats, and Dane backs out of the parking lot. The sun is low on the horizon as we drive the short distance to the haunted house. Cars are already pulling in, and laughter and screams echo in the night sky. I spot a bunch of teenagers running around. "I guess this isn't really for kids, is it?"

Dane takes my hand as I snuggle into him. "At nighttime, it's not."

Jesse speaks to a few people he must know, and then we all head to the front door of the house, cutting across the lawn like everyone else. As we walk, something tickles my ankle and I nearly jump into Dane's arms. Josie screeches from behind me.

"What was that?" She searches the ground.

"I don't know," I answer, but let's get off the grass.

Dane arches a brow. "Are you sure you want to do this?" I nod at Dane in reply. "If you don't find this fun."

"I won't know until I do it," I tell him with a small lift of my chin.

"Okay then."

The house is dark as we enter and follow behind a teenage couple who are clinging to one another. Groans and creaks fill the air, and streamers, or at least I think they're streamers, brush against our heads. I whack them away, and just when I think it might not be too bad, a coffin lid opens and a corpse jackknifes up.

I yelp, and back up, nearly knocking into Josie. "Ohmigod," I yell, and take in the corpse's hideous mask of a decomposing body. Dane pulls me against him. "Did you know that was going to happen?"

"It's different every year, but there's always a casket."

"What else should I be prepared for?"

"Are you afraid of spiders?"

"Why?" I ask, and as soon as I do, a great big spider drops down in front of my face, and when I scream, and it dangles, I nearly get a mouthful. I clamp my hand over my mouth, and Dane whacks the thing out of our way.

"Afraid of spiders," he says. "Duly noted."

We continue through the haunted house, and while it's scary, it's also fun too. Or at least I think it is until we reach the end, and a bunch of zombies chase us out the back door. I don't think I've ever run so fast in my entire life. Dane and I are laughing—and screaming—okay, I'm the only one screaming as Josie and Jesse come running out behind.

"That was so much fun," Josie says. "Can we do the corn maze now?"

I stand there bent over, hands on my knees trying to catch my breath. "Can you give me a minute? My heart is about to explode."

Dane bends forward to check on me. "Are you okay?"

I smile at him. I'm not sure if I'm okay. After we're over, I might not ever be okay again, and I'm used to existing that way anyway. But right now, tonight, being here with him, that makes me happy, and I'm simply going to enjoy it.

"I am," I tell him and push upright. I poke his hard belly and glance down at my own, which has a bit of a pudge. I need to stop eating pizza and pasta. "I'm out of shape."

As Josie and Jesse head toward the maze, Dane puts his mouth close to my hear. "I like your shape. Play your cards right and later I'll show you just how much."

"We're playing cards?" He angles his head, staring at me like I might be serious, and when I give him a teasing grin he laughs.

His big hand engulfs mine and he tugs to set me into motion. "The only cards I'll play with you is strip poker and we don't need to do that for me to get you naked. You're kind of easy like that."

"Hey," I whack him. "It's true, but you didn't have to point it out."

"It's okay, when it comes to you, I'm easy too."

"When it comes to me. Pfft. I know your reputation, Dane. You're easy with everyone."

He puts his hand over his heart, like I just pierced it. "Ouch."

I roll my eyes. "It's not a dig. You're a single guy. You can be with whoever you want."

"I want you, Kendra," he says, everything about him so serious, it pierces my heart.

I swallow against the lump rising in my throat. What the hell are we doing?

Having fun, Kendra, enjoying this while you can.

Is it a mistake though? I mean, I could be ruining this man's future, everything he's fighting for—all for my own selfish reasons.

"Hurry up guys," Josie calls out, and I swallow down the fear rising up inside me.

"We better move."

He nods and I fall quiet as he goes somber. We hurry our steps and catch up with Josie and Jesse. "Are things going to jump out at us in this maze?" I ask.

"You can count on it," Jesse answers, and I don't miss the way Dane has gone quiet. Should I have told him I wanted him too? Would he read more into that? Actually, maybe I'm reading too much into his words.

"Do they change the maze every year too?" I ask Dane.

His somber mood shifts, and there's playful mischief in his eyes. "Not enough that I don't know a few secrets."

"What's that supposed to mean?" We enter the maze, and scary moans come from a nearby speaker.

"It means I want to make this a fun experience for you."

We walk in the dimly lit maze, losing our friends, and I brace myself, waiting for something, anything to jump out at me. Catching me by surprise, Dane snatches my hand and takes me down a long path, taking turns I'll never find my way out of. We come to a dead end, and he turns, leans against a bale of hay, spreads his legs and pulls me against him. He brushes my hair from my face, and puts his mouth on mine. His kiss is hot and hungry, and so damn needy my legs weaken. A low, agonized moan rumbles in my throat as I sink against him.

"Oh, yes, this is fun," I murmur.

He breaks the kiss, still holding me close as he repositions and puts a knee between my legs. "If we want to scare the others off, I'm going to need you to moan louder."

"You want me to moan?"

He rubs his leg against my aching sex. "Yes, and I'm going to help you with that."

19

DANE

"You could have slept in," I tell Kendra as she yawns beside me. Unlike me, she's not used to early morning practices at the rink, and while I like having her watch me, she looks tired and pale this morning. I'm not surprised. After all the fun we had at the haunted maze, we went for a walk by the lake and didn't get in until late. She'll have to return home to classes to get a break from this weekend away.

She stretches her legs out. "No, I want to watch." Her grin is cute and playful. "I know how much you love it when I watch." I wrap my fingers around her thigh and give it a small squeeze.

"I like it. I think I perform better when you're watching. I didn't play so great during our away game last Thursday night."

"You kill it when I go to your home games."

"Maybe you're my good luck charm."

She laughs. "Do you have any superstitions? I know my brother said a lot of guys on the team do." She cringes. "One guy wears the same underwear every game and never washes them."

"Yeah, it's me."

"Dane, no!"

I laugh. "I'm kidding. I don't really have any superstitions." Probably because hockey isn't really my passion. I don't get into it like the other guys do. "Do you have superstitions?" I ask.

"I never used to, but now I do."

I arch a brow. "Oh?"

"Yeah, I cross at the crosswalk now. If I don't, it can lead to uncertain consequences, bad luck like—"

"Getting run over by a bike."

We both laugh, and I squeeze her leg again. "But that brought you luck."

"How?"

"Maybe what I'm trying to say is, you got *lucky* after getting run over." I wink at her. "We both got lucky."

"I'm not sure I needed to get run over first," she jokes.

We pull into the rink, and Jesse pulls in beside us, his car all fixed. We hop from my car and I move our bags—we're headed back to the city after the game—to grab my gear from the back. I always have spare gear and honestly, I'm surprised my parents aren't here to check my progress, make sure I'm on the top of my game. I probably wouldn't play well if they were watching. Unlike Kendra, they follow my moves with critical eyes.

"How are you this morning, Kendra?" Jesse asks, and I turn to her. Does she look pale to him too? "Nightmares after the haunted house and maze?"

She stifles a yawn. "I slept okay."

He arches a disbelieving brow. "Doesn't look like you slept at all." He turns to me. "You either."

I put my hand on his back. "On that note," I tease, giving him a shove to set him into motion. He doesn't need to know that Kendra and I are tired because I spent the better part of the night with my mouth on her body.

As we head inside, the girls follow behind, chatting quietly, and I'm sure Kendra is getting all caught up on what's going on between our friends. Fingers crossed they like each other. Yeah, okay, I have guilt. Jesse is doing me a huge favor, and I can only hope I'm doing him one in return.

"Hey, how's it going with you two?" I ask Jesse. He opens his mouth but before he can get the words out, the doors to the rink are flung open and the high school team we're playing all start slapping us on the backs. I'm sure, with Jesse being drafted, they're all anxious to say hello, and get pointers. I'm still a nobody.

We follow the guys in, and meet up with our old high school coach. We chat for a bit, and I find myself more interested in Kendra sitting in the stands than the game we're about to play. Jesus, that's not conducive to making the NHL. But she is my good luck charm and when push comes to shove, she makes me a better player because I'm playing for something important. I heard her last night when I left the restaurant.

She might not be willing to admit it to me, or herself, but I won't be good enough if I don't make the NHL.

The coach leads us into the locker room and there's excitement in the air. I look at all the NHL hopefuls, and I wish them all the best. I wish I had their enthusiasm. But to me, it's a need, not a want.

After we gear up, we head onto the ice, and Kendra and Josie stand and clap. I laugh as I lift my stick to them. Jesse pats me on the back. "Head in the game, bro."

I drop my stick and slap it on the ice. "Right." I do a few warm-ups, as do the rest of the guys and once we're done, we all take our positions, the coach putting Jesse and me on opposite teams, and for the next hour we play. I give it my all, even though it doesn't seem to be good enough today, but it's kind of fun, actually. With no scouts watching, I can just be me, and enjoy the game for what it is. We all have a great time, and Jesse and his team end up winning. I still think I played my best. Unfortunately, at times my best isn't good enough. Which means I have to play better than my best if I want to keep Kendra in my life.

After the game, we head to the locker room and hang out with the guys for a bit, and Jesse gives them advice. I pipe in once in a while, although my advice isn't worth much at this point. Once we're done, we head outside, and Kendra and Josie are in deep conversation.

"Hey," I say as I approach. A smile stretches across Kendra's mouth and I'm sort of disappointed that I lost. I want to make her proud of me.

"Great game," she says and kisses me, which makes me feel a lot better. I put my arm around her waist.

"Thanks, want to get a breakfast sandwich?"

She laughs. "Is there anywhere around here to get one?"

"We can stop on the way home."

"You played great," Josie says to Jesse as he comes up behind me.

He smiles. "You ready to hit the road?"

She nods, and Jesse pats me on the back. "See you back at the dorm. Talk to you later, Kendra."

They head toward their car, and I turn back to Kendra. Her brow is furrowed. "Everything okay?"

She puts on a smile. "Everything is good. Ready?"

We start toward my car and I cast her a fast glance. "Josie is good?"

Her smile reappears. "Yes, I think she really likes Jesse. Has he said anything to you?"

I laugh. "What, are we back in junior high?"

She threads her hand through my arm as we walk. "You're right. I just worry." Her top teeth press into her bottom lip, and I get it. We don't want to use our friends for our own benefit. I look up and spot Jesse tossing his gear into the back of his car. "I think he's happy."

We reach my car and I put my gear away as Kendra slides into the passenger seat. She's yawning when I climb in beside her. I put my hand on her leg. "Why don't you have a nap, and I'll wake you when we get to the drive-thru."

"I don't want to fall asleep on you."

I give her a playful wink. "I'm the reason you're so tired."

She chuckles. "I might be responsible too." She yawns again. "I don't know why I'm so tired lately."

Probably all the sneaking around is playing havoc with her. It sure as hell is with me. I'm definitely more tense than usual, the pressure to succeed even more predominant. I start the car and she settles back in her seat as I aim my car toward the city. She sleeps and I drive for about a half an hour before I find my favorite breakfast spot. I order and I'm almost reluctant to wake her.

"Coffee," she murmurs, and inhales as she sits up a bit straighter.

I chuckle and hand over her extra-large cup, made just the way she likes it. She takes a big sip. "So good."

I reach into the bag and pull out the sandwich I got for her. "Do you think you could eat?"

Her hands go to her stomach. "I don't know."

"You barely got any toast down this morning." She frowns, and I take in the tightness of her body. "I think you might be coming down with something."

She takes the sandwich from me. "I'm okay." What, is she trying to prove she's not sick? She doesn't have to pretend with me. Unlike her brother, I know she's strong and capable, but hey, people get sick.

I reach back into the bag and grab my breakfast sandwich. Since I'm an expert at eating and driving—considering I'm always eating—I tear down the wrapper and make my way back to the highway. Every now and then I cast Kendra a quick glance and while I devoured my breakfast in four big bites, she's still nibbling on hers.

"How's your week looking?" I ask, hoping I can see her again before the weekend.

"Busy. Test coming up. You?" She keeps swallowing, and I'm beginning to suspect something is terribly wrong.

"The usual. School, hockey...you." I smile at her and she smiles back. "Are you coming to Friday's game? It's against the Islanders so it will be a close one."

"Definitely."

She folds the paper back over the sandwich and puts it back in the bag. "I don't usually have much of an appetite in the morning."

Up until now, she had a fine appetite in the morning, but I let that go. She closes her eyes again, and I turn the radio down, so she can sleep for the rest of the drive. A little over a half hour later, I pull into her driveway and she stirs awake.

"We're here," I say quietly and she sits up. A second later, panic moves over her face. "Kendra."

"I'm going to be sick."

She bolts from the car, her key in her hands as she hurries to her front door. "Fuck." I kill the ignition, unbuckle and pocket my keys as I follow her inside. Heaving sounds reach my ears as I shut the door behind us. "Kendra," I say and walk down the hall, stopping outside the closed bathroom door. "Kendra, can I come in?"

"No," she yells and then goes back to vomiting.

I stand there for a second, and glance around, searching for her roommate. She's not back yet. I shift from one foot to the other. I hate feeling useless like this. I want to help her. If I open the door will she be mad?

I walk to the kitchen, and pour a glass of water. "Kendra," I say quietly, back at the bathroom door. "I'm coming in, okay?"

She doesn't answer, so I open the door and find her on the floor, her blue eyes stark against her pale face. My stomach lurches. I drop down next to her. She groans and tries to turn away. "I don't want you seeing me like this. I'm disgusting."

I brush her hair back. "Babe, I want to help, and nothing about you is disgusting." I hand her the water and she rinses her mouth. I notice the small cabinet, and open it to pull out a clean cloth. I run it under cool water and press it to her forehead.

"That is nice," she moans and leans against the wall, and I note the way she's cradling her stomach.

"Do you think we should go to the clinic? It can't be food poisoning from bad pasta. It's been too long." She shakes her head and I use the cloth to wipe her mouth. "You haven't been feeling good for a while. It wouldn't hurt to get a checkup."

She moans. "I don't want to go."

I sit next to her and we stay like that for a long time. I wish Josie was here. She'd know what to do. When Kendra starts vomiting again, I realize we can't let this go on any longer and make the decision to take her to the clinic.

"We need to get you checked out, babe."

"I'm sure it's the flu." It's not flu season just yet, but okay. "I've been run down," she adds, her dark lashes blinking weakly over her big blue eyes. "School. Stress. No sleep. A weekend away. Swimming in the lake."

"I know. I'd just feel better if you had a quick checkup."

A not so humorous laugh crawls out of her throat. "Nothing is quick at the clinic, and I have studying to do."

I lightly run my finger over her wrist. "You can't study like this anyway."

She goes quiet for a long time. I'm about to push again when her shoulders slump in defeat. "You're right." She blows out a long, slow breath. "I guess I'm going to the clinic."

I rinse the cloth again to wash her up. Once she's feeling strong enough, I help her to her feet and she takes a moment at the sink to rinse her face and brush her teeth. I carefully help her outside, back into my car and drive the short distance to the waterfront clinic.

"This is going to take forever," she groans.

Worried that she's going to bail, I pull her to me and hold her tight. "Let's just go see. If it's really bad, we can come back tomorrow."

"You don't have to come back with me."

I don't argue, instead I lead her inside, and take in all the people waiting. Kendra registers as I snag us two chairs, and she sits beside me. I take her head and put it on my shoulder, encouraging her to rest. Our wait is long, and Kendra is rest-less, but at least her stomach has settled. I really shouldn't have pushed that sandwich on her.

Hours pass, and her name is finally called and I'm about to stand and go into the back room with her. "I'm okay," she says weakly, and I nod and sit back down as the heavy black door leading to the offices falls shut behind her. I try not to feel a pang of hurt that she didn't want me with her. Christ. I'm not her boyfriend, so why would she?

I pull out my phone and scroll as I wait for her. Fifteen minutes pass and the door leading to the back room opens and the second I set eyes on her, take in her horrified expression, I jump to my feet.

"Kendra, what is it?"

20

KENDRA

My legs are shaking as I step into the waiting room. I take one look at Dane, my heart pounding in my throat as he jumps to his feet. How do I tell him?

What do I tell him?

I take deep breaths, hoping to fuel my constricted lungs as he comes toward me, his warm hand doing little to heat my chilled blood. I stare up at him, unable to find my words. He repeats my name, and that's when I notice we're drawing attention from those in the waiting room. I take the piece of paper in my hand—a follow-up appointment for an ultrasound, which will take forever since our health care system is broken—and shove it into my pocket. Dane's gaze follows the action, and his eyes, when they fall back on mine, are brimming with questions and worry.

My news is going to ruin his future.

"Can you...take me home please?"

"Right, of course." He puts his arm around me and I fight back the tears as I force one leg in front of the other. How could I have been so damn stupid? I should have listened to my brother. I never should have started anything with Dane. This is just a reminder that I don't make good decisions and I should have left them all in my brother's hands.

My God, my brother. What is he going to say?

The afternoon wind is nice on my face and I lift my chin to the October sun. Dane falls quiet, and I owe him an explanation. I just need a moment to gather myself. Honestly, all the signs were there. How could I not have put this together.

He helps me into his car and we drive the short distance back to my place. The front door is locked, and when we get inside I call out to Josie, but she's not back yet. I might be a little grateful for that.

"You want to go to your room?" Dane asks quietly, tentatively, as he stands by the door. My heart wobbles at the vulnerability on his face. He has no idea if he should stay or go, and right now, after I tell him the news, I'm not sure which one he'll want more.

I nod, and he puts his arm around me and guides me up the steps and to my bedroom. I sit on my bed, and he stands there, scrubbing his face. "Kendra?"

"Dane," I begin and he exhales and drops to the floor in front of me. He moves between my legs, and my throat squeezes tight. I have to tell him. It's his right to know. Is he going to hate me?

"Are you...hurt?"

I shake my head, and cup his cheeks. "I'm sorry," I say.

"For what?"

A big, hiccupping cry catches in my throat, and I cover my face as I begin to sob. "Hey." He removes my hands from my eyes, puts them on my lap and touches my chin until my eyes meet his. "Whatever it is, I'm here for you."

"I'm pregnant," I blurt out, and he goes still. Too still. I search his face, and try to see past the shock.

"I thought..."

I nod quickly. "The implant didn't work, and there is a chance of ectopic pregnancy."

"That's dangerous."

"The doctor took the implant out, and they're getting me in for an ultrasound as soon as possible." I swallow. "I'm sorry, Dane. I never meant for this to happen. If you don't want to have anything—"

"We're in this together, Kendra. I'm not going to let you do this alone. I'm here no matter what you decide, and...what do you want?"

"I don't know. It's all coming at me so fast. I'm going to have to think about this. I just don't want this to affect you. You can't let anything interfere with the NHL."

"Kendra." My name comes out a breathless whisper. "We need to think about what's best for you right now." His hand goes to my stomach, and he flattens it. For the briefest of seconds, I think I spot a tiny smile on his face. I must be mistaken. He doesn't want this. A shiver goes through me and I hug myself. "Why don't you lay down for a bit?"

I nod and look longingly at my pillow. "Okay."

He pulls the blankets down and helps me crawl under them. For a second, I think he's about to leave, but then he crawls in beside me, and I'm the little spoon to his big one. Exhaustion pulls at me, despite sleeping in the car, and I sink into his warmth.

He holds me tight, and for a moment, I think everything is going to be all right. Until I realize how stupid that is. Fresh tears fall and he makes soothing sounds behind me until sleep pulls me under. When I wake, a burst of panic invades my body, and I try to move, but can't. That's when I realize Dane is still beside me, his heavy arm around me, holding me down. I take a deep breath and let it out.

He's still here.

That thought almost makes me laugh. Was I worried he'd flee? I guess maybe I was. This is a pretty big bomb to drop on him, especially when it could easily pull him off the path he's determined to travel. Even though I'm pretty sure it's not the path he wants. Still, the decision is his, not mine, and I don't want this baby to be something he comes to regret later. I won't have that.

"Hey," he whispers quietly, his breath warm and comforting on my face. "How are you feeling?" His arm loosens and I turn to see him. My heart lurches as I take in the deep concern in his eyes. I don't think he slept. Nope, he probably laid here the whole time worrying and I hate that.

"I'm feeling much better." I swallow against a tight throat. "You don't have to stay. You probably have a million things to do."

His body tightens, and a line forms on his forehead as he frowns. "Do you want me to go?"

"No, it's just… I don't want to keep you if you have things to do. It's not like there's anything you can do, and we don't need to make any decisions today."

"I can get you some crackers, or some soup. That's what I always had when my stomach wasn't good."

As soon as the words leave his mouth, my stomach grumbles. "Actually, that does sound kind of appealing." He's about to roll and I touch his arm. "Dane."

"Yeah."

"We can't tell anyone." More secrets for us to keep close. Goddammit, I'm so tired of the secrets. "It's early, and things can happen, you know."

"You're not telling Josie?"

"No, and please don't tell Jesse. I know it's a lot to ask, and it's not that I don't trust him. Things have a way of leaking."

"I won't. You can trust me." He touches my face, before he pulls me to him. His heart is beating fast, pounding against his ribcage. "I want to be here for you, Kendra."

I inch back, and scan his face. "Promise me you won't let this interfere with your hockey, or your plans for your future." I quickly do the math. My brother graduates and goes off to the NHL in April. I'll be like eight months pregnant then, and there'll be no hiding it. God, I have so much to figure out. I dig deep, and work to find a strength inside me that I'd always suppressed. Dane is going to be in my life no matter what now, and no way am I going to let my brother ruin his future.

Dane glances down for a moment, his struggles all over his face. "Dane, please. Don't veer off your path because of this."

"What about you, your path?"

"I have an inheritance which will help with expenses, and women have babies in college. It won't be easy by any means, but it's doable." My stomach cramps and I bite back fresh tears. What do I know about being a mother? Heck, I killed my own family. How can I keep a baby safe, and cared for? "It's a lot to figure out," I say, trying not to sound breathless and anxious for Dane's sake. "One day at a time." I lean in and kiss him as I work to push down another bout of anxiety. Why didn't I realize what was going on with my body? How could I have been so stupid? I've just turned our lives upside down. Dane and I aren't even a couple, yet here I am with his child inside me.

Nate was right. I make bad decisions. I never should have had sex without a condom.

"One day at a time," He agrees, his voice is shaky and it's easy to tell he's trying to remain calm for me. Heck, I'm trying to do the same for him. I'm not sure either of us are pulling it off. He rolls and stands. "I'll run out and get you some soup. What kind do you want?"

I force a smile. "Chicken noodle sounds about right."

He laughs in response, but it's rough and labored, and heavier than he intended, I'm sure. "My favorite." His body shifts, like he's about to turn, but then he goes still. "I want to be involved, Kendra," he says quietly, but firmly.

"Okay."

His chest rises and falls quickly, his adrenaline pumping as fast as mine. "No secrets. I know we're keeping secrets from others, but not between us, okay?" I nod, and he continues with, "The paper you put in—"

"It's the ultrasound. I'm waiting on dates. You want to come?"

"Yes." His body relaxes. "Just let me know when."

"Dane."

"Yes."

"I'm sorry I made a mess of things."

His throat makes a sound as he swallows. "Hey, Kens. It takes two. Right?"

It does take two, but he's not disagreeing that this is a mess. Neither of us wanted or are ready for a child.

I nod and his back muscles are tight, his shoulders around his ears as he disappears out my door. I lay there, still, the sound of his engine revving reaching my ears. My stomach grumbles some more as I roll over, my mind a chaotic mess as I wait for Dane to come back.

I somehow drift off to sleep, exhaustion getting the better of me until footsteps on the stairs pull me awake. My heart squeezes tight as Dane comes into the room, a bag of food in his hand. I can't let this mess up his future, can't let him come to resent me. The way I think Nate might resent me. I sit up and cross my legs as he pulls soup, and rolls and crackers from the bag.

"Soup," I murmur. "Jesse's nickname."

He grunts out a laugh and hands me a bottle of vitamin water and it makes me laugh. Wait, why does he suddenly look so sheepish, so embarrassed?

"I thought." He shakes his head and averts his eyes. "I don't know what I thought." He runs his fingers through his hair, shifting from one foot to the other. "I don't know the first thing about pregnancy or supplements, or...anything."

"Neither do I, but I do love vitamin water. Come here." He sits next to me, and I lean forward and kiss him. "You're sweet, Dane." I open the water, take a sip and another burst of panic invades my body. What am I going to do? I start taking deep gulping breaths.

"Hey."

"I can't..." I lift my head to meet his worried eyes. "I can't even take care of myself, how am I going to take care of a child?" My mind goes back to my childhood, and the results of my mistakes. I begin to hyperventilate, and with my free hand I grip the bedding and fist the sheets. Dane quickly takes action and removes the drink from my hand. He climbs into the bed and leans against the headboard, pulling me between his legs, so I can rest my head on his thigh.

"Breathe, Kens." He takes deep breaths, and I breathe with him until I'm somewhat calm. "None of what happened in your childhood was your fault," he says again. "You were a child. You're not a child anymore. You're a responsible adult, and you make good decisions." He's trying to remain calm, but there's a hitch to his voice. I understand. I'd basically told him he wasn't a good decision. "It's not your fault the implant didn't work. Sometimes mistakes happen. Sometimes bad things come from mistakes, and sometimes good things come from them, too." He brushes my hair from my face in a soothing manner.

"I just..." I can't believe I'm having a baby. I take a deep breath and let it out.

"One day at a time," he whispers quietly. I nod, and hold onto him like he's my lifeline, and after a long while, his voice breaks the quiet. "Do you want to try to eat something?" I nod, sit up and brush my hands over my face to wipe away the wetness. "I can reheat the soup."

"No, I'm sure it's fine."

He props up a pillow and I lean against it as he stands, opens the soup container and hands it to me. I breathe in the delicious smells, happy it's not making me nauseous. He takes the spoon from the bag, dips it into the container and holds it out for me to taste.

"Delicious," I tell him.

"Kens?"

I glance at Dane, as his eyes flicker over my face, a nervous gesture I've never seen him do before. Then again, no one has ever told him he was going to be a father either.

"What?" I ask.

"Will you be my girlfriend?" I stare at him for a second, my brain absorbing his words. "Secret girlfriend, I get it. It has to be a secret," he adds quickly. "But girlfriend, none the less."

A laugh bubbles out of my throat. "Yes, Dane. I'll be your girlfriend," I tell him, just as my phone pings. I stiffen, knowing it's Nate from the chime. I stare at Dane, and he reaches for my phone and holds it out to me. I read the message and the soup I just swallowed threatens to make a resurgence. A noise crawls out of my throat.

"Kens?"

"My brother is on his way over."

21

DANE

I pound the steering wheel as I drive back to Storm House. Goddammit, I wanted to stay there and talk to Nate. I wanted to stand eye to eye with the man, and tell him I would become everything he wanted me to be, so he'd accept me as his sister's partner. Only problem was, Kendra didn't want that, and right now, with so much to deal with, I have to respect her wishes. Plus, I need to prove myself. Once I get drafted, we'll have the conversation we need to have. The rest Kendra and I will figure out afterward.

I'm going to be a father.

Jesus. My brain swims as a million thoughts come at me so fast, the street before me blurs. I blink to clear my head, even more determined to become the man Kendra needs me to be. A laugh bursts from my throat. It was easy to tell my father thought she was a distraction, but at the end of the day, she's the reason I needed to succeed.

I pull into Storm House and glance around for Jesse's car. It's nowhere to be found. I usually tell him everything. Fuck knows I hate secrets. While I want to tell him, I can't. I'd never betray Kendra's trust like that. Hell, she doesn't even plan to tell Josie.

Trust is important to me, and I'm glad she told me about the pregnancy. For a brief moment there, when she came from the clinic, I wasn't sure she was going to tell me what was wrong, and I understand. She's worried about my future. She puts everyone else's needs above her own, which means I need to put her above mine. While I know she's capable of taking care of herself, I plan to be there for her.

I exit the car, and my body is tired as I head inside Storm House. I check my phone, worry gnawing at me. I'd like to know what Nate wanted. I guess I'll find out soon enough. Until then, I need to hit the books and later hit the gym. I plan to work twice as hard at practice and exercise. With that plan swimming in my brain, I enter Storm House and I'm about to dart up to my room when Andre comes from the kitchen, his face red. Shit, did I do something to piss him off?

"What's up?" I ask, stopping on the first step.

"My best friend Gabe just fucked me over. We've been friends since we were kids, for fuck's sake."

I drop down onto the step. "Jesus, what happened?" He makes a fist, and paces back and forth. "I fucking came home." He shakes his head. "My sister, Elise. My best friend, Gabe. What the fuck was he thinking? He's lucky I didn't fucking kill him."

I don't really know much about Andre, other than he comes from Quebec and has a younger sister he's very protective of.

I have no idea what's going on here, so I simply say, "Yeah, man, I don't know."

"Now my sister isn't talking to me. She said she never wants to see me again."

I try to wrap my brain around his words and piece things together. "Your sister and your best friend?" Ah, I get it. There seems to be a lot of hook ups between player's friends on the team and their sisters. I wouldn't know anything about that. I only have an older brother.

"Motherfucker." He drops down onto the step next to me. "I just want what's best for her. What the fuck ever happened to bro code, dude?"

Bro code, yeah, I get it. Every player on the team is supposed to abide by it. I never was one to play by the rules, but this time not playing could tank my career, and I need my career more than ever. What a fucking mess I've gotten myself into. Guilt swamps me.

"I'm sorry, Andre."

"Why would Gabe do that to me?"

"Did you ask him?"

"No, I told him to get out and that I never wanted to see him again." I give a low slow whistle, mainly to hide the storm brewing inside me. "What, do you think I did the wrong thing?"

"I don't know, man. I wasn't there."

"He betrayed me, Dane, and is out of my life. I also lost my sister. Family is important."

Guilt once again hits harder than a hockey stick to the face. "Yeah, family is important." I swallow. Christ, I might live in my brother's shadow, but I can't imagine a scenario where we never spoke to one another again. Is that the scenario I'm putting Kendra in? Jesus, she can't lose her brother, not after all the loss she's had in her life.

"I know you don't have a sister, but imagine if you did and imagine if your best friend Jesse betrayed you like that?" My throat clamps tight. Am I betraying him? Asking him to be with someone to cover my own deceit. Wow, I'm a real piece of shit, aren't I?

With my earlier mojo deflating, I try to summon a bit of energy. "Actually, I'm going to hit the gym."

He stretches his arms over his head. "Even better."

"Speaking of Jesse, have you seen him?" I glance around when I hear noise coming from the kitchen.

He shakes his head and pushes to his feet. "Not since the game. Why, what's up?"

I grab hold of the banister. "Oh, nothing."

"I haven't seen you either." He starts up the steps. "Where have you been?"

Oh, just betraying everyone and ruining lives.

"Had to go back to Bass River, drove Jesse home to get his car." Not a lie. Not the whole truth but not a lie either. "He's probably just hanging with his family a little longer." He likely circled back to see them. Me, well, I couldn't get away fast enough and it kind of sucks that I never got to show Kendra how to make cheese. Will she still want to go to the wine and cheese show coming up? Not that she can eat the soft cheese or drink wine. Not when pregnant. Damn, maybe I do know a little something about pregnancy.

His head lifts, his eyes hopeful. "Did you bring back any cheese?"

I laugh. "No, next time."

"Cheddar would have brought back cheese."

Yeah, of course he would have. He's better at everything. I stand and we head up the stairs, my legs a little heavy with guilt as I climb. I can't come between Kendra and Nate.

"I like that jalapeno gouda," he informs. "It's got that hot bite to it." He rubs his stomach. "Delicious."

"Noted." I glance at him and while he's seems like he just got a load off his chest, I realize I didn't help him with anything and he likely has a long, hard road ahead of him with his sister and best friend.

I go to my room and check my phone again. How is Kendra going to put on a brave face for her brother, and pretend nothing is wrong with her? Then again, hasn't she been doing that her whole life? I snatch my workout gear from my dresser and pull it on. Back in the hall, I meet with Liam and we head back outside, walking the short distance to the campus gym.

I glance out at the running track. "I think I'll go for a run before hitting the weights."

"Catch up with you later, man."

"Andre, I really am sorry about your sister and friend. I hope things work out for you."

Sadness invades his face and my heart clenches. "Yeah, thanks." His shoulders go slack as he walks into the gym, and I head to the track, needing to fill my lungs with fresh air. It's been a crazy day, a crazy fucking week. Actually, it's been a crazy fucking month.

I do a bit of mental math. Kendra can't be very far along. Sure, we've been having sex like crazy, but she must have gotten pregnant that first time we didn't use a condom. Was that my idea or hers? I can hear my fucking brother now. How many times did he warn me to use a condom—warn me to stay away from Kendra? He'd tell me she had an agenda I knew nothing about. He'd be wrong.

The truth is, he's seen guys get trapped and baited by women wanting to get their claws into a hockey player—wanting the money and lifestyle that comes with the NHL. He doesn't know Kendra like I do. She's not like other women on campus. I get that she wants me to be a hockey player, but that's for me, because it's my dream. Sort of. Although she did tease me about opening Bike and Bries. That was a joke though, I'm sure. She was pretty adamant that I not let her pregnancy interfere with my goals.

Because she's all about the jersey, dude.

As my brother's words, not mine, jump into my brain, I stretch out on the grass and glance around. I peer into the distance. Are those Lance's asshole friends gathered at the other end of the track? I shake my head. What did Kendra ever see in that asshole and how dare he fucking make her feel bad about herself. I should punch the motherfucker in the face.

Yeah, and that's going to help you keep your feelings for Nate's sister a secret, asshole.

After I stretch out, I put my ear buds in and hit the track, pacing myself at first, but the run feels good, helps clear my head, so I pick up my pace. I run by Lance's friends, and they're saying something to me, but I can't hear them. I'm not about to stop either. I don't care what they have to say to me. As long as they're leaving Kendra alone, that's all that matters.

I circle the track, and on my next pass two of Lance's friends flank me, keeping pace on the track. Okay, this is interesting. I continue to ignore them, until I can't, and the reason I can't is because one of the guys, I think his name is James, bumps into me.

I slow and pull my earbuds out, my body preparing for what I think is about to come—a fight. "Hey Jimmy," I say. "You're supposed to stay in your own lane."

He laughs. "It's James and you're one to talk. Isn't that right, Brent?" he says to the guy tight beside me on the left.

"That's right."

"No idea what you're talking about," I say, but suspect he's about to enlighten me.

"Going after Lance's sloppy seconds."

It takes every ounce of control I have to keep my anger in check. These guys don't get to talk about Kendra like that.

I force myself to stay calm and it takes a hell of a lot of effort. "Kendra and I are friends."

"Yeah, is that why you wouldn't let Becca blow you?"

How the hell does he know about that? "Go fuck yourself," I say and slow down even more, my hands fisting at my sides. I really can't get into a fight. That could get me suspended but goddammit, I am not putting up with this bullshit.

"Wait, are you a fudge packer? You like cock, Dane?"

At least when he's picking on me, he's leaving Kendra alone and that I can handle.

"What part of go fuck yourself didn't you understand?"

"I'd rather fuck Kendra." He snorts and runs his fingers through his blond-tipped hair that could only have been done by a professional. "But she's Lance's, and watch your fucking mouth." He cracks his knuckles. His threats don't scare me.

"Does Lance know you talk about Kendra like this?" He stiffens for a second, and now it's my turn to smirk. "Yeah, I didn't think so, which means you're the one who needs to watch his mouth. Also, in case you didn't know, they broke up and Kendra can be with whoever she wants."

Careful, Dane.

"They might have broken up, but when he wants her sweet pussy back, he wants it available." He snaps his fingers. "He can have her back anytime he wants, and I think he wants it very soon."

"Fuck you."

Unable to help myself, I stop abruptly, and throw my arm back, ready to knock the fucker's perfect white teeth from his face. Unfortunately, his buddy Brent grabs my arm, and James gets the first hit in. I shake Brent off my arm and the next thing I know, the two of us are trading punches. The fucker is stronger than he looks, but I've got the upper hand here— until Brent jumps me, knocking me to the ground.

James kicks me in the ribs, knocking the air from my lungs, and stands over me. "You're nothing like your brother, Dane. So stay in the fucking loser lane and out of Lance's way."

"Tell your pussy friend, the next time he wants to send a message, not to be such a chicken shit and bring it himself."

Those words earn me another kick to the ribs. But dammit, it was worth it.

22

KENDRA

Lying to my brother yesterday wasn't fun. He grilled me on where I was and who I was with and I told him I was with Josie, not a lie, at her family's cottage on the south shore. A total lie. As I underwent his inquisition, there were times I wanted to blurt out that I was with Dane, tell him I wanted to run my own life, only for me to realize that would be a colossal mistake for a couple of reasons.

One, I can't and won't do or say anything to risk ruining Dane's future, and two, guilt over all Nate's done for me flooded my veins and prevented me from telling the truth. How could I be so callous when he acts the way he does because he cares so deeply about me, and has done so much to get me where I am right now?

And where is that, Kendra?

Oh, I don't know. Just pregnant with a guy I barely know. A guy he doesn't think is suitable for me.

If I had listened to Nate from the beginning, I wouldn't have made this mistake and our futures wouldn't be at stake. Damn, what the hell am I going to do? I'm not sure. I glance at my phone, and the messages Dane and I exchanged last night. I love that he was worried about me and my conversation with my brother. Something seemed off, though. He didn't seem himself. Naturally I wanted to chalk it up to the news we got, but there's something else. I can feel it. Then again, I could be projecting, and it's easy to read things into texts that might not be there.

"Good morning," Josie says as she comes into the kitchen, a little lighter on her feet than I'd ever seen her before. She takes one look at me and goes still. "Are you okay?"

"Just tired." Totally understanding, she grins, a sweet, satisfied lift of her lips that lets me know just how well she and Jesse are hitting it off and at least that lessens some of the guilt ballooning inside me. "You didn't get home until late last night." I'd heard her come in, and pretended to be asleep. After my brother's visit, I wasn't up to talking to anyone, not even my bestie, who I don't normally keep big secrets from.

"Yeah, we hung around a bit longer at Jesse's place after the game." She stares off into the distance, a dreamy look on her face. "He has a big family."

I nod, a feeling of happiness and envy coming over me. The only way I'm going to be a part of a big happy family is if I have one myself. My stomach rolls at the reminder that I'll soon have a small family, and not a traditional one.

"You liked them, huh?" I ask, trying to sound normal. I reach for my coffee and take a sip, but it actually turns my stomach. Please God, don't let coffee be one of the things I can't drink during pregnancy. I take another sip and set the mug down.

"They were so nice and welcoming." She stretches her arms over her head. "They're really proud of him getting drafted."

"I'm sure they are." I put my hand over my stomach and Josie frowns.

"Are you feeling okay? Still a bad stomach from the pasta?"

"Yeah, I think so, and just stress from classes." I plaster on a smile. "I had a great weekend, though."

"I'm glad. Are you going to tell Nate about Dane?"

"I think eventually."

She puts her hand on mine and gives it a squeeze. "Good. I'm here for you, you know that, right?"

"I do."

"Okay, I need to get to class." She hops up, drops a pod into the machine, turning back to me. "Thanks for setting me up with Jesse. I owe you one."

Actually, I owe her one.

"You don't owe me anything. Just well, if my brother asks, we were at your cottage on the south shore this weekend, okay?" I toy with my mug. "Not that I think he'll ask."

She angles her head, worried eyes moving over my face. "Kendra—"

"I'll tell him. When the time is right."

She nods, and takes her cup from underneath the machine. She goes quiet as she adds milk and sugar. Once done, she says, "It might be fun to go to the cottage, actually. I can take Jesse out on the boat. I owe him a lesson."

"That sounds fun."

"Come. You and Dane. As soon as they have another free weekend."

"It does sound fun. I'll check with him."

On that note, Josie darts back upstairs to get ready for her class. My phone pings and my heart leaps, hoping it's Dane. The second I see a message from Lance, my blood runs thick. What the hell?

Lance: Want to come by after classes?

I stare at the message. Is he kidding me right now? After the way he talked to me, practically threw me off his steps as his ex-girlfriend sat there and watched, he thinks I'm going to go running back to him—and not to even start this conversation with an apology. Am I really surprised? No, but I do wonder what he's really up to.

Me: No.

I sit there, my heart in my throat as three dots appear and disappear. His message finally comes through.

Lance: I miss you, babe.

Anger fills every pore in my body. He misses me? What he misses is his study buddy, someone who is willing to drop everything to put him first. My thoughts race to Dane. Could the two be any more different? Dane drops everything to put me first. That thought tightens my stomach. I'm going to have to be very careful about that. I can't come first over his career. I'd never forgive myself if he didn't get drafted because of me, and in the end he'd only come to resent me, and our child.

I run my fingers over the phone, ready to tell him what I really think, only to delete my message. It's better not to engage. I drop my phone and a rap sounds at my door. That had better not be Lance. I push to my feet, and head down the hall. Honestly, I shouldn't worry about Lance showing up. I'm the one who always had to run to him. My heart leaps at the sight of Dane.

I swing open the door, take one look at him and before I can get any words out, he holds his hands up to stop me. "It's not as bad as it looks."

"Dane," I say as I wince, pulling him inside, partly to get a better look at his split lip and bruises and partly so no one sees him at my door. "What happened?"

"Lance's goons happened."

My jaw drops open. "Are you kidding me?"

"Afraid not. Don't worry, I got a few punches in too."

I take his hand and lead him to the sofa. "Why would they do this to you?" He sits, braces his elbows onto his knees, and I drop down onto the coffee table to face him.

"They were warning me to stay away from you." His gaze moves over my face. What is he looking for? Signs that I've gone back to Lance? Jeez, I hope he knows me better than that, and when could I have done that? I've been spending all my time with him.

"I'm not with Lance," I state. "What right did they have to do that, now that we're broken up?" Anger floods me. "He doesn't own me, and has no right to say who I can and can't be friends with, or even more," I add. Dane and I aren't just friends anymore. I'm not sure we ever were.

"No one has that right," he says quietly, and I know he's talking about my brother.

I examine his face, and consider what to put on his cuts. "Wait, did they see us together?"

His eyes narrow and he shifts uncomfortably, sliding his hands down his thighs. "They saw us at Salvadori's," he reminds me.

My body tightens. "No after that. Do you think they saw us?" Would they say something to Nate. Is that why he interrogated me last night? I'm sure he would have come right out and said something. It's not in Nate's nature to play games.

"Not that I know of. We've been careful."

"Not that careful. Where is your car?" I turn to look out the window. If he parked it in the driveway...

"Down the street," he says, and leans toward me.

"That was smart." I truly appreciate that he's respecting my wishes to keep things between us quiet for now. It's not like we'll have long before the world knows what we've been up to.

"I'd never want to come between you and your brother, Kendra." There's a deep worry in his eyes that nearly takes the air from my lungs. Dane might be a joker, and can be reckless at times, but there's profound depth about him too. Sometimes I wonder if he's too good to be true. "I'm trying to be careful, and I will be, until…" He swallows, his words falling off.

"Until what?" I ask quickly, suddenly anxious. A hard, uneasy quiver goes through my body and he puts his hand on my leg.

"Until we don't have to be," he finally says.

I meet his glance, and he looks like he wants to tell me more, but isn't sure how. I wait, but no words come. I have something to tell him too. Since he's not speaking, I'll go first. He's not going to like it, but he's always been honest with me so I want to extend the same to him. No secrets between us. That rule is important to both of us.

I sigh, take my phone from my pocket and set it on the coffee table like it might now be diseased. "Lance messaged me a few minutes ago, asking me to come over."

He scrubs his face and winces as he moves. They clearly did a number on him. "Motherfucker."

I note his stiff movements. "Can you take your shirt off for me?"

"You want me naked, babe?" he asks, making a joke of this, but it's not a joke. It's serious. He could have really been hurt and not be able to play hockey and that all falls back on me. I'm the one responsible for this. My stomach squeezes tight.

"I want to check your ribs."

"My ribs are fine." I put one hand on my hip and glare at him.

"Are you a doctor, or a nurse?"

"Yup, didn't you know? I got my degree in my spare time."

"Dane," I warn in my best hard-ass voice, which isn't that hard at all, but it gets him moving.

"Fine." He winces again as he works to lift his shirt. I stand, helping him get it over his head, and gasp as I take in the blue and purple bruising on his ribcage. A new sense of anger rips through me. How dare they do this to him. I am not Lance's possession, and this isn't the way to solve it.

I bend forward and look for a contusion. "I'm going to touch, okay?"

"I like it when you touch." I glare at him again and he sobers. "Fine."

I lightly check his ribs for breaks or fractures. Touching ever so carefully. "Can you take a deep breath for me?" He sucks in air and his chest expands without added pain. "I don't think anything is broken, but maybe a trip to the doctor wouldn't hurt. They might want to do an x-ray."

"Nah, I'm just a little bruised up. I've taken punches before."

I sit on the coffee table again and face him, my heart thumping in my chest. Tears threaten as I take in the state of him. "Dane, I'm so sorry." Maybe I should push him out of my life. I'm not good for him. I struggle to keep my eyes from watering as I wave a finger back and forth between the two of us. "I don't think we should—"

"Oh no, hell no," he swears quickly, and tenderly pulls me onto his lap, and that has to hurt his ribs. Ignoring the pain, he says, "None of this is your fault. I'm a big boy. I can handle anything Lance throws at me. I just wish he'd come at me himself."

"Why did they do this?"

"I think he wants you back, and he obviously thinks I'm a threat."

I sniff. "He said horrible things to me and kicked me out. God, he practically threw me off his steps. Why would he all of a sudden be doing this?"

"The only thing I can figure out is that he's a spoiled rich kid who always gets what he wants, and now he wants what he can't have." I nod and go quiet as I think that over. Dane touches my chin, and lifts it. "He can't have you, right?"

I take in the vulnerability in his eyes. He's so unsure of himself, of me...of all of this. I touch my stomach. Hell, I'm unsure too, but my heart aches as I study the worry and pain on his face. I cup his cheeks and tenderly kiss his mouth, not wanting to irritate the cut. "I'm not going back with him, Dane. I'm with you. You're the guy I want to be with." He glances down, the pain spreading.

"I'm not—" He takes a breath, and holds it for a second.

"You're not what?"

He shakes his head, and puts his hand on my stomach. "How are you feeling?"

If we're not keeping secrets, why does it feel like there's so much he wants to say, but isn't? I don't press. We're both going through so much right now.

"I'm good," I tell him. Well, I'm as good as one can expect after the news yesterday and opening my door to find out my ex had my new boyfriend beat up. "Do you think we should report this?"

He crinkles up his face. "I tried to throw the first punch."

My chest squeezes tight. "Why did you do that?"

"Let's be real here. It wasn't even James I wanted to punch." He laughs like it's nothing. I have no idea what was said, but he clearly doesn't want me to know, so I keep quiet, for the time being.

I shift, and put my hands on his lap. "I have some ointment for the cuts. Is there anything else I can help you with?" His grin is playful, as I look over his body and note the bulge in his pants. Good God, he's all beat up and one touch from me has him hardening.

"Do you really want to know?" he asks playfully.

23

DANE

I glance up into the stands and find Kendra and Josie watching us warm up for the game. My stomach squeezes tight. What the hell is she doing here? She was sick all day, and she should be home in bed. When will this morning sickness pass? Here it is December already and it's been going on for months. I get that she thinks she's my lucky charm here on the ice, and it's important for me to play exceptionally well, as many important people are watching, but at the moment, her health is more important.

She smiles at me and I smile back, but I also give her a look that lets her know I'm not too pleased about this. I realize it's only morning sickness that lasts all day for Kendra, and it's nothing serious. Still, she should be home resting.

"You good, bro?" Jesse asks.

"Yup." As anxiety pulls at me, I stretch, thankful that my ribs have healed from the beating, and I shouldn't have any more trouble on the ice, pretending I was just fine when it hurt to breathe. I'm distracted though, by Kendra being here, by her pregnancy, by the secrets we're keeping from everyone. I just don't want her to see it or feel it. My main goal is keeping her healthy and easing her fears—despite the fact that I have a million of my own.

I finish stretching, and as we line up, I find myself casting glances Kendra's way. Fuck, I need to clear my head and get it into the game. This is my—our—future at stake here, and I can't fuck it up. What am I saying, all I've been doing is fucking up. I have more than myself to think about, which means I need to get my shit together.

I scan the ice as the game starts at center ice. The ref drops the puck and Jesse scraps with the opposing player, shooting the puck to our left winger. I move, around, keeping a close eye on the game. The puck is intercepted in a play and shot my way. I handle it easily and pass it to our left winger. Okay so far so good. There was nothing stellar about my play, but at least I turned it around, and put the puck back in our possession.

I glance up at Kendra, and someone on the ice calls my name as the center on the opposing team, along with their right winger, zip right past me. What the fuck? I spin, and while I'm fast on the ice, I'm not as fast as their center and before I even know what's happened, they score. Their team goes crazy while boos erupt from the local fans.

"What the fuck, dude?" Nate asks, grabbing my helmet as he comes skating up to me. "Two minutes in and you let one past you."

It takes every ounce of strength not to look up at Kendra as her brother tears me a new one. "Yeah, fuck. I'll do better."

I reposition and the game resumes. Only problem is, I don't do better. I play like total shit until I'm taken off the ice, with my fucking tail between my legs. I sit with the guys, and while some tell me shit happens, others aren't happy. Can they tell I have the weight of the world on my shoulders? That weight is making me play worse, instead of motivating me to play better.

Maybe you're doing it on purpose, Dane.

What the fuck. I have to do this. I have to get scouted and ultimately drafted. Kendra wants and needs me to make it. It's the only way I'll be worthy and I know that. I only get put out once again, and because I'm playing like shit, I'm benched again. I can't even imagine the lecture I'm going to get in the locker room.

The game ends and we lose three to one, and I hang my head as I stomp back into the locker room. I spot Nate and Coach Jameson talking and I don't need to ask to know it's about me. They part and the coach comes in and gives us a talk as I drop down onto the bench, taking everything he's saying personally.

Once he's done, I strip and prepare to head to the shower and get the hell out of the place, until Coach tells me he needs to see me in his office. My entire body chills. Jesus, if he kicks me off the team, I'm fucked.

I keep my head low as I shower. "Grab a beer?" Jesse asks.

"Nah, I think I'm going to go for a bike ride." I need something to clear my head and I want to check on Kendra. It's cold but there's no snow, so it's easier going to her place on my bike. It's easier to hide.

Hide.

Christ, I'm sick of fucking hiding, but I have to play the game until we no longer have to. I turn the shower off and wrap a towel around my waist. Jesse does the same. We walk back into the locker room and the mood is somber.

"You seeing Josie later?" I ask not wanting to come off looking like a sulking asshole. I really wish I could tell him what is going on in my life.

"Yeah. Are you going to go to her family's cottage next weekend after the game? She's going to teach me how to drive the boat. The lake isn't frozen yet."

I put on a smile. "Sounds fun. Not sure if Kendra is up to it." He angles his head, concern in his eyes. Shit, I shouldn't have quite put it that way.

"She's still sick?"

"Flu season," I tell him, as good of an excuse as any.

"Okay, well, I hope you can come." He puts his hand on my shoulder for support. None of us want to get called into coach's office. "Should be fun."

"I'll let you know." I get dressed and push my way through the locker room and head to coach's office. I knock and he calls for me to enter. He waves to the chair, and I plunk down.

"What's up?" I ask, as he leans back in his chair and slides a few inches back.

"Just checking in to see how things are going with you."

"Good, things are good," I say, trying to stay positive.

"Anything going on in your personal life you want to talk about? Anything that gets said here stays here."

"I'm good," I assure him.

"Just want to make sure my players are all doing okay." A pause and then, "I couldn't help but notice you were distracted tonight. If you have something on your mind or need help with someone." His gaze goes to the cut on the side of my face. It's mostly healed, just an ugly red scar that will fade over time.

I run my fingers through my hair. "Nothing I can't handle." Can I though? Can I handle not living up to the expectations of others? Can I handle being a failure? Heck, what kind of father would I even make? I wouldn't even be able to give my child someone to look up to.

Fuck.

He slides back in, and asks, "How's Rhys?"

"He's doing great."

"You've been watching his games?"

Oh boy, here it comes.

"Yeah." I haven't, not really. Mom and Dad text to let me know the results all the time.

"Good, good," he says with a nod. "Lots of pointers you can pick up."

"You're right about that," I agree.

He stands and indicates this conversation is over. "Okay, if you need anything my door is open." He holds his hand out and I shake it before hurrying out of his office. I lean against the wall for a second to pull myself together, the pressure building inside of me. I've never had a panic attack before, and I'm not sure what one feels like, but if it feels like someone is squeezing the air from your lungs, and your entire body is shaking, then yeah, it's possible I'm having one.

I suck in a fast breath, hoping to refill my lungs and get my shit together. My phone pings, and I tug it from my pocket to see a message from Kendra. Will she be disappointed in me? I read her text, asking me to come over, and I text back that I'll be there soon.

I make my way back to the dorm—and since there is no victory celebration tonight—I grab my bike and go for a hard ride along the water. It's windy tonight and spray from the Halifax harbor falls over me, chilling my body, but I don't mind. I'm sweating and it's kind of nice.

The bike ride is great, and while I wanted to think about nothing other than the breeze, my thoughts go to Kendra and her brother. When I asked her if she thought I wasn't good enough, she denied it. My gut squeezes tight.

If you were good enough, why is she holding out, not telling her brother?

Jesus Christ, she's pregnant with my child—and no way am I allowing anyone to push me out of her life. But while her words say one thing, her actions say another. I'm not good enough. I head to the commons and race my bike up and down the ramp, being a little careless and reckless, simply because I'm a hot mess.

Once I'm done, and have exhausted myself, I bike to Kendra's, carrying it up her stairs and knock. She comes to the door, her face flushed, and my heart jumps.

"Are you okay?"

She backs up and lets me in. "Actually yes, I was just rushing around."

"Why?"

"I made us dinner."

I glance past her shoulder and smell something delicious. "I'm sorry. I would have come right away. I went biking. Needed to clear my head."

She frowns. "I'm sorry you had a bad game, Dane."

She doesn't know the half of it. "It happens."

"I thought I was your good luck charm." She glances down. "I guess the charm wore off."

I pull her to me. "No, it didn't. I just had things on my mind."

She shakes her head, and wiggles from my hold, and my heart thumps. "Dane, you can't...I can't mess this up for you."

"What are you saying, Kendra? We're in this together. Nothing is your fault."

I reach for her and her tears start to fall, her emotions all over the place tonight and I can only assume it's from the pregnancy. "Dane, no. You...you should go. I mess everything up."

"You're not messing anything up."

I hold her tight and she tries to escape. "Dane, please." She makes a fist and lightly pounds on my chest. "You have to go."

"Kendra," I whisper and take her hands. I lead her into the living room, set her on the sofa and sit on the coffee table facing her. "What's going on?"

She wipes her eyes and snorts out a laugh. "Oh, just that I'm making one bad decision after another."

I take a couple deep breaths. Getting pregnant wasn't the plan, but it guts me when she keeps telling me I was a mistake. Maybe I should go. Maybe she really doesn't want me here. But I'm not going to abandon her or our baby. That's not who I am.

"You were never a mistake," I whisper and her head lifts. Her eyes go big.

"Dane," she begins and touches my face. "I'm not saying you were a mistake. I'm just saying…" She exhales and shakes her head. "I don't know what I'm saying, or even doing."

"That's okay. But what I think you're trying to do is find your own way, make your own decisions and have your own thoughts. You don't need your brother to run your life. You're allowed to make mistakes. That's how we learn and grow."

"That's how people die," she chokes out as her eyes water.

I sit next to her and pull her to me. "You're strong and capable. More than you realize, Kendra. When you saw that I was hurt, you stepped up and knew just how to take care of me."

I hold her for a long time, until she stops shaking. A little laugh bubbles out of her throat when my stomach grumbles.

"We should eat."

"You didn't have to cook for me. You weren't even feeling well."

"It passed, and I'm kind of hungry now too." She pushes off me and stands, holding her hand out to me. "Come on."

"What did you make?" I breathe in and familiar spices fill my nostrils.

She grins, like she's up to something. In the kitchen, she goes to the oven, and pulls out a meatloaf.

"No way."

"I'm sure it's not as good as your mother's, I'm not a great cook, but you didn't get to eat your favorite childhood food when you were home, so I thought I'd make it for you."

"Are you serious." I glance at the stovetop. "Are there mashed potatoes too?"

She laughs. "Of course. Who serves meatloaf without mashed potatoes, Dane? I'm not a monster."

I laugh as she lifts the lid to the pot and I take in the creamy buttery potatoes. "Wow, you sure know the way to a man's heart."

"Oh, is that the way to your heart?"

She grins, and I drop a kiss onto her mouth.

I am ridiculously, out of my fucking mind, in love with this woman, and goddammit, I need to be the man she needs me to be.

24

KENDRA

hristmas music blares from an overhead speaker, as the nurse calls my name. I jump to my feet, quickly gathering up my books and shoving them into my backpack, not that I could concentrate on studying. I'm kind of a hot mess right now. I hated to miss class this morning—I have a test coming up. But I had to be here. I got notice yesterday there was an opening today for an ultrasound and I really needed to jump on the appointment.

Dane wanted to be here with me. He's going to be so upset that he missed it. I really like that he wants to be a part of the process, but he had practice early this morning. He was going to skip it, but I refused to let him do that. He can't be missing time, and we don't need Nate or the coach grilling him on his absence. Also, he had his own classes afterward. He was sure he could make it here on time, but apparently not, and I'm not upset with him.

With my bladder full and desperate to be emptied, I walk toward the nurse, who seems in a bit of a hurry, and turn and search the hall behind me, hoping to see Dane come running in. My gaze turns up empty, and there's a measure of disappointment and nervousness in my gut.

You've got this, girl.

I take a breath to pull myself together. When he goes off to the NHL, I'll be as good as a single mother, and I need to get used to doing things on my own, without needing to consult anyone. Honestly, I've come a long way in a short period. I never make big decisions without running them by my brother and getting his opinion. I never trusted myself. Now here I am pregnant and ready to find out the due date of my baby, all by myself.

I follow the nurse with my file, and take slow steps, because my bladder is so full. She asks my name and birthday and leads me to a locker room. She hands me a gown and robe and points to a change room.

"You can put your belongings in this locker here."

"Thanks." I change quickly and lock my things up, and then I'm led to a small room with a bed and ultrasound machine.

"Go ahead and lie down. The technician will be with you in a moment."

I make myself as comfortable as I can on the bed, and in walks a different woman, dressed in a white coat. She picks up my chart and smiles at me and I smile back. "Hello, Kendra. I'm going to be giving you your ultrasound this morning. Are you comfortable?"

"I am, thank you."

She grabs a tube of lube and shakes it. "This might be a bit cold."

"No worries." I slide my hands under my backside, and work not to sound or appear nervous. The machine beeps and she puts a little wand on my stomach and starts moving it around. I crane my neck, glancing at the screen, but I can't figure out what I'm looking at. She presses some buttons and takes some pictures. There's a swishing sound, followed by swoosh, swoosh, swoosh.

"That's the heartbeat," she tells me. Tears instantly fall and there isn't anything I can do to stop them. She hands me a tissue and I wipe my face.

"Sorry, I'm just emotional."

"That's okay. It's an exciting time."

Exciting time?

Up until this moment, I wasn't sure I was excited, but now, I have this odd little flutter in my stomach. Dane and I are going to have a baby. I still can't quite wrap my brain around that. What will everyone think? We haven't known each other that long, and let's be real, we are so not ready for this, yet there's excitement mixed with the panic as I listen to the baby's heartbeat. This is scary but I'd said a while ago, I was tired of being afraid of everything. I just didn't think I'd be facing something as momentous as this.

There are still so many things I need to consider, like child-care and finishing my nursing degree. Money isn't an issue. I have my inheritance. My stomach knots at that thought. I'd rather have my parents here. The technician continues to scan.

"Is everything okay?" I ask, knowing there was a chance of ectopic pregnancy because I was using Nexplanon.

"Everything looks great." She takes the wand off my stomach and wipes the goop off my body, but I still feel slimy. "The results will be sent to your primary care doctor, and you two can discuss. Bathroom is right there."

After she leaves, I hurry to the bathroom, feeling pretty good about the appointment. I walk back to my locker and dress quickly. Still in the stall, I reach for my phone to text Dane, and see there's a message from him letting me know he's running late. I send a quick message back that it's over and things look good. By the time I finish up, and make my way back outside, I find Dane hurrying toward me. He's frowning, and I give him a big smile to ease his worries.

He runs his fingers through his messy hair and I think he might have been anxious and tugging on it all morning. "I'm sorry I missed it, Kens."

"It's okay," I tell him. "I'm just happy everything is okay."

"Me too." He takes my hand. "How are you feeling? Did it hurt?"

"No, it was just an ultrasound. I'll make an appointment with my family doctor next week to find out more. Right now, I need food."

"You're feeling better?" I nod. "Let's get you home, and I'll make you something to eat, unless you'd rather pick something up."

"I think I just want to go home." We start walking and I follow along having no idea where he parked. "I'm so sorry. I wanted to be able to drive you to your appointment."

"It was a short walk, and I could have taken an Uber." Honestly, I could buy a car if I wanted to. I just never wanted to drive before. Maybe I was too scared, and everything is so close and accessible in the city it was always just so easy to walk. I suppose with a baby, I'll have to get an SUV or something suitable like that.

I stifle a yawn. "I am so tired, all I want to do is go back to bed and stay there until the weekend." I can't, of course. I have classes.

"I'll have you home in minutes," he assures me and my heart wobbles at his sweetness.

We reach his car and he opens the door for me. I slide in and buckle up, admiring the sight of him as he circles the front of the car and gets in beside me. Honestly, I still can't believe he wants to be with me when he has so many puck bunnies vying for his attention. Warmth wells up inside me. No man has ever made me feel so special before.

"This baby is kicking your ass," he jokes playfully as he climbs into the car. "It will be nice to get away to Josie's cottage for the weekend. You can put your feet up and do nothing."

"Three more sleeps," I tease. Dane has an away game tomorrow night, which I won't be going to, but I will be cheering him on from home. I know things have been tough for him lately. His stress levels are high and it's affecting his play. I really hope a few days away will help relax him and get him back on his A-game. "I'm looking forward to a bonfire."

"Josie said there are some great hiking trails."

I put my hand on his lap and give his thigh a squeeze. "Hopefully I'll feel well enough. I really enjoy hiking those trails." He goes quiet for a bit. "How do you feel about tomorrow's game?"

"Good," he says, and I think this might be the first lie he's ever told me.

"Speaking of kicking ass..."

"Yeah, I'll kick some Brunswick ass," he says, adding a bit of enthusiasm to his voice. "Do you have any more classes this afternoon or can you sleep?"

"Sleep," I moan as he drives the short distance to my place. He pulls into my driveway and I reach for the handle, noting that he hasn't turned the car off. "Are you coming in?"

"I'll be right back." He jerks his head to some spot in the distance. "I'll just park down the street."

I nod as my stomach squeezes tight. God, I hate this so much. "Do you have classes this afternoon?"

"Nope, done. I'm napping with you."

My insides do a little happy dance. "Nap date, I love it."

I exit the car and hurry into the house. It's quiet. Josie has been spending time with Jesse at his dorm. I think she's been absent to give Dane and me privacy. She likes the idea of the two of us together. I wish my brother could see what a good guy Dane really is. It's crazy. I know I'm pregnant, but things are going well between us. I don't want to jinx anything, but with the way my life is, I'm almost waiting for the other shoe to drop.

I head to the kitchen and open the fridge as Dane comes in. I actually gave him a key last week. Not that he needed it today, but if there's a baby emergency, he needs to be able to reach me.

He drops his backpack on the table, and steps up behind me, putting his arms around my body. I moan and lean against him, enjoying his warmth and comfort and the way his strong heart beats against my body. We haven't had sex since I found out I was pregnant. One, I've not been feeling great, and two, I think Dane might be worried he's going to hurt the baby or something.

"Sit, and let me make you something," he says around a groan. "How about a grilled cheese?"

"That sounds just about perfect."

"Go on up to bed, and I'll bring it to you."

"I'm actually going to jump in the shower and rinse off really quick."

"Wait, before you go." He walks over to his backpack, opens it and hands me a notebook.

I take it. "What's this."

"Notes from today's class you had to miss."

I stand there on shaky legs and stare at the man I'm in love with. "Dane..." I whisper, my words falling off. What the hell? "You went to my class, and took notes?"

He nods like its nothing. "Yeah, that's why I was late. The class is on the other side of campus. I'm sorry I missed the ultrasound, but I know you hated to miss this class."

I swallow against a tight throat, unable to even push a thank you past my lips. "Dane," I repeat and glance into his backpack to see a book on pregnancy. I reach for it, and pull it out. "You bought this."

"Yeah, I actually went over to Dartmouth Book Exchange. I didn't want anyone on campus seeing me buy it."

"This is so.... sweet."

"Hey, we're in this together, Kens," he says, taking the book from me and putting it back in his bag. "Go get that shower." He gives my backside a playful slap, and emotions flood me and nearly bring on tears. He's going through as much as I am and is still trying to keep things stress free for me. How could I not fall for a man like Dane? I am so over denying my feelings, and next week, after I find out my due date, and have all the information I need from the doctor, I'm going to put on my big girl panties—I sort of have to anyway because my clothes are getting tight—and tell my brother everything.

Dane deserves that.

So do I.

As that thought settles in the back of my brain, and I pray it doesn't interfere with Dane's game, I listen to a pan hit the burner and head upstairs for a quick shower. I note the bulge in my tummy as I strip off and jump under the warm water. I spend a long time under the spray. So long that Dane comes into the bathroom to check up on me. He opens the curtain to peek in and my heart swells with everything I feel for the man.

"Sandwich is ready," he says, and instead of turning the water off, I reach out and tug at his shirt.

"Join me."

"But—" he jerks his thumb over his shoulder.

"I'll eat it cold. Right now, I want something else in my mouth."

"Jesus," he moans and quickly and starts ripping his clothes off. Once he's naked, he jumps in with me, and his lips find mine for the hottest, sexiest kiss. Our tongues tangle as he tastes the depth of me. I think he missed me. I know I missed him.

His hard cock, primed and ready in seconds, presses against my stomach. I put my arms around him and hold him tight. I love how fast I can make him hard. I turn in the shower, putting him under the spray, and reach between our bodies to take his hard cock into my hand.

"Kendra…" he groans. "Are you…I mean, I don't know a lot about pregnancy."

"It's fine, Dane," I assure him, loving how much he cares and that he's working to understand my body and the whole process.

"I mean, I read that we can have sex. I just worry."

"Talk about role reversals," I tease. "I think I'm rubbing off on you and you're rubbing off on me."

"You're rubbing something," he groans as I run my hand along his long length.

I chuckle. "Maybe we're both changing, and that's healthy for us. You're sliding toward being more cautious, and I'm sliding toward being open to more things." He grunts as I cup his balls and gently massage.

"Yup," he agrees as I drop to my knees and take his cock to the back of my throat. The second his deep moan echoes around me, I grin, pretty sure he's onboard with sex during pregnancy.

25

DANE

"Want to jump in?" Dane asks as we walk toward the dock, where Josie's parents dock their boat.

Kendra wraps her arms around her body and shivers. "It's December and a lot colder than last time." She touches her stomach, and my heart does a strange little flip. Over the last couple of weeks, I've been warming to the idea of having my own little family. It's crazy and nothing I planned on, yet here I am, wanting to take care of Kendra and our growing baby.

"I was kidding. I'm not letting you in that water." I've been pampering her, it's true, and reading all about the first trimester, wanting to get everything right. I point to the two Adirondack chairs as Josie and Jesse head toward the boat.

"Are you two coming?" Josie asks, looking at us over her shoulder.

I cast Kendra a quick glance, and she telegraphs me a secret message. The waves will likely make her seasick. I drop down into a chair and pull the other one closer. "Nope, we're going to watch from here. With Jesse steering, I have no idea what you're going to crash into."

Jesse offers me his middle finger. "Hey, have a little faith, bro."

I laugh and Kendra sits next to me, exhaling a relaxed breath as she does. "It's so gorgeous here."

Following her gaze, I glance out at the lake and admire the gorgeous yellow and red leaves reflecting in the water. "It's perfect."

Another deep breath and then she says, "I want a place just like this someday."

"In the middle of nowhere?"

"Yup. No noise, no pollution, no people."

"Not even me."

She smiles and reaches for my hand. "Of course you."

My chest expands with happiness, then deflates again. Is she still going to want me if I don't make the NHL? Jesus, I've been playing so craptastically, the coach keeps benching me. I give myself maybe a one percent chance of getting scouted now, and while I know that's what everyone wants and needs from me, there's a part of me that wonders if I'm self-sabotaging.

But I don't want to think about that right now. I just want to enjoy this view, help Kendra bring her stress level down and be at her beck and call all weekend. Maybe then she'll see there's more to me, that I'm worthy for other things.

Are you though, Dane?

As old demons rear their ugly heads, I give her hand a squeeze. "Feeling okay?"

"I don't remember the last time I was this relaxed." She turns to me. "How about you?"

"I'm good." She arches a brow like she doesn't believe that. She knows I've been playing badly, and word is getting around.

With the sun low on the horizon, the air begins to chill, and she tugs her coat tighter around herself.

I shift forward in my chair. "Want to go for a little walk before the bonfire?"

She nods and pushes to her feet. "Yes, let's go while I'm feeling well." We walk back toward the house, and she veers off to the left, following a path through the woods that follows the water.

As nature closes in on us, no matter the mess of things right now, I can't help but feel happy. It's nice being here with Kendra, the world outside moving at a different pace. In the trees around us, squirrels call out warning signs as we approach and something big moves in the underbrush. Off in the distance, waves lap gently and through the trees, I see Josie's parents' boat making its way to the middle of the lake.

Life isn't perfect, even though all seems right with the world at this moment.

Kendra stops walking and I bang into her. "Sorry," I say and slide my hand around her waist to hold her.

"Look," she whispers and points, a huge smile on her face. "A pheasant. He's gorgeous."

The bird struts and crows, and I shift to get a better look. My foot crunches on a stick and the bird lifts its head, and takes off, moving at lightning speed on those little legs. I laugh at how funny he looks running. "Did you see how fast he was?"

She whacks me. "You scared him. That's why he ran. Did you know when startled they can run up to sixty miles an hour?"

"Too fast for me to catch him for dinner."

Her mouth falls open. "I would never eat a pheasant."

"Okay fine, you clearly like pheasants. Let's see what else we can find out here in these woods."

"I am not eating anything from nature, Dane."

I chuckle, and put my hand on the small of her back to set her into motion. I stop abruptly. "Not even that." I point and she follows my gaze to the deer about twenty feet away.

She goes quiet and squeezes my hands, a smile on her face. I slowly reach into my pocket and grab my phone, snapping a quick picture. The deer slowly walks away, moving deeper into the woods and within seconds, we can no longer see it.

"So pretty," Kendra whispers. I show her the picture. "Let's see how many animals we can find and in answer to your question, no, I am not eating a deer."

I chuckle, and we walk. "Why is it in nature all the males are so pretty?" She casts me a fast look and then goes back to walking over a tree root carefully. "You saw that pheasant. Gorgeous. Look at the peacocks, mallards, and even lions."

"They have to compete to mate."

"Unlike the guys on the hockey team. They have women throwing themselves at them."

I shrug. "True. In nature though, the female must choose wisely. The males only provide the sperm and then they are out of there." I jerk my thumb over my shoulder. "Leaving the female to raise the offspring alone."

A fine shiver goes through her. "I'm glad it's not like that with humans."

"Women are way prettier than men." I wave my hand down my body. "Nothing to look at there. Just some farm parts."

"Farm parts."

"The business end of things," I say and she laughs hard and whacks my chest. I grab her hand and kiss it.

"I don't know." She grins playfully. "I think you're kind of pretty."

"Hey, watch your mouth." I glance around, like I'm worried someone overheard her. "I have a reputation to uphold, you know."

She grins and goes back to walking. "I think the females in nature are plain to avoid predators. When they're re incubating their eggs, the bird needs to blend in, so she can protect them. She's all on her own out there. The males have a harem, you know."

"Why do you know so much about pheasants?"

"When I was young...before, you know. Every spring I'd hear the male pheasant marking its territory and searching for all the single ladies." She does quotes around those last four words as she sings them. I laugh at that. "I was kind of fascinated, and Mom got me a book. We read it together. I don't have that book anymore." That fond memory brings on a little smile.

"What was it called?"

"I don't know. I think it was something like facts about the ringneck pheasant. It was mainly a picture book and some facts."

I nod as I picture little Kendra tucked up in her bed with her picture book. "That book told you they had a harem. That's a bit much for a children's book, isn't it?"

"It didn't use the word harem." She eyes me. "Wait, why do you say harem like you might like the idea of it."

I hold my hands up. "Nope, that sounds like an awful lot of work. Women are high maintenance," I tease. Kendra is anything but. "And there's only one woman I want to be with."

She puts her hands on her belly, and a wave of anxiety comes over her face. "Animals in nature have strong instincts to protect their families." I'm beginning to see I have those strong instincts too. I'd do anything for those I love.

"Do you think we're going to do okay, Dane?"

I put my arm around her. "I do. One day at a time."

She nods, seemingly reassured by my answer. "I'm not a pheasant who's about to let you do this all on your own." As the path grows darker, I catch her hand. "Come on, it's getting dark. We should head back before we get lost out here."

"Fire?"

"That's the plan."

She turns with me and I retrace our steps back. The cottage comes into view and I look out over the lake to see the boat still bobbing in the middle. "Do you think they're coming back?"

"Josie has been known to camp out on the boat all night."

"So, if I take all your clothes off and make you scream, no one will hear us."

She laughs. "I'm not sure. I do know sound travels over water easily. Those on the other side of the lake might hear."

I grin as I think about that and toss some dry wood into the fire pit. Neither of us are ready to go inside, and there are s'mores to be eaten. I dart inside and grab the lighter and paper Josie showed me earlier, along with two bottles of water and everything we need for making s'mores.

"Thanks," Kendra says cracking hers and taking a big swig as I crinkle paper and toss it into the pit. Five minutes later, I have a roaring fire and Kendra leans in, holding her hands out to warm them. I drop next to her and hand her the bag of marshmallows.

"Dessert before dinner. I like the way you think."

"We do seem to put the cart before the horse a lot, don't you think?" She grins, and holds her stomach.

"Apparently." A moment of quiet and then she says, "I'm going to tell Nate when I get back."

My heart jumps into my throat. "Really, I thought you didn't want to, that you were worried about how that would be for me on the team." I guess she knows I'm playing like shit, and it no longer matters. Does that mean making it into the NHL doesn't matter to her? Or has she changed her thinking. If she's pregnant with my baby, maybe that will force Nate to help me out, and get me scouted. Maybe this is a new tactic.

My stomach sours.

"I can't do secrets much longer, Dane, and I'm already show-ing." She cups her belly. "I'm so big so early, I thought for sure we were having triplets or something."

"If you think it's the right thing to do, I do too." I sit back, my stomach in knots. This isn't going to go over well at all.

She shoves a marshmallow onto a stick and holds it over the fire until it's golden brown. She holds it out to me and I shake my head. She pops it into her mouth and the resulting moan curls around my dick and squeezes. I groan, my cock thick-ening at the sexy noises.

"Something wrong?" she asks, a teasing edge to her voice. I grin. She knows exactly what she's doing to me and she's doing it on purpose, maybe to lighten my mood. Setting my worries aside—hell this is our last secret weekend, and I want her to enjoy it—I stand.

She laughs as I start strutting and crowing. "Dane, what are you doing?" She practically shrieks.

"I'm peacocking." I glance up and to the left. "Wait, that's not the right word when it's a pheasant calling all the single ladies, right? Hmm, is it called pheasant-cocking?" I strut and crow some more.

She shakes her head at me. "You're crazy, you know that?"

I pull her to her feet and wrap my arms around her. "Crazy about you," I say and warmth moves into her eyes.

"Come on." She takes my hand and starts up the path to the cottage.

"It worked?" I ask, like an excited Labrador retriever. "My pheasant-cocking worked?"

"Yes, it worked." She chuckles and shakes her head again.

"You're kind of strange, Kendra." She angles her head and eyes me. I crinkle up my face. "This weird pheasant fetish you have," I tease. "I'm not sure that's normal."

"You're the one crowing and calling all the single ladies."

I pick her up and she yelps. "Nah, there's only one single lady I want." And...if I play my cards right—or my game right—maybe someday I can put a ring on it.

26

KENDRA

I leave the doctor's office and walk outside, my legs barely moving, my mind a chaotic mess. Small flakes of snow begin to fall and I drop down onto the curb and just sit there, unable to wrap my brain around the words that just came out of my doctor's mouth. My chest is so tight, I can't breathe, which might be why the world is spinning around me and the contents in my stomach are jumping into my throat. Chances are it's the ultrasound results that are making me nauseous and dizzy though.

I pull the paper from my pocket, and stare at the due date the doctor wrote down. May 2. Which means I didn't get pregnant in September, I got pregnant in August.

This is Lance's baby!

A noise crawls out of my throat, half moan, half cry and an elderly woman stops as she's about to walk past me.

"Are you okay?" she asks, tugging her purse tight.

"No," I say quickly, and tears flood my eyes. What the hell am I going to do? How am I going to tell Dane. I didn't even tell him about this appointment, because he would insist on coming and I refuse to let him miss any more classes taking care of me. I was going to tell him the due date tonight, when we went to the wine and cheese festival.

Over the past few months, he's been so sweet and caring and attentive, putting my needs before his own, which is why he's not been sleeping and has been doing poorly in hockey. He's even talked about our future as a family, and I could sense the growing excitement in him. I was even going to tell my brother about us this week, but now... This will destroy Dane, and once I tell him, there will be no us.

"Can I help you with something? Call someone for you?"

I swipe at my face. Who do I call? I'm not ready to hurt Dane, and for the last couple of days, Josie has been avoiding me. I'm not sure what I did to her, but a couple of days after we got home from her cottage, she began going out of her way not to be in the same room as me. Then again, maybe it has nothing to do with me and more to do with her and Jesse and she doesn't want to talk about it. Lord knows I don't want to talk about what's going on with me right now. And Nate, well he's going to lose his mind at the mess I've made of things, reminding me that I should have listened to him, as he knows best.

My world is falling apart right before my eyes.

The elderly woman shifts, blocking the late day sun and that's when I realize she's waiting for an answer. "No, it's okay." I push to my feet and try not to wobble. "I'm okay," I lie. She eyes me for a moment, and I force a smile. "Thank you."

I force one foot in front of the other and struggle to take in air as I head home. A million questions dance around in my brain. I have to tell Dane. Heck, I have to tell Lance. I don't want to, but he deserves to know he's going to have a child. Neither of them are going to take this well, and the one thing I'm sure of is that I'll be raising this baby alone. My phone pings, and I glance at it.

Brie: Can't wait for tonight. Wine and cheese and my girl.

I stare at my phone, and my tears blur the words. God, Dane is the last person on earth I want to hurt. I love him and this is going to destroy him. My breathing is rough and ragged as I wipe my eyes and shoot a message back, pretending I'm not once again about to lose a person I love.

Me: Same. See you soon.

He's about to hit the rink for practice. I can't say anything to him right now. I tuck my phone away and keep my head down, not wanting to run into anyone as I make my way home. Once inside, I listen for sound, but Josie isn't home. I hurry to the bathroom, making it just in time to lose the contents in my stomach. I sit on the bathroom floor, a hot mess as I work to pull myself together and figure out a way to tell Dane. But no matter what, I don't see a scenario where he's not going to hate me.

A car horn sounds on the street and off in the distance a dog barks, and I glance at my phone to realize I've been sitting on this floor for a very long time, and now Dane will soon be here. After a long while, I push to my feet and climb into the shower, hoping the water will wash away this whole mess.

I clean myself up, scrub my body until my skin hurts and stay under the spray until it turns cold. I shut off the water and dry myself off, checking my red eyes in the mirror. Will Dane know something is wrong simply from looking at me? Do I tell him before or after the festival? He's been looking forward to it, and well…I just don't want to hurt him.

I head to my room and pull on a pair of black pants, which are pretty much too tight to wear, but they'll have to do, and a loose sweater that hides my bulging belly. I guess now I know why it's so big. I'm further along than I ever knew.

The front door opens and closes quietly, and I glance at my phone, not sure if it's Dane or Josie. I listen quietly, the heavy footsteps on the stairs letting me know it's Dane. Panic erupts inside me and I pinch my cheeks to give them a bit of color. I turn at the noise outside my bedroom door, and the second I set eyes on Dane, I nearly fall to my knees. Worry and sadness mingle in his eyes as he stands there, his hands in his pockets.

Does he already know?

"Dane," I say, my words coming out shaky. "What is it?"

He takes a big breath. "Coach benched me until he sees improvement at practice. If he doesn't, I'm off the team. It's over, I know it in my heart."

I hurry across the room, and wrap my arms around him. I breathe in his familiar scent, and hug him tight. "I'm so sorry, Dane." His big hands grip the back of my sweater, and as he holds me, there's a part of me that wonders—has always wondered—if not making the NHL is a blessing in disguise.

I know he's stressed, yet my gut tells me he might have been purposely failing, wanting to do—be something different—something, in his eyes, that is more fulfilling than becoming an NHL player. Sure, his parents are paying for his college education and had worked to give him everything, but doesn't he have the right to choose the path he wants to walk. He's just so worried about letting others down. Doing what he's expected to do, and he doesn't want to let anyone down.

You're going to let him down, Kendra.

I back up, take his hand and lead him to my bed. "What now?" I ask.

"I don't know, Kens," he says and scrubs his face. "One day at a time, I guess." His gaze searches my face. What is he looking for? "I'm sorry."

"Don't be sorry." I hug him again. "You could always open Bike and Bries," I say.

His laugh is tortured. "Yeah…"

He doesn't think I'm serious, but I'm dead serious, and maybe there is a way I should show him that.

"Fuck," he curses.

"What?"

"It's over. I'm nothing but a disappointment."

"Your parents," I say quietly, knowing exactly where his thoughts have gone, and knowing I can't tell him about my appointment today. Not when he's hurting so horribly. "I'm not disappointed in you, Dane." He searches my face again.

Does he not believe me. "I think things happen for a reason." As soon as I voice that, I fight back tears, unable to find a reason for the mess my life is in right now. Am I being punished for my mistake as a child?

Tenderness moves into his face, and he cups my cheek. "I'm sorry, Kens. I didn't even ask how your day was? Are you feeling okay?"

Oh, God, when he looks at me like that...

"I'm okay," I lie. "If you don't want to go out tonight, we don't have to. We can order a pizza and watch a show."

"No," he says. "You've been looking forward to this, and maybe getting out will take my mind off things." He frowns and glances down.

"What?" I ask.

"Are you...still going to tell Nate about us?"

God, does he think I'm going to toss him away because there's little to no chance of him getting drafted now? This man's demons definitely run deep. Another thought hits like a brick. I blink and avert my gaze as my brain races. What do I tell Nate? I can't tell him I'm having Dane's baby, because I'm not, and once I tell Dane the truth, why would he stick around to raise another man's child?

"Kens," he says quietly, his voice low, rumbling with vulnerability.

I glance at him, and because I can't stand to see him hurting more than he is, I whisper, "Yes."

He swallows, his throat making a bit of a tortured sound as he stands and swipes his hand through his mess of hair. "We don't want to be late."

I nod and stand. As we head down the stairs, I try to keep my thoughts focused, even though I'm a mess inside. "Have you talked to Jesse?" I tug on my coat, and pick up my belt bag.

"Saw him at practice."

"Is he okay?"

Dane opens the door and I step out onto the stoop. He locks up behind us, and I glance down the street to where he parked his car. Will I ever see it on my street again, once I tell him the truth?

"Yeah, I think so, why?"

"I don't know. I think Josie has been avoiding me. Are they having troubles?"

"I'm not sure. I can ask him if you want."

"No, I don't want to get into their business if Josie doesn't want me to know." We walk down the sidewalk, and I put my arms around myself to ward off a chill and keep myself from shattering. My world is falling apart around me, and I don't know what to do about it.

Dane opens my door for me, and I slide in. After I buckle up, I hug myself again. Dane circles the car and gets into the driver's seat. He seems a bit off tonight, and I'm not entirely sure it's because he was benched.

"Cold?" he asks.

"A bit." He starts the car and turns on the heat. He drives us the short distance to the waterfront and parks. I take in the stiffness in his body. "Are you sure you want to do this?"

"Yeah," he says, half-heartedly. I exit the car and he circles it to meet me. His mood seems to pick up a bit when we step inside and he hands over our tickets. The crowd is lively, and well, there's cheese.

"Now remember, you can't eat the unpasteurized or soft cheese."

"I know." Our knuckles brush and my heart squeezes tight. I love how he's always looking out for me and the baby. How am I going to tell him?

He winks at me. "No brie."

"No brie," I agree. "Just the hard stuff."

"That's what the cheese said," he jokes and laughs quietly. I grin and he pokes his chest. "Unless, of course it's this brie you want."

I force a laugh and from the way he's angling his head and staring at me, he can tell it was fake. I tug on his coat. "Come on."

We go from table to table, and I watch Dane come to life as he talks to the vendors, sipping wine and cheese. I stick to water, but gobble up all the cheese that won't hurt the baby. As I watch him, I once again think getting benched was a blessing. I wish he'd take my Bike and Bries idea seriously. What can I do to show him I really support that?

We spend the next couple of hours wandering, and Dane really seems to be having a good time, telling me about a bacon cheese and a dill pickle cheese he tried to talk his parents into making years ago. I try to smile and listen as he describes how he'd like to create it, although I catch him watching me a few times, and I'm not sure I'm pulling off happy. I'm not surprised. I'm seriously just trying to keep myself from breaking down.

I stifle a yawn, my feet growing tired after walking all night, and Dane puts his arm around me. "Tired?"

"I'm okay," I say. "We don't have to go."

"I'm ready to go. If I eat any more cheese I might explode."

I force a laugh, and once again he looks at me strangely. I zip my coat up, and we go back to his car. I glance at him as he drives. Do I tell him tonight? He'd already gotten bad news today. How can I possibly add to that? He pulls into my driveway and I glance at my phone to check the time.

"Are you coming in?" I ask.

Just then my phone pings and I glance at it again. I frown as I read the message from Lance.

"What is it?"

"Lance...he passed his exam and has been accepted into law school."

Pain flashes in his eyes as they stare at me, holding numerous questions. "Why is he still texting you?" The underlying accusation in his tone tightens my stomach. He's not in a good place after getting benched, so I let it go.

"I don't know," I say honestly, and glance away, my stomach tight, knowing I have to tell both these men the truth, and soon.

How could I have gotten myself into this situation? More importantly, is there anything I can do to make it all right again?

● 27

DANE

I shoot Kendra a text and wait for a response. When none comes, I sit back in my chair and try to focus on my lecture. At the festival she seemed a bit off and now it feels like she's avoiding me. I get she's busy, and has a lot on her mind. I want to blame it on the pregnancy. It's a lot we're dealing with, but I suspect something else is going on with her. We vowed no secrets, and I have the sneaking suspicion she's keeping a big one from me.

Then again, I was off my game at the festival too, in more ways than one. I was off in three ways, actually. I got benched, and when I asked Kendra if she still planned to tell Nate about us, she hedged. She actually freaking hedged. Fuck, I don't know what to think about that. Is she having second thoughts because my career is in the toilet? Lastly, what the hell was the text from Lance all about? Why would she care that he passed and is going to law school? Talk about rubbing my failures in my face. I clench and unclench my hands, unable to concentrate, and when the class ends, I'm the first one out the door.

I check my phone again as I walk home. I have a break between classes, and need to get something to eat. Off in the distance, I spot Lance. He's standing outside his car, his back to me. He's talking to someone, but his big body is blocking my view. I turn to go the other way, unable to figure out why I'm suddenly uneasy. I shoot another text to Kendra, asking if she's home, and if she's feeling okay. I wish she'd answer me.

I walk toward home, and halt abruptly, deciding I'd better check on Kendra. Maybe she's home in bed sick. I spin, and when I do, I spot Lance getting in his car, and the person he was talking to disappears into the crowd headed into the main campus building. My heart leaps. Was that Kendra? I pick up the pace, and hurry toward the building. Inside, I glance around, but she's nowhere to be found. Maybe it wasn't even her. I'm pretty certain she doesn't have a class right now.

I go back outside and double time it to her house. I rap and wait, and when she doesn't answer, I use my key. I have to make sure she's okay. Inside, I dart up the stairs quietly. If she's asleep, I don't want to wake her. Her bedroom door is ajar, and I peek in, to find her bed sheets mussed. Is she under them? I walk closer for a better look, but she's not here.

Me: Hey Kendra, are you around? I'm at your place.

Three dots appear and I sink onto her bed, relief flooding my veins. I glance around her messy room. Dishes sit on her desk, and papers are everywhere. She's not been feeling well, and I left her alone last night to get a good night sleep. I stand and decide to clean up a bit for her.

.   .   .

Kendra: On my way.

I shrug out of my jacket and drop my phone onto her bed and gather up the dishes and take them downstairs, setting them in the sink. I go back to her room and put the mess of papers into a pile. I reach for one, not meaning to read it, but I can't help but notice it's from her doctor. She was supposed to tell me about this appointment.

My gaze races over the page, and my heart thunders, a mixture of excitement and nervousness invading my gut when I see the due date. Jesus, that makes this all so real. On May second, I'm going to be a father. I shake my head and take a couple of deep fueling breaths. Just then the door downstairs opens and Kendra comes racing up the stairs in a big hurry. She bursts into her room, her blue eyes wide and full of...fear?

"Kendra," I burst out. "Are you okay?" Her gaze goes from me to the paper in my hand, then back to me, and a tortured groan catches in her throat. "You didn't tell me about the appointment."

She swallows and something uncomfortable niggles in the back of my brain. "I know. I didn't want you missing any more classes or practices."

I shake my head. "I wanted to go. You know that." I sink down on the bed. Why would she hide this from me? I had a right to be there. I wanted to be there. That wasn't fair of her. She starts shifting, her fingers tugging at the hem of her coat, and as I take in her nervousness, I turn my focus back to the paper.

"Holy fuck," I swear, and Kendra drops down into her desk chair, tears pooling in her eyes. I jump to my feet. "Kendra. What the fuck?" I'm good at math. Great at it actually. I can't believe I didn't put this together the second I looked at the paper. I guess I was just anxious and excited, thinking about a future with Kendra and our baby. My stomach clenches so hard, I think I might vomit. "Kendra," I practically shout as I walk up to her and point at the date. "How does this make sense?"

"Because....because..."

Holy shit. "Because it's Lance's baby." I stumble back, and grip a fistful of my hair as the world tilts on its axis. "Were you with Lance today?"

"I told him about the baby today..."

"Holy fucking hell."

Jesus, she's getting back together with Lance. Was this planned all along, with him messaging her behind my back. Or did this just start up again—and she finally told him—because I just found out I'm not going to make the NHL, and Lance is going places? This is what her brother wanted all along and she always does what her brother wants.

"I've always been the mistake, haven't I? If you listened to your brother, none of this would have happened."

She's crying hard now, her words a jumbled mess that I can't decipher.

"I guess Nate is getting what he wants." I pace her room as anger floods me. The fucking baby isn't mine, and she was pretending it was—she was unwell for a long time before we found out she was pregnant, and clearly knew—and now that I'm not going to be who she thought I was going to be, she went running back to Lance. I guess I know why she didn't want me at the appointment.

What the fuck has my life become?

I work to get my thoughts together. "Okay, so it's Lance's baby, and you were pretending all along it was my baby." Was she even on birth control? Did we purposely not use protection so she could trick me? Anger floods me and I can't keep my voice from shaking as I add, "I was excited by this, Kendra. I mean, sure I was shocked at first, but the idea of having our own little family was growing on me, and I was even thinking maybe someday we could have a farmhouse of our own. I wanted it all, whatever you wanted. It didn't matter to me where we lived as long as I was with you." She stands there pale and shocked and I shake the paper. "Why would you do this to me?"

"Dane...I...didn't..."

"I asked for no secrets."

She covers her face. "I know, and it's not...well, I mean...I told Lance because he cornered me on campus."

"Let me wrap this up. Lance didn't want you a couple of months ago, so you latch on to me to be your baby daddy, hoping I'd make the NHL so I could support you. Now he wants you back, and he has a good future ahead of him, so you're choosing him. Wow, Kens, this is some pretty fucked up shit."

Shock and hurt lives in her eyes as they meet mine. "Is that what you think?"

"I can do math, Kendra."

"Dane, please..."

"You've been avoiding me."

"I just didn't know how to tell you."

"You didn't seem to have trouble telling Lance."

"Dane, please..."

I shake my head, and the room spins around me. I put my hand on the doorjamb. "No. I can't hear anymore. I can't listen to any more lies." She's pregnant with Lance's child and I'm not part of her small family. With my insides feeling like they were just ripped apart by a cheese grater, I stumble back and out the bedroom door.

I did everything I could for Kendra, treated her like she was the most important person in the world, because she was my whole world, and yet she's running back to an abusive asshole because I'm not the success story she needed. I'm not worthy of her love. Would she even have told Lance the child was his if I made the NHL? Would I have ever known it wasn't mine?

I leave Kendra's place and head back to the dorm. I don't go in. Instead, as rage prowls through my veins I hop in my car, and drive down the street, heading toward the direction I saw Kendra coming from the night I ran her over with my bike. I scan the streets, going slow, looking for Lance's car.

What are you doing, dude?

Ignoring that inner voice, I creep along the streets, and just when I'm sure I'm never going to find him, I spot his car in a driveway. I pull in behind him, slam mine into park and stomp to his door. I knock, hard, and repeatedly until the door flings open and an annoyed Lance stands there staring at me. His annoyance turns to shock, and maybe fear.

"What the fuck do you want?" he asks.

"I'm only going to say this once. If you so much as lay a finger on Kendra, or hurt her in any way at all and I'll find out, I'll be coming for you." My nostrils flare as my hands fist at my sides. He backs up and inch. "You can send your assholes after me, I don't care. I'll go through every one of them to get to you if you hurt her."

"You can't threaten me like that."

"I just did."

His head lifts an inch, but he still has to look up to make eye contact with me. "Do you know who I am, who my family is?"

"Don't care. I expect you to treat Kendra and your child with respect and love. That's all I'm saying."

He holds his hand up, palms out. "Fuck, the kid's not mine. She's been pregnant for how long now, and then after her appointment the other day she decides to tell me, it's mine? I don't know what she's trying to pull, but no way is the kid mine. I told her that."

"Of course, the baby is yours. Kendra can easily prove that with tests, or even math."

He shakes his head, a new kind of fear in his eyes. "Kendra said she didn't want to do tests. She said she was going to raise her child and that she didn't want anything from me." He steps a bit closer and glances out on the sidewalk, like he's worried someone might hear. "My family can't hear anything about this."

"Are you fucking serious?" I always knew he and his family were assholes.

She just found out the date, dude. She didn't know all along.

"Look, she told me she was pregnant, and the child was mine. 'Allegedly'." He does air quotes around that one word. "Because she felt it was the right and honorable thing to do. She said she didn't want anything from me, man. So you can back the fuck off. She's all yours. I don't want anything to do with her."

I frown and scratch my head, completely confused. Kendra wasn't trying to get back with him? He cornered her and she ended up telling him. "I thought you were trying to get her back."

"Well, she's good for a fuck, but I'm not having anything to do with the baby shit."

Anger shoots through me like a flyaway puck and the next thing I know, my fisted hand is connecting with his jaw. He flies backward and lands on his ass in his hall.

"What the fuck?" Blood oozes from the corner of his mouth.

"Don't talk about her like that. Ever."

"Jesus Christ, I'm going to sue your ass."

I snort. "Yeah, I'm pretty sure you're not. Don't go near Kendra ever again."

With that, I turn and stomp back to my car. I sit in it for a second, going over today's events. I pound the steering wheel. Jesus Christ, I had it all wrong. I was so caught up in my own demons, so sure I wasn't good enough for Kendra, that I blew up at her, and accused her of things that weren't true. Fuck, how could I have done that? She must hate me for the things I said, and I can't blame her.

Before I start the car, I shoot a message to Jesse, and find out he's in his room. I tell him to stay there, start the car and back out of the driveway. Ten minutes later, I'm climbing the stairs at Storm House, and walking into Jesse's room. I take one look at his pained expression and my heart sinks.

"Are you okay?"

He looks like he wants to answer but he points to his chair. "Sit, tell me what the fuck is going on with you. You're a fucking mess."

I plop into his chair and tell him everything, from the pregnancy to Lance, and all my insane accusations. "I had it all wrong, Jesse. All fucking wrong. She only just found out herself, and was avoiding me because she was terrified of telling me. She wasn't going after Lance because he was going to make something of himself and I wasn't."

"You'll make something of yourself," he quietly assures me. "You never wanted the NHL anyway."

I barely hear him as my mind races. "I can't believe the things I accused her of. What a fucking asshole. I screwed everything up."

"The baby still isn't yours, Dane. No matter how much you want it to be."

The truth is, I do want it to be. I want so much with Kendra. "I love her."

He nods like he knows. "Then you need to figure out a way to make things right between you and Kendra."

"How?"

"Only you can answer that question."

KENDRA

I try to go back to feeling numb, like I used to before I met Dane, but this time it's far too difficult. My love for him has shattered the walls protecting me, and now he thinks I was tricking him, letting him believe he was the father of my child when all along I knew the difference. I had planned to tell him. I was just so afraid that the fallout was going to turn out exactly like it turned out.

I walk to class, forcing one leg in front of the other, and keep my head down. My eyes are so puffy, I'm sure people will think I've been in a fight. I've not seen Josie for days, and while I'd like to talk to her, she doesn't seem to want to talk to me. Nate has been calling, and I've been avoiding him. I'm sure he doesn't know anything about this mess I'm in. It's not like Lance is going to breathe a word of it. He's completely in denial and doesn't want anything to do with the baby, and that's probably for the best. For all our sakes.

I have no idea what Dane will do with himself now, or what will become of him. He might hate me, but I still want what's best for him. I lift my head for a split second, to open the lecture hall doors and I hurry to class, sit in the corner and work to concentrate, a difficult task when my life is in shambles. I barely take in anything my professor had to say and as soon as class ends, I walk to the next, and the day continues like that until it's time to head home.

Christmas decorations are everywhere, gorgeous wreaths on each lamp pole. I stare but take no pleasure in it. I find myself searching the street for Dane's car. Will I ever stop doing that? Maybe I'll have to move. I trudge down the sidewalk, cool air brushing over my body. Up above, the sky is dark, a snowstorm threatening—which is pretty fitting for my mood. I shove my key into the lock, but the door is ajar. My heart leaps. Has Dane come back? Or is Josie home?

"Hello," I call out as I enter and I find my brother at the end of the hall, his big body eating up the kitchen entranceway. I quickly straighten my shoulders and leave my coat on, wanting to hide my bulge, even though he's going to find out soon enough. Just not today. I can't deal with any of this today. Why the heck didn't I think to hide the paper in my bedroom? Honestly that was no way for Dane to find out. I guess I didn't expect him to just show up when I wasn't home.

Would it have been different if I told him myself?

"Hey," Nate says as I close the door behind me, not bothering to lock it. He stands in the doorway eyeing me. "Have you been avoiding me?"

I shake my head. More lies and secrets. What a tangled mess I have going on here. "No, I've been really busy."

His head dips and he has that serious brother look on his face. One he always gets when he senses his loss of control. "Too busy to answer my text."

Exhaustion pulls at me, and all I want to do is crawl in bed. "What's going on? Why are you here, Nate?"

"I've been worried about you." His face softens and my heart pinches tight.

I don't want to hurt him. I'd never want to hurt him but I can't take this anymore. "I'm a big girl. I can take care of myself."

He arches one brow, and it's a reminder of what I'd done as a child. The fight drains out of me and my shoulders sag. I walk down the hall and he moves to the side, making room for me to slide past him.

I grab a glass from the cupboard, fill it full of water and slowly sip it. I turn back to face Nate, and lean against the counter. "I'm sorry, Nate. I'm sorry you had to grow up without a mom and dad and take on those roles for me."

His face softens even more. "Kendra..."

I shake my head. "I'm so sorry. I made a mistake. Over the course of my life, I'll probably make many more mistakes, but the only way I'm going to grow and learn is from mistakes. Granted, I hope none of them lead to such horrible consequences, and if I could change the past, I would. I can't, though, and both you and me, well, we need to find a healthy way to move forward. I can't live with this guilt." Tears fall down my face, and I sniff, turning my back to him to refill my glass.

"Kendra, no." His boots sound on the floor as he crosses the room, turns me around and pulls me into his arms. "I'm the one carrying all the guilt. None of what happened was your fault, it was mine. I should have made those noodles for you." He gulps and his voice cracks when he adds, "You were a child. You were *my* responsibility. I'm the one who fucked up."

I stare at him and realize that all this time he's been blaming himself, too. Something Dane once said to me jumps to the forefront of my brain. "No, Nate. You were a child too. A child taking care of a child. It wasn't your fault, either. It was an accident, and sadly accidents happen." I inch back as his eyes flood with water. "I'm sorry you've been carrying this, and I know you worry about me."

"I just..." His voice cracks as he speaks. "I can't lose you too, Kendra."

"I don't want to lose you either, but you can't keep me in a bubble anymore. I'm suffocating."

He swallows and pinches his eyes shut tight. "You're right, I know."

"I need to be able to pick who I want to love, Nate."

His eyes narrow in on me, his chest rising and falling rapidly. "Kendra, I just want—"

"I know you want what is best for me, and I love you for that. More than you'll ever know. But maybe you don't know, Nate. Maybe you just don't know what or who is best for me to love."

"Who is it you want to love?" he asks, but as he looks deep into my eyes, I sense he already knows.

"It doesn't matter now," I choke out. "He doesn't love me."

Just then my front door flings opens and in storms none other than Dane. I'm shocked to see him, but I'm more shocked at what he's holding in his hand. My vision goes blurry as my legs threaten to give out. Ohmigod, is this really happening?

Nate and I break apart, and Nate's gaze goes back and forth between the two of us. "What the hell is that?" Nate asks, his voice sounding a little broken from our talk. But I think if Nate is ever going to be whole again, he needs to break completely so he can start rebuilding from the foundation up. Hopefully, like me, he'll find someone who loves him enough to help with that. But Dane doesn't love me anymore. My heart cracks a bit more, aching with pain and loss.

Dane tries to put the baby's bicycle seat behind his back. It's too late for that. Worry and fear dance in his eyes, and he glances behind him, like his fight or flight instincts are kicking in. "Shit, I'm sorry, Kendra."

Nate folds his arms across his barrel chest when I ask Dane, "What are you doing here?"

"I wanted to talk." He stands on shaky legs, not knowing what to do. "I'll wait outside," he tells us, not fleeing but instead hanging around to fight. Is he fighting for me...us? Do I dare hope?

"No," I say quickly, my heart racing, desperate for answers. "What do you want to talk about?"

"Kendra," Nate pipes in. "Why is he carrying a baby's bike seat?"

Dane's groan is deep and full of regret, and I take a fueling breath and turn to my brother. "Because...because I'm pregnant, Nate."

Nate stands there stunned, and it's an appropriate response. He opens his mouth and closes it again, unable to get the words out. I take a fast glance at Dane and he mouths the word *sorry*.

"Whose child?" Nate finally asks, and my stomach cramps. Saying Lance's name in front of the two guys I love the most hurts my heart and my brain.

I open my mouth. "It's—"

"Mine," Dane says quickly and my gaze shoots to his as my heart jumps into my throat. What is he saying? He stares at me, love, pain and heartache all mingling in the depths of his eyes. "The baby is mine," he states, his voice stronger this time. "I'm going to raise the child with Kendra." That last sentence comes out more like a question. My heart pounds harder, full of love as Dane stands there, hope in his eyes as he waits for me to respond.

He drops the bike seat and crosses the room. He puts his arm around me, and pulls me close, and when his strong heart beats against my cheek, I know I'm home, and the man who is holding me is the man I want to love...forever.

"Kens?" he whispers into my ear and I hear the fight in his voice.

"Yes," I say, and turn to my brother. "The baby is Dane's." Dane's body relaxes, and I put my arms around his back and hug him. "I love him, Nate."

"I love her right back," Dane says, lightly touching my belly. "I know I'm not what—"

"No, you're not," Nate says, and I turn to stare at him. I thought after our talk he might see things differently. How can he not feel the love in this room?

"Nate," I begin, needing to make him see and understand that I'm a grown woman and can make good decisions.

"No, he's not what I wanted and that's on me, Kendra," Nate says. "I've made mistakes and if you chose Dane, then he must be a good guy. The right guy. I need to trust that."

I don't say anything about him choosing Lance and that he turned out to be an asshole. I think he already knows that.

I put my hand on Dane's chest. "He's the best guy, Nate, and the only guy I've ever wanted or loved."

Nate nods, and Dane says, "I'll always love her and take care of her..." he puts his hand over my stomach. "...and our baby."

Nate swallows and his voice is low when he murmurs, almost to himself, "I'm going to be an uncle."

I grin. "Yeah, you are."

"I'll be a good uncle," he tells him.

I grin and put my arms around him and hug him. "I know you will be, and you're not losing me, Nate. I'll always be your sister and now you're gaining a niece or nephew, and a brother." I smile at Dane as the two nod, agreeing with that, but then suddenly Nate's eyes go wide, like he just had a lightbulb moment.

"What about school, and nursing, and—"

"One day at a time," I say to him. "One day at a time." I move back beside Dane and he puts his arm around me in a show of support.

"Nothing is going to stand in the way of Kendra's career," Dane says. "I'll be here to support her through everything."

"I...I'm going to go," Nate says a small grin on his face, like he's enjoying the idea of being an uncle. "You two look like you need to talk."

"We do," I agree.

Nate leaves and I turn back to Dane. The warmth and love in his eyes fills my soul with happiness. Happy tears spill down my cheeks. "Is this what you want?"

"It's everything I want. I'm so sorry, Kendra. Sorry for what I said, for thinking you knew and were hiding it from me. I just…I thought I wasn't worthy, and when I didn't make the team, and Lance…Old demons…I was stupid."

I go up on my toes. "None of that matters now. I love you and you love me, and now we move forward."

"I want that more than anything," he says quietly.

I cup his cheeks. "I have something for you."

"You do?"

I wink at him. "It's your Christmas present. I'm giving it to you early. This will prove I never thought you weren't worthy."

His shoulders sag. "I know you never thought that."

I hurry to my stack of papers on the counter, and hand him a piece of paper and he stares at it, confusion all over his sweet face. "What is this?"

I point to the words Bike and Bries. "I registered the name. You were always the man I needed, Dane."

He blinks and water fills his eyes. "Kens…you really registered the name?"

"Yeah, just so no one took it. I wanted it to be yours, for when you're ready to open your bike and cheese shop."

His chest rises and falls quickly. "I can't believe you did this."

"I wanted to show you that I care about you and your passions, and hockey didn't matter to me."

He pinches the bridge of his nose, a sobbing sound in his throat. "This means…I love you so much, Kens." He picks me up and hugs me so tight I can barely breathe.

"I can't believe you bought a baby's bike seat," I tell him.

"I wanted to show you that I was all in. That I want this between us, and that the baby is mine." He glances over his shoulders to where the seat sits by the front door, and chuckles. "You never know, our child could be the next Tour de France winner."

"How about we let our child be whatever they want to be? No pressure. No comparisons. No bubble wrap."

He laughs. "I like the sound of that."

I blink up at the man I love. "Just for the record, you were my best mistake."

"Good." He continues to hold me and heads toward the stairs. "Let's make more mistakes together."

"It's not like I can get pregnant again," I tease with a laugh.

"No, but we can practice for when we're ready for baby number two."

"Baby number two?"

"If we're going to get a big farmhouse, Kens, we have to fill all the bedrooms. I believe that's a rule."

"A rule, huh? Since when have you ever followed the rules?"

"Never and it's a good thing, or I never would have run into you crossing in the middle of the street."

"You mean run me over."

His grin is sexy and mischievous. "Right. Did I ever make that up to you?"

I tap my chin. "I don't believe so."

"Well, I'm going to." We reach my bedroom and he sets me on the bed. "Right now, and for the rest of our lives."

"I like the sound of that, Dane."

"Good, now get naked."

Christmas Eve, Bass River,

I glance at Kendra in the passenger seat beside me and take her hand into mine. It's crazy really. It was last Christmas when I was visiting Storm House with my brother Rhys when I met her, and now here we are heading to my place for Christmas, with her brother in the back seat, joining us.

I couldn't be happier, although I'm pretty sure shit is going to hit the fan when I tell my folks that I quit the team, and Kendra and I are going to start a family. Nate came around quickly after we shared the news with him—he loves the idea of being an uncle and getting all the free cheese he can eat. But seriously, the baby has brought us all closer.

Fingers crossed my parents warm to the idea as fast as he did, and that a baby will soften them. Basically, when it comes right down to it, my parents have two choices. Kick me out of their life, and never see their grandchild, or accept that for the first time in my life, I really am happy.

Kendra gives me a nervous smile, and I squeeze her hand before I bring it to my lips and kiss it. I'm really happy that she and Josie had a long talk and worked things out. She has enough on her mind, and she needs her best friend by her side. My phone pings and I glance at it. It's Jesse inviting us over to his place for some holiday cheer. I'm sure Kendra and Nate will enjoy that. As long as Nate stays away from Jesse's sisters.

"Do you think your parents will have some of that jalapeno cheese at the shop?" Nate asks, and I grin.

"Pretty sure. If not, I'll make you some over the holidays."

"Are you still going to make the bacon and dill pickle cheese?" Kendra asks, her lips twisted like she'd just eaten something sour.

Last time we were here it was a quick visit and I never got to show off my artisan skills. This time we're here longer, and I plan to get into the shop—well if things go according to my plan, and we all work things out. "It's going to be good, and aren't pregnant women supposed to crave pickles?"

"Yeah, pickles, but not dill pickle cheese."

"I can't wait to try it," Nate says.

"At least someone has faith in me."

Kendra laughs as we pull into the snow dusted driveaway. "I have all the faith in the world in you, Dane."

I glance up as I park, and that's when Rhys comes out the front door, not bothering to pull on his winter coat, despite the single digit temperature outside. I called him the other day, and filled him in on my relationship with Kendra, and

I'm looking forward to working on my relationship with him. I want us to be close.

"Hey bro," I say and jump from the car when he comes around my side. I give him a big hug and he holds me tight. I really have missed him, and I really hope Mom and Dad aren't going to pressure me, wanting me to remain in his shadow. "Is Leeza here?"

"She's coming a bit later." He grins, that same goofy smile he always gets on his face when he talks about Leeza and I'm happy the two are in love.

"Nate, Kendra," he greets as they get out of the car and then he shakes his head, like he still can't believe Kendra is my girl-friend. It was only a year ago, he warned me to stay away from her, otherwise Nate would make my life a living hell.

"Mom and Dad inside," I ask quietly.

The afternoon sun shines down on us, and Rhys folds his arms to keep himself warm. "Yeah, let's go in and have a drink. I'm freezing my balls off."

"Bro," I say quietly as Kendra takes my hand and Nate goes for the bag. "There's something I need to tell you."

His eyes narrow in on me. "Is everything okay?"

I smile at Kendra, my heart full of love. "Actually, it is, but—"

"Dane," Dad says, zipping his coat up as he comes outside, Mom following behind. "What's taking so long? Do you need help with the bags?"

"I got them," Nate calls out as he closes the trunk and I quickly do the introductions. I can feel Rhys's eyes on me, as I square my shoulders. Does he sense the change in me? I really wanted to tell him in private, but I'm no longer able to do that. I guess I just needed to know I had an ally in him, and I'm pretty sure I do, anyway.

"Let's all head inside, then," Mom says. "Rhys was in the middle of telling us a funny story about when he was in Detroit."

"I'm sure you must have some good hockey stories to share too, Dane," Dad says.

I straighten to my full height. "As a matter of fact, I do, but I'm not sure you're going to think it's a good story."

A small noise crawls out of Kendra's throat, and I put my arm around her, ready to tear the band aid off so to speak, before we go inside.

"Oh, is that so," Dad mumbles as his gaze goes between Kendra and me. "Is there a problem?"

"Actually no, not a problem Dad. Not for me anyway." He eyes me, his body tensing. "I'm no longer on the team," I say and brace myself for the backlash. But it's okay. I'm ready for it, and have thought this day through in my mind numerous times. "I gave up my spot for someone who really wants to be there." My parents go quiet, like they're trying to wrap their brain around what I just told them, and I suppose they are. "You see," I continue as silence falls heavy. "Hockey is Rhys' passion, not mine. He's good at it, great at it, and I couldn't be happier that he's in the NHL, but it's not for me."

Rhys hand lands on my back and I'm grateful for the support. I smile at him, and he gives me a curt, understanding nod.

"I'm going to really concentrate on my business degree."

"Dane, what is this all about?" Dad asks gruffly, and that's when I notice something in my mother softening. The fine lines around her eyes smooth out, and when she glances at Kendra, who has put on baby weight since our last visit, I'm almost certain she knows.

"Someday, down the road, I'd like to follow in your footsteps, Dad," I say to him, meaning every bit of it. "You're the best artisan in the province, and I think with time, effort and maybe a little help from you and Mom, I could take that title away."

Did he just smirk?

After a long moment of silence, Dad says, "I don't think so, son."

"That sounds like a challenge to me," I tease to lighten things. Mom takes a tentative step closer and my heart pounds a little harder. "I love you both," I say. "I'm sorry I'm not going to be in the NHL, but I think one NHL player in the family is enough. We all know Rhys doesn't like to share the spotlight. He's kind of a media hog like that."

"Hey," Rhys says, tugging me in to rub his knuckles in my hair, and Kendra gives a nervous laugh.

I go serious again. "Making cheese and biking make me happy, which is why I want to pursue my own business someday."

"Son," Dad says, as he shifts from one foot to the other. "You were groomed for the NHL. All the time, money and effort we put into your future."

"I know, Dad. I know. I appreciate everything you've done for me. I truly do. I realize you loved it—me—when I was going to be something great, like Rhys, but I don't want to be in Rhys shadow anymore, I want to follow in your footsteps."

"I didn't know. We pushed you because..." He glances down and I'm pretty sure I've never seen my dad so confused before, and that's when I realize why they've been so hard on me. They truly thought hockey was what I wanted, and because I can be reckless they've been trying to keep me on the right track.

"Because we love you," Mom says, stepping up to me and taking my hand. "If we ever led you to believe you could only be loved if you followed Rhys, I'm sorry." Tears pool in Mom's eyes and beside me Kendra sniffs. I swallow against the lump in my throat. Never in my life did I think a conversation with my parents would go down like this.

"There's more," I say. Mom nods, like she was waiting for this. "I love Kendra, and...we're having a baby."

A little squeal catches in mom's throat as Dad's eyes go wide. His gaze drops to Kendra's stomach as I put my hand on it. "You're going to be grandparents."

"Dane, when, how..." Dad stutters and I laugh.

"The how I'm not going to get in to," I joke. "But we're due in May and we're really excited about it."

"I...I don't know what to say," Dad says.

"Say you're happy for them, Bill," Mom pipes in. "Say you can't wait to be a grandfather." Mom takes Kendra's hand. "Let's get you in out of the cold, and get you some hot chocolate."

Kendra glances at me and I nod. I stand there as Mom leads her into the house, and in my heart, I know they're going to be the best of friends.

"Dad…"

He stands there for a moment, and scrubs his hand over his chin. "You really think you can be a better cheese artisan than me?"

My body relaxes, as I fight back tears, because that right there…that was acceptance. "Yeah, I have some great ideas, too. Remember when I was young and I talked about bacon cheese, and dill pickle cheese?"

"I do."

"Maybe over the holidays we can experiment."

He nods. "We could do that."

We nod to one another a new understanding that fills my heart with love.

"I better get these bags inside," Nate says breaking the quiet.

Rhys takes one of the bags. "Come on. I'll show you where to put them."

As they walk away, my gaze goes to Rhys and for the first time in my life, I see only one shadow behind him. I chuckle quietly.

"Coming, son," Dad asks.

"Yeah, I'll be right there."

He turns, his big boots leaving tracks in the snow. I glance down, and follow in his footsteps, knowing that I'm finally on the right path in life and I couldn't be happier.

. . .

* * *

Thank you so much for reading Kendra and Dane's story. To find out what happens with Jessie and Josie, and why Josie has been avoiding her best friend, check out **Fake Out**.

ALSO BY CATHRYN FOX

Scotia Storms

Away Game (Rebels)

Warm Up (Rebels)

Crash Course (Rebels)

Home Advantage (Rebels)

Shut Out (Rebels)

Deal Breaker (Rebels)

Moving Target (Rivals)

Face Off (Rivals)

Scoring Fast (Rivals)

Opposing Teams (Rivals)

Hard Burn (Rivals)

Fake Out (Rivals)

End Zone

Fair Play

Enemy Down

Keeping Score

Trading Up

All In

Blue Bay Crew

Demolished

Leveled

Hammered

Single Dad

Single Dad Next Door

Single Dad on Tap

Single Dad Burning Up

Players on Ice

The Playmaker

The Stick Handler

The Body Checker

The Hard Hitter

The Risk Taker

The Wing Man

The Puck Charmer

The Troublemaker

The Rule Breaker

The Rookie

The Sweet Talker

The Heart Breaker

In the Line of Duty

His Obsession Next Door

His Strings to Pull

His Trouble in Talulah

His Taste of Temptation

His Moment to Steal

His Best Friend's Girl

His Reason to Stay

Confessions

Confessions of a Bad Boy Professor

Confessions of a Bad Boy Officer

Confessions of a Bad Boy Fighter

Confessions of a Bad Boy Doctor

Confessions of a Bad Boy Gamer

Confessions of a Bad Boy Millionaire

Confessions of a Bad Boy Santa

Confessions of a Bad Boy CEO

Hands On

Hands On

Body Contact

Full Exposure

Dossier

Private Reserve

House Rules

Under Pressure

Big Catch

Brazilian Fantasy

Improper Proposal

Boys of Beachville

Good at Being Bad

Igniting the Bad Boy

Bad Girl Therapy

Stone Cliff Series:

Crashing Down

Wasted Summer

Love Lessons

Wrapped Up

Eternal Pleasure Series

Instinctive

Impulsive

Indulgent

Sun Stroked Series

Seaside Seduction

Deep Desire

Private Pleasure

Captured and Claimed Series:

Yours to Take

Yours to Teach

Yours to Keep

Firefighter Heat Series

Fever

Siren

Flash Fire

Playing For Keeps Series

Slow Ride

Wild Ride

Sweet Ride

Breaking the Rules:

Hold Me Down Hard

Pin Me Up Proper

Tie Me Down Tight

Stand Alone Title:

Hands on with the CEO

Torn Between Two Brothers

Holiday Spirit

Unleashed

Knocking on Demon's Door

Web of Desire

ABOUT CATHRYN

New York Times and *USA today* Bestselling author, Cathryn is a wife, mom, sister, daughter, and friend. She loves dogs, sunny weather, anything chocolate (she never says no to a brownie) pizza and red wine. She has two teenagers who keep her busy with their never ending activities, and a husband who is convinced he can turn her into a mixed martial arts fan. Cathryn can never find balance in her life, is always trying to find time to go to the gym, can never keep up with emails, Facebook or Twitter and tries to write page-turning books that her readers will love.

Connect with Cathryn:
Newsletter https://app.mailerlite.com/webforms/landing/c1f8n1
Twitter: https://twitter.com/writercatfox
Facebook: https://www.facebook.com/AuthorCathrynFox?ref=hl
Blog: http://cathrynfox.com/blog/
Goodreads: https://www.goodreads.com/author/show/91799.Cathryn_Fox

Pinterest http://www.pinterest.com/catkalen/